The Croviss Girls

BY THE SAME AUTHOR

NOVELS:
She's Alone
Both
Kingswinford Sunset
Lydgate

SHORT FICTION:
'The Cold'
(Available via Amazon Kindle)

POETRY:
'Grene Woddenesse'
(Published in *The PoW-WoW Book of Ghost Stories*)

The Croviss Girls

Richard Bruce Clay

First published 2024 by Tenebrous Texts

Copyright © 2024 by Richard Bruce Clay

Cover painting by Kat

Photographed by Phil Cervi

Cover Layout by AJ Pilkington

ISBN 978-1-914246-40-1

AUTHOR'S NOTE

The song 'Meurglys III' by Van der Graaf Generator contains funny time signatures and anyone attempting, in reality, to perform a striptease to it is in danger of doing themselves a proper mischief.

Prologue: Satansfist

What happened, Dad?

PART ONE:

GOOD

(BABALON KYLE)

1: Lon Kyle

Grey-black January trees clutched at the clouds, seeming desperate to claw a way through the swirl – the swirl grey-white as half-set concrete.

What kind of blue Heaven did they expect to find beyond?

In the midst, Saint Paul's Church glowered chronic disapproval. Of trees or of cloud-covering? Of both, surely: dark bricks, dark slates and narrow windows tut-tutted, unceasing righteous at the world. The graves, many broken, all in muted colours, leant respectfully one way or the other in silent assent. West, the main road (Dudley to Halesowen) grumbled with internal combustion. North, the green railway cutting, damp and mostly quiet, now and then exploded with the glass and metal rush of a Stratford-upon-Avon to Malvern or a London Marylebone to Kidderminster, disappearing into the Blackheath Tunnel, single-minded, heterosexual – one more thing for the old church to disapprove.

About three on a Friday afternoon: not much daylight left. The sort of time and the sort of place where you might expect a ghost to show up.

One grave caught my attention – I wasn't sure why but my hunches about such doings had a history of being spot-on. The churchyard was packed with the dead and the grass was long – you'd not have thought any single monument would stand out and there seemed nothing special about this one – though I could tell it had more than one name on it: maybe two, maybe three. I started to walk towards it; I felt attracted to it. Or maybe repelled by it. Or a bit of both.

'I sort of like it round here.'

I stopped and turned. 'Really?' I said. Or thought. One or the other.

'Yeah,' he replied. 'I like the atmosphere. I like the trees.'

He was about two metres from me, looking up into those trees. There'd been a time when this would have pissed me off – a time when anyone in my presence looking at anything that wasn't me would have pissed me

11

off. Like any half-decent occult magician, I'd been brought up to be narcissistic.

He did love his trees though, did this bloke – really loved them.

'There's a load of my family buried here,' he said. 'So I suppose... a fair old chunk of my flesh has found its way into the wood by now. Crovisses over there, mostly.' He pointed at the northwest corner, close to where the main road grumbled over the tunnel's mouth; one of the graves he indicated was the one that had attracted me. 'Griefsticks over there –' he added, pointing to the dark brick of the south wall. 'None of my mum's lot, though. They're all in Kidderminster.'

Kidderminster: yes, you could hear it in his accent. I'd not started to fall for him – not exactly, though I could sense he was someone who might wind up important to me. And, though I knew he hadn't intended the things he'd said to be chat up lines, the spell they'd cast was powerful. I was okay with that.

'So these trees are family?' I asked.

'Yeah. I guess.'

I looked up at him. A tall bloke and he needed to shift a bit from round the gut – not a problem: give him to me and I'd have him doing forty lengths of the pool inside a week. He must have been my sort of age (I'm thirty-four), but not someone whose life was settling down into thirtysomething tedium. The hair was a dead giveaway: it was like mine – ginger, lots of it and frizzy as anything.

He wore denim – no leather, but a lot of denim. With patches promoting just about every rock band who'd ever referenced JRR Tolkien or Mario Bava. That is indeed a lot of patches.

'And when you wander round here,' I said – and I think I smiled at him – 'you can hear "Planet Caravan" in your mind's ear.'

Now he looked at me, ever so pleased at my choice of words.

'"My mind's ear,"' he said, turning to another tree, then back to me as if starting to see me properly. 'I like that.'

'Full of such witticisms, me,' I said.

What kind eyes he had! I noticed them quite suddenly. Blue green like underwater sunlight. Not a trace of fear or sneer about them.

'Got a few bits of family here myself,' I ventured. 'The Tulpers – Mom and her lot. The Kyles are mostly in Scotland; lost touch with them years ago – or rather Dad did.'

'Kyle..?'

I wasn't going to make him work for my identity: 'Lon Kyle,' I said. 'Lon, short for Babalon: Dad's idea, not Mom's.'

'The Death of Wallenstein!' he said, delighted.

Stourbridge-based rock band. Keyboardista me. Audibly influenced by a number of German groups from the early 70s. Three out of five of us – not me, obviously – were old enough to have seen those bands live in their prime. 'The Death of Wallenstein', or 'The Wallies' as some snarky sods called us, was the most successful musical thingy I'd ever been involved in; if we'd had any sew-ons or iron-ons made, I'd have been miffed that he didn't have a patch bigging up our back catalogue.

'Moog, Korg microsampler, Akai sequencer and…' said I – tapping the guitar case slung across my back – 'occasional twelve string. The DX7 finally conked out last year.' I briefly whipped off my orange woolly bobble hat and stared gravely at the ground – I can do mock solemnity really well.

He laughed. 'I do love *Antidisestablishmentarianista Jones,*' he said. 'It's so spacey.'

'That was the intention.'

'And...' He hesitated, nervously. 'Years ago... er... my dad's cousin was in your band. Before your time or mine of course. Early seventies.'

'What... Martin?'

'Yeah. Martin.'

Well, we were off to a good start, weren't we? So we began to talk about the band. About *A Right Madam: The Death of Wallenstein Live at Greensforge, 2011* – our acknowledged masterpiece, recorded at the open-air wedding reception of a couple of friends – one of whose description of yours truly had given us the title. We'd sold dozens of that one! We didn't say much about Martin, though. We both knew what had happened to him, what had happened to his wife. And we knew what had happened to his daughter and...

Hang on a bit – had anything happened to his son? Suddenly I wasn't sure, yet I felt I ought to be.

Much more muzo chat – and why not? I enjoy muzo chat; a lot of people don't think a woman can – but stuff them.

He told me he was a 'crap guitarist' and a writer. His name was Warren Griefstick. He'd spent years on a big thick fantasy trilogy, *The Chronicles of X'Vath* – though he didn't tell me how *'X'Vath'* was spelt on that occasion. He'd bunged this on Kindle – where it had seen very little action – but anyway, these days he was getting more into local history.

We wandered out of the churchyard and took a right, heading through Blackheath and up Rowley Hill towards Dudley.

After a while, I found myself waiting on my own at a bus stop at the top of the hill. Warren Griefstick had said his friendly goodbyes a few moments or minutes before – though I couldn't quite remember him doing so.

Peculiar, that.

But I was sure we'd shaken hands. And his grip had been firm and warm with life. Yes, life. Definitely life.

But the evening was getting dark and sodding chilly so I was glad when the bus eventually turned up. I started to read one of the paperbacks I'd picked up in Blackheath Market, changing buses at Dudley (another long wait) and finally getting off near Neil the guitarist's place in Upper Gornal.

It was band practice night.

You won't find many English suburbs further above sea level than Upper Gornal; the Russia-bound wind was as icy and vindictive as usual: *'I'll-have-you-human-wankers-'cause-for-me-it's-next-stop-the-Urals!'*

I rang Neil Haines's front bell. His missus, Sarah, came to the door just as I was knocking the last of the churchyard muck from my new pair of Docs (orange, to match my flowing ginger magnificence. Did I mention I was narcissistic?). She let me in with one of her crooked little smiles and a brusque 'He's in the back.'

A lot of people would have described Sarah as 'long-suffering'. As wife of the lead guitarist in a band that had been going forty-eight years with various lineup changes but no sign of making a profit, her life might, in such folk's minds, be summed up by that one word: 'suffering'. But the thing was, she managed a charity shop in Dudley and had done lots of other work for Macmillan since she'd packed in the nursing herself, so she'd got her own bit of personal not-Neil space; neither of them had wound up being a cage for the other.

'The back' was Neil and Sarah's garage. It stood at the bottom of their garden and its main door opened on to a still-unpaved back lane that served a row of such car shelters. There was a smaller metal door into the garden, which made a scraping noise like an arthritic robot as I opened it. Inside, doors, walls and ceiling were all covered with manky old mattresses that we'd nailed and hung up a couple of years before – as much for the sake of the sound quality as for the neighbours' peace of mind. We'd done quite a bit of recording in Neil's garage and some of it had turned out well. But when the weather got too warm or too wet, those mattresses started to get pretty pongy; I could see us having to swap them for new ones in the next year or so.

Goddess knew how long it had been since Neil or Sarah had kept a car in there.

Dougie Cayle had his kit set up and was tapping cautiously at the floor tom. Dave Calper the bassist and Neil, our two founder members, were sat tuning up. No sign of Andy Reynolds, the flautist. We were a cross-generational band: Andy and me in our thirties, Dougie in his early sixties and Dave and Neil neither of them too far shy of the big eight-oh. Wilf, Andy's granddad, veteran bluesman and the original drummer, would have been over a hundred by now. I liked that about us.

We said our ' 'Owdo's and I unslung my twelve-string. The keyboards were already here, in their cases, propped against a workbench. I started to set them up.

'You alright?' asked Dougie, with a serious edge in his voice. I'd learned to hear that seriousness of his and to take notice of it.

'Think so,' I said. 'Why?'

'Dunno. You've got a funny vibe about you.' 'He picked up a pair of brushes and pattered out an intricate little pattern on the snare, by way of explanation.

'I met this really nice bloke in Blackheath Churchyard,' I said.

'Might we know him?' Dave chipped in.

'Warren Griefstick. His dad was Martin's cousin.'

15

I didn't tell them I was attracted to him – I wasn't sure if that was the right way of describing it, but I'd been playing with these guys for fifteen years on and off, so they were bound to suss something was up. Back when I'd first joined, the principle that *He or She whom Lon Doth Desire to Shag, She Almost Inevitably Shaggeth* had been as reliable as the laws of physics. But something had happened and I'd quietened off. Quietened off a lot. Quietened off to the extent that I didn't even have a stud in my tongue anymore.

Still, the only human being who'd ever actually turned me down was now sitting next to me, twiddling with the butterfly screws on his hi-hat.

I saw, with a lurch of surprised fear in my guts, that a single large tear, lit from within by a spark of silver blue, was making its way down his cheek.

'Dougie?!'

He looked up at me, noticed the tear and wiped it away, puzzled.

'That's weird,' he said, 'I've no reason to be upset.'

A silver blue spark. We didn't talk about it, but we both believed such a spark was the sign of a presence – of Dougie's spirit guide. Perhaps the whole band needed guidance that night.

There was a tap at the big door. Neil tugged it open; Andy stood there, flute cases in hand. His usual grin was missing.

'Bloody Greyshirts,' he chuntered. 'Half a dozen of them out the front reading the riot act to some kids. Decided I'd come this way.'

He'd been right to keep out of it. Though he was mostly an affable chap, when it came to Ronsardist Greyshirts, Andy was not the sort who saw them as salt-of-the-earth neighbourhood watchers. No, he was an obstinate old-school anarchist who'd call them fascistic vigilantes to their faces. Oh, and by the way (he wouldn't leave me out of it, if he got wound up enough) did they know that their glorious Gaffer Charlotte, the Leader of Her Majesty's Opposition, had, ten or eleven years back, been the other 'arf of the girl – yes *girl* – who played keyboards in the band he was in?

It was true: the Leader of the Ronsardist Party was one of my exes and that party, the most toxic manifestation of British Fascism since Mosley, was in a state of complete denial about its boss-gal's sexuality. This state of denial would have been funny if the Ronsardists didn't go round killing people.

There'd been a stage in my life when, like my favourite fictional character, I'd believed that all the problems of the world could be solved by shagging them. An occult magician will usually believe as much, especially if she's a disciple of Spare, Tremayne, Crowley and, most of all, of Alex Chaplain (creator of said favourite fictional character). Seven months, three weeks, five days, three hours and eighteen and a half minutes as Charlotte Ronsard's girlfriend had broken that spell sufficiently for me to realise it wasn't necessarily true.

It had also been the reason why I'd quietened off.

Andy got his flute out and through it he exorcised himself of a long entanglement of shrieks and flashes, all full of affronted justice. Then he breathed in and out a few times and, that done, he got his mic stand sorted and effects pedals (he had a lot of them) plugged in.

Neil and Dave looked up from their tunings. They were very fussy buggers about their tunings but they'd got them ready at last.

That was when things started getting weird.

***

Just how weird I don't think any of us knew straight away. We were playing for a couple of hours all told, sometimes with ferocity, sometimes with a kind of sunshine softness – very very gentle.

We'd parted quite happy and even Sarah, who came in towards the end, told me that 'parts of that sounded quite nice.' We didn't get that kind of praise out of her very often.

So – back home for one last cup of tea and then bed – where I should have been out like a light but wasn't.

My waking mind hung around, sourly and sexlessly, and it was soon pretty clear that I wasn't going to get past it until I'd picked apart some of the knots that the music had tied in my insides.

I hadn't intended to use so many samples from Martin's tapes – the birdsong, the pumping station, the electric cables, all ordinary noises and all so much more than that. It had never been easy using them, especially not if I'd manipulated them – as I'd done on the *Right Madam* album.

17

But back then, it had seemed necessary – a joyful release. Now, it felt like heading back in a direction I was scared to go.

Martin Icement had been my predecessor in the band: he'd never used keyboards, hadn't even known much about playing them, but we both made it our main business to tape or sample sounds. And we used them – manipulated, distorted or placed in the most exteme states of counterpoint – as a key part of the music. Mostly, I did this with my Korg microsamper but Martin had got unexpected and otherworldly tones and textures from mucking about with tapes on a couple of portable cassette decks and on a reel-to-reel that had been, Neil and Dave both agreed, pretty knackered when they'd got hold of it in 1970.

There'd been a gap of about thirty years between Martin leaving and my joining. Since then, I'd been digging into the mysteries of how he'd got those effects. I'd made progress, but there was still work to do – lots of it. And, like it or not, that work had created a bond between Martin and me, even if he'd been dead since 2010 and we'd never met. It was a bond that was only enhanced by…

I sat up in bed. My heart rate had shot up and I was gasping for breath. Something was very wrong.

'Had' anything happened to Martin's son? To Lee Icement, the painter who'd called himself *'Satansfist'*? Of course something had bloody well happened to him! In the spring of 2011, his boyfriend, Lewis Gladrell, had smashed his brains out with a lead pipe. And I knew this because I'd been writing to, and sometimes visiting Lewis in prison for the past five or six years. I could be in no doubt of that!

I could be in no doubt of that – not now, not here. But in Saint Paul's Churchyard, I *had* been in doubt of it. In the presence of Warren Griefstick, I had almost seemed to be standing in another world – a world in which Lee Icement still lived…

But I had only met Lee once or twice; we'd hardly spoken and not really got on. I'd grown to love his art, but when we'd met, we'd not really got on.

And yet I felt somehow that we knew each other far better than that – that we knew each other to this day and he had some kind of nickname for me that pissed me off no end.

Shrill as Andy's flute and insistent as Dougie's floor tom, my gut

18

instincts were singing that this other world was real. And that this was all to do with Warren Griefstick...

I needed to take another look at Lee Icement's art. Some of it was still muralled up on the walls of public spaces in the West Midlands – and some further afield. But there was one place that held his most powerful work – and though I knew I could get in there if I really had to, I was, at that point, reluctant to try. There was a good album of his stuff and I knew Dave had a few copies. I'd go over and look at one of them tomorrow. As good an excuse as I needed to visit my bass playing bandmate and his legendary second-hand bookshop... And to have one or two of his legendary cuppas...

Should I give him a ring now and let him know I was coming? Nah – by now, even Dave would be... asleep...

Finally, I was beginning to nod off.

Still, I couldn't stop myself dwelling on Lee. And on Martin. And on Warren. All part of the same family. And, as I drifted out of myself, it seemed to me that this family existed under a kind of shade – the shade of something unutterably toxic. And that it was down to me to push through that shade, as if I was pushing through the concrete skies over Blackheath. Push through, to something beautiful... Something so utterly utterly beautiful...

Beautiful...

Beautiful...

My beautiful...

2: Dave Calper

'There's stuff,' said Adil Muhammed Shah, 'There's stuff as wants stopping. That's what the Old Gaffer used to say. And that's what I'm a-saying to you lot right now. There's stuff as want's stopping and we – I'm a-telling you now, *we* – we'm a-gonna stop 'it!'

Cheers from his audience. There were a lot of them: you could rely on a Ronsardist rally to fill a good-sized football stadium with slack-jawed, grey-shirted goons. This one was on the radio from the Villa. Two weeks before it had come from Coventry and the week before that from the Hawthorns. In each case, the fans of the football teams had included a fair number who'd not been happy about this but, in each case, they'd done the sensible thing and shut up. These days, people had learned to do the sensible thing and shut up.

And on he pontificated. And on. And bleeding *on*. Still treading a fine line between veiled threats and open boasts of what him and his mates had got up to. And were going to get up to. Much laughter still when he reminded them about the office of *The Guardian* newspaper going up in smoke the year before – but with nothing that could pass for an admission it was anything to do with them – not in court anyway. Bloody hell, it was amazing how cunning these sods could be! Despite the actual content of all their speeches being so relentlessly bleeding thick. 'I'm not saying anyone should go round burning stuff down.' *No, of course you're not.* 'All I'm saying is this: them as says we shouldn't give them Jockos the boot,' (loud cheers) 'and them Micks the boot,' (louder cheering) 'and them Welsh the boot,' (louder cheering still) 'and them Cornish bastards the boot,' (the loudest cheers of all – the Ronsardists really seemed to have it in for Falmouth these days) 'Them as goes round opening their big blabbering mouths and coming out with rubbish like that, I've got one thing to say to 'em. And that thing is: KEEP YOUR BIG MOUTHS SHUT! Or you'll find there's a-gonna be somebody as'll have stuck the boot in 'em! And where's your teeth a-gonna be then? Ay? Where's your teeth a-gonna be then?'

A rousing chorus broke in:

> *Where's your teeth*
> *Where's your teeth*
> *Where's teeth a-gonna be?*

At which point I decided I'd had enough I and turned the set off. To think: just two years before – 2017 wasn't it? – we'd still been getting *The PM Programme* at this time and I'd never used to think much of *that*: hadn't realised how lucky I was.

January and bleeding cold, so I put a few extra bits of wood on the fire. It was past five o'clock; I could have shut the shop up and gone in the back for my tea but I wasn't in the mood. Running low on firewood and one or two second-hand booksellers *have* been known to stick some stock on the blaze when it gets chilly. Granted, it's almost always an out-of-date phonebook or an L. Ron Hubbard but still, *I* never burn books. Never did in the past and, in these days of the Ronsardist Greyshirts, I never ever will. I'd sooner burn a Greyshirt.

Adil Muhammed Shah or 'Big Mohammed' as his white mates called him, had put me in a rotten mood. I'd been noticing him for a few years now – from the movement's beginnings. He wasn't part of the leadership but he'd been among the first to sign up; this had been back when Charlotte Ronsard's dad, Harry, was running the show. And by God, this Adil Muhammed Shah, he was a true believer! Most of the Ronsardists had always been plain idiotic. These days though, a growing minority were opportunists, hitching a ride to money and to power. Neither was true of Big Mohammed! All the guff about England's National Destiny– you could hear that he was convinced of its righteousness. And this conviction arose not from stupidity but from boundless self-deception, which only made him more dangerous. Because here was a fascist whose convictions shone so brightly that it burned away at the edges of your own. You could feel your own morality curl up and disintegrate, even as you knew the bugger had had plenty to do with that busload of left-wing WiGIiE saps going over the edge of the cliff at Bridgnorth, week before last. He'd looked smug when he'd been on telly that night: there'd been no hiding it.

At the same time, his grandparents had been born in the Punjab. And I'd been noticing how the proportion of Blacks and Asians among the Greyshirts had been going down lately; the petty prejudices that had been meat and drink for fascism in decades gone by had been absent from Ronsardism in its early days. Now those prejudices were reasserting themelves. Would most of the Greyshirts tolerate Adil Muhammed Shah for much longer? And, despite her apparent celibacy in recent years, would they even tolerate Charlotte herself?

There'd be no telling Adil himself as much. I bet there'd been some ructions up the mosque over his loyalty to Charlotte and to Harry: you couldn't square their ethics with those of any religion remotely Abrahamic. But such things were going to have been kept strictly in-house: I wouldn't have expected to hear a peep about them and, indeed, I had not.

I went in the back and found some copies of *Satansfist* – the big album of Lee Icement's art that Taschen had put out a year or so after he was killed. Lon had got me on the blower that morning, asking if she could have a look at one? Leafing through the images, from the harshly abstract to the post Burne-Jones heroism, I got tearful, as I often did over anything connected with Martin. Tearful, and full of premonition. Then I heard someone come in. I looked up. Neil Haines.

We stared at each other for a bit.

'What' he asked, 'the fuck happened last night?'

I didn't have an easy answer to that one, so I just looked down at the photographed paintings. Then back up at him. He noticed what the book was.

'Martin's son?' he asked.

'Yeah,' I said, and nodded towards the back room. He picked his way through the piles of stock and went in there. I stayed where I was. He paused and was silent; he could see I'd got the computer turned on, internet open at an ancestry page. I heard him sit down and look at it.

After a bit, the chair creaked and he came back into the front.

'They didn't have much luck, did they?' he said.

'Hey?'

'The Croviss sisters. Martin's mom and her sisters.'

This hadn't been the thing I'd been paying attention to but, suddenly, I was curious.

'How d'you mean?' I asked.

'Well, the youngest one – what was it? – Jennifer – she dies aged nine or ten. Martin's mom, Frieda, only lasts till she's forty. Not quite forty, even. Martin's her only kid. And he and both his kids go within a year of each other.'

It was true: Alice from smack, Martin a stroke and Lee murdered.

But...

'That's not the strangest thing,' I said.

'Oh?'

'Go and have another look.'

He went in the back again and, this time, I followed him.

Jennifer Croviss: the name gave me a funny feeling. I couldn't explain why. I didn't know anyone with that name... Didn't *think* I did...

The light from the computer screen turned Neil's face ghostly pale as he stared into it.

'Oh,' he said, 'I see.'

He had, indeed, seen.

The third Croviss sister, Janice, Frieda's twin according to the dates, had one child, Anthony Griefstick, born 1950. Anthony Griefstick himself had one child, Warren, born 1982.

And died 1982.

'Warren Griefstick died in 1982. Aged two weeks. Can't be him then, can it?'

'You wouldn't think so,' I said.

'Still... poor sodding Janice.'

I saw his point: it looked like Janice never remarried and it even seemed she might still be alive. That would be grim. Starting off one of three, with Frieda and Jennifer, and ending up being just the one – being just the one for so bleeding long! That'd do your head no good at all... And added to that, you'd lost your one and only grandchild, your little Warren. Who had definitely died in 1982,

So it *couldn't* be that Warren Griefstick that Lon had met – could it?

Except that – let's not bollocks about here – of course it bleeding well was.

'You look at stuff like that,' said Neil. 'and it almost seems like the whole family wanted to wipe itself out...'

'Just one sad ballsup after another,' I said. 'It happens. But you're right: there's probably only the one of them left.'

'Anthony Griefstick.'

'Yeah, Anthony Griefstick. Hang on, do I know that name from somewhere?'

I turned to him. The look on his face mixed puzzlement with worry and aversion.

'Doesn't seem like it's anywhere pleasant,' I said.

'No – but – I don't know... It'll come to me,' he sighed.

He got up and we went back into the front.

'So,' said Neil, making himself comfortable on a large pile of Catherine Cooksons that squeaked a bit under his weight, 'Lon starts playing last night and...'

'I know. She ain't used so many samples from Martin's tapes since... I dunno, not for five or six years. Really freaked me out.'

'I think we were all freaked out. Dougie was having one of his haunted turns and all. And Andy's never looked so much like his grandad.'

We were quiet. The fire crackled.

'And she seems,' Neil went on, 'to have just met Martin's cousin's son. It'd be a funny coincidence, even if he wasn't dead.' He paused again, then added: 'Looks like our little Lonnie's fallen for a ghost.'

'Well they were out in force last night weren't they? Ghosts.'

'You could hear it in the music,' he said. Then paused. Then, 'We're going to have to tell her.'

'I don't suppose she'll need us to. I mean, she's going to notice. First time she tries to shag him – there's going to be some sort of a difference when you shag a spook. Well – I'd have thought there would be.'

'So would I.' He sighed. 'I'm pretty new to this kind of thing. I know you've... seen some weird stuff...' His voice trailed off. 'Hang on, though,' he said, 'I'm sure I can remember something about a kid of that age – one who died round about then. Two weeks old or so. People were grumbling about whether it had been an accident or not. I don't think

24

anything ever got proved but for a while it looked bad for somebody. Might have been his mother…'

We went and looked at the websites of some local papers but we found nothing from 1982 that fitted the bill. No place of death had been listed on the ancestry website – so it might have been outside the area.

I made us some tea and put on an old Jack Parnell ten inch that had Wilf on congas. Then I had another look at Lee Icement's art; there was a photo of the suburban bathroom he had decorated just before he got killed. A suburban bathroom that belonged to Charlotte Ronsard and to her dad, Harry. It was divided diagonally in half: below the line – the straight and absolute line – walls and floor were painted with a confused grey swirling. Above, the ceiling and walls were black. And there was something about that black that I was drawn to. I remembered Lee's words, scribbled on a notepad in his car, perhaps only minutes before the end – the last words he wrote, describing his last painting:

There is something universal, final and all-consuming about this particular darkness. It is a darkness in the face of which no re-emergent light ought to be possible. It is a darkness that ought to be the end of all things.

And that had been it.

I wasn't sure I'd agree, somehow. It was the 'ought to be' that was the giveaway.

Because I could sense something about that darkness that was different. It wasn't kindness or happiness or anything that was going to come easy. It was a hard, painful journey into death itself. I looked up at the shop window and, though it was softened by orange streetlight, there was something similar in that January dark outside. It looked like pain. Pain and redemption.

3: Lon Kyle

I woke about midday (very late for me), sat up in bed, stared at the two piles of unedited typescript crouching next to the laptop and wished evil things at them. All the same, they were my ticket to a few hundred quid.

I'd inherited a shedload from Angus and Cynthia McSaddin, my ex-boyfriend's aged parents who'd unofficially adopted me after he was dead. Nineteen had been a funny age to get adopted but there you go: two more graves as well as Mom's that felt parental enough to shed tears over. It also meant I had a house in suburban Glasgow, formerly theirs, which I was mostly renting out to students. So I was better fixed than I'd ever thought I would be. I'd spent a few grand on the place where I now lay yawning – an upstairs flat in a Pedmore semi – but, if the Ronsardists started making things any scarier south of the border, I had a Scottish passport to get north of it.

I knew myself well enough to be sure that, if I wasn't careful, I'd soon blow all the cash on glad rags and musical instruments, so I was forcing myself to do paid work: freelance editing.

I got up, ran my hands through my hair and shook it. Did a few stretchy exercises and scratched my pubes. Then I took off the string vest I used as a nightie and went for a shower.

After that, I gave Dave a ring to let him know I'd be over that evening. 'About seven,' I said. 'And if you've still got any copies of *Satansfist,* could I have a look at one?' He had several, and said I'd be welcome.

That done, I put a couple of rounds of wholemeal in the toaster and grabbed some over-garlicky homemade hommous out the fridge. Ten minutes munching got me adequately anti-social. Unfit for much save four or five hours of ploughing with *Piers*-like virtue through the soon-to-be-self-published.

Starting with *Why I **Know** They're Out to Get Me*. Never mind who'd written this cantankerous internal memoir that claimed to be a book of poetry. Enough to say that it did what the title promised. Repeatedly.

And then I was faced with *Castrate Them All!!!*: in prose, this one, and a perfect example of why I don't always like calling myself a feminist. But the attitudes might not have been so much of a problem had the writer any awareness of the possibility of a full stop. Eight pages in, my head exploding with 'ands' and exclamation marks, I broke off, brewed up a litre of Fairtrade Columbian and changed into a burlesque cozzie that was all bows and twiddly bits and things that took an age to undo, with a pair of purple flock paisley-patterned hot pants, all crowned by a purple top hat with peacock feathers stuck in the band. Then I got my three full-length mirrors set up so that, wherever I looked, I could always see *me*. Then I put on *World Record* by Van der Graaf Generator and performed a striptease to 'Meurglys III' for my own sweet benefit, spontaneously orgasming at the eventual sight of my glorious unadorned Self. (Unadorned apart from the top hat that stayed on top throughout – though one of the feathers had got lost somewhere during the proceedings and it took me an age to find the bugger afterwards.)

So there. Yes: when I said 'narcissistic,' I meant *that* narcissistic: so narissistic that I was narcissistic about my own narcissism. And anyway, if you've been brought up by ritual sex magicians, stuff like that is what you do in such circumstances.

I necked the coffee with not a trace of milk or sugar and had another shower.

Then, back to the grammarless bile it was. Fucky Nell! By five o'clock, I was only about fifty pages in. Two hundred left to go.

No chance of going any further without seriously damaging my mental health, so it was time to get down the gym, which I did on my bike in a big fluorescent orange overcoat, lighting up the Pedmore nighttime. An hour of low-weight-high-repetition was enough to get my circulation feeling like an irresistible force. It also made my third shower of the day an absolute necessity. In the past, I'd sometimes relished the state of being *'sweaty'n''orrible'*. This had usually been when on the receiving end of cunnilingus or anilingus from a certain kind of lover: male, hairy and reeking of engine oil. These days, though, the idea of cleanliness was beginning quite seriously to grow on me.

From the gym, I biked round to Dave's.

It was only then, dismounting outside the bookshop in a rainy Brettell Lane, that I had a flashback of my dream from the night before.

There had been a most beautiful man. No – not a man – a boy. Fifteen or so. Still just about a boy. And he'd been saying '*Oh Mother, for God's sake!*' Very crossly. She'd clearly pissed him off, this mom of his. Odd. How had that happened? God oh God, though – how beautiful he was! The most beautiful thing I'd ever seen or dreamt or imagined. Hair and skin like mine, though the hair was shorter, face a similar sort of shape but his eyes... What kind eyes he had!

How had his mom pissed him off? She had, you see. She hadn't meant to but she had. She'd been a bit drunk, I thought... a bit drunk and going on about her sex life. Which I sensed she did quite a lot. And, though he was sort of used to it, she'd gone on a bit too much this time...

God God God, though, he was beautiful! I was sorry to think his mom had pissed him off so much. What had she been like, this mom of his? I tried to sense it, though my dream seemed reluctant to let that pass into the waking world: very short, hair ginger and lots of it – like mine though with more grey bits, goofy teeth, forties or early fifties – but looking bloody good for her age. She...

Oh.

Oh.

Ah.

I saw.

And Dave was clunking around inside as I saw. And he was getting the door open as I said, silently, insistently to myself: 'This wasn't a dream, it was a PREMONITION!' And he was looking a bit worried when he saw the tears start, as start they did.

This boy was...

This boy would be...

God God God, how beautiful he would be!

'What's the problem, Lon?'

I just stood there for a moment, like a dimwit.

'I've... I've just had a premonition, Dave,' I sniffed as I began to chain the bike to his front drainpipe.

'Oh yeah?' He stepped back from the door and stood aside to let me in. His little fire was blazing and he went into the back to get the tea on. I

28

sat in that battered but comfy easy chair in the middle of all the piles of books.

Dave returned.

'So what's gonna go wrong?' he asked, putting a mug of his usual brew under my nose.

I took the mug from Dave and sipped at it.

A lot has been written about Dave's tea and it's all true.

'*Refreshing*' is one verdict.

'*Best used as paint stripper*' is another.

'*As dark and as corrosive as the stygian depths of the nightmare undersea city of R'lyeh*' is a third – my dad's.

Whatever, it's certainly a brew that's good for bringing your thoughts into focus.

'*Go wrong,*' he'd asked. Yes, usually premonitions meant something was going to go wrong. That wasn't the case here.

'I think I'm going to have a son.' I said.

Dave paused. 'Is that necessarily a problem?' he asked.

I looked down into the dark brown, took a bigger swig of it and felt my face twist into the lopsided thoughtful look I know I do. The one where my tongue pokes out of the corner of my mouth and that some people find oh-so-bloody-funny. Dave kept his face straight.

'I don't think so,' I said, 'not in itself. It came as a bit of a shock. Never really considered kids – thought there'd always be a lot of other stuff for me to do.'

'I've found there is,' Dave nodded.

'I had this picture come into my head last night, in a dream. But it was too clear to be that. It wasn't a face I could have made up. It looked like me, a bit, but... his teeth were more normal.'

'Idealised, then?'

'No. It wasn't idealised at all. It was too... just too real...'

Which was true.

'And he was really pissed off at me. He was about fifteen, I think. I hadn't known he was there and I'd been going on about... Hmm... Some sexual escapade or other I'd had. Anyway – this boy, I can remember him saying *"Oh, Mother, for God's sake!"* And he was looking furious. But his eyes... He had the loveliest eyes. The kindest eyes – *Oh!*'

I froze. Then I necked my tea. Dave could tell I needed a second mug, so he went to get one. I sat, silent, astounded and suddenly, entirely, in love. The fire crackled.

More tea in front of me; I sipped, gingerly.

' *"Oh"* what?' asked Dave.

'Oh I think I know who the dad is.'

'Ah.'

I looked up at him. He looked worried.

'It's not Warren Griefstick, is it?'

I felt myself smiling, tearfully. It concerned me that Dave wasn't smiling back.

'Because Neil was round a couple of hours back and we was trying to find out about his family. There's something you really need to have a look at.'

I didn't like the sound of that at all. I felt my eyes go very wide, begging to know and dreading to know.

Dave sat on an old piano stool he'd brought in from the back. 'I've searched all over for "Warren Griefstick" on the web. As far as I can find out, there's only been one.' He paused again. 'He died in 1982. He was two weeks old. And he was the son of Martin Icement's cousin.'

I thought about that.

'Well, that's what this Warren Griefstick was,' I said, finally. 'He told me. And I don't think this could have been any sort of identity theft: he'd have picked a less conspicuous name. And why mention he was related to Martin? It'd just make it easier to find him out.'

'True. But ghosts and demons don't get to be the parents of human children.'

'They do get to be the parents of demon children,' I said, smiling at old memories.

'They do. But this son of yours sounds very human.'

I didn't reply. I searched inside me for the sinking feeling of abandonment I get when some vision or prophesy is about to let me down – as they sometimes do. I felt no such sinking. Somewhere out there, I knew, was a real human Warren Griefstick. Father of my real human son.

Dave took me into the back and showed me family tree. I didn't pay much attention to most of it – which was maybe a mistake: if I had done, the things that I was soon to learn might not have come as such a shock. As it was, I had eyes only for three names: Anthony Griefstick, Martin's cousin, had married Frances Chessil in 1980, and they'd had one child, Warren Griefstick – this *other* Warren Griefstick – this *dead* Warren Griefstick.

But it couldn't be my Warren Griefstick; my Warren Griefstick was *alive*.

Once I got back home, I went to bed early in order to get stuck into *Castrate Them All!!!* and to have done with the bloody thing as soon as I could.

Up at seven the day after, full of vim and determination. Toast, hommous and black coffee down my neck, to the desk I did go. And I slew the thing. Every shite bit of sentence structure, every tiny misspelling spotted and put right. It was three thirty in the afternoon by then but, as I attached it to an email and sent it back to its perpetually seething author, I allowed myself a cheer. I changed into a tracksuit and went for a run.

I should have headed downhill to Stourbridge Junction Station, maybe done a circuit of Mary Stevens Park and dropped in on Ith and Dougie. Instead, I legged it down to Lye, where all the curry houses used to be and a couple still clung on. Then, over the main road towards Quarry Bank and Merry Hill.

My mind was still full of that beautiful boy. Of *my* beautiful boy. What particular shenanigan had I been recalling that had annoyed him so much? There were a few to choose from. Had it been that time when..? Yes, I thought it probably had been that time when...

Okay, out with it: I'd very probably been going on about how I'd given a moderately famous rock star a blowjob on the top deck of a bus in Lower Gornal and the bloke had told me – get this – that I'd brought him more pleasure than anything, second only to having his first two solo albums remixed in Five-Point-One Surroundsound by Steve Wilson. I mean. Wow. Five-Point-One Surroundsound by Steve Wilson...

It was the sort of thing I'd be prone to let slip after the odd glass of dry white wine but I could see that most fifteen year old sons would get a *BIT* on the narked side if their mothers started going on about it. Might not have been so bad if it had been in Upper Gornal.

A possible problem jerked me back to the here and now.

By the Cedric Hardwicke memorial, a bunch of Greyshirts. All male, all quite young, all scowling. Looking for a stray WiGIiE or some other poor sap to pick on. If I hadn't been focussed on other things, I might have changed my route to avoid them, but probably not: having been Charlotte's girlfriend, though a long time ago, I wouldn't have thought they'd have wanted to start anything with me. But the Ronsardist movement had grown over the past three or four years and the old directive that they should *leave Lon Kyle alone and ask no questions* had got lost in the internal mail.

I was about to learn that I wasn't immune to them anymore.

'Ey!' I heard somebody shout as they turned to face me. *'It's that lezzer bitch!'*

I kept running – straight past them – but inside, I was stunned.

It was obvious that *'Bisexual, actually'* wouldn't cut it as a comeback, still less my preferred *'Omnisexual actually'*. I'd be wasting my breath and wasting breath right now was a bad idea.

But however little they wanted to acknowledge Charlotte's sexuality, I'd never thought the Ronsardists were a shabby enough bunch of tyrants that they'd start giving gays or bis any actual grief.

Don't get me wrong – they were evil. Their original gaffer had been possessed by Lucifer and Lucifer's shadow still hung over the movement. Not everybody believed that but I *did* believe it and I was right. I'd done time as Charlotte's girlfriend so I knew my stuff here: I was *right.*

'She says she bin lickin' out the Gaffer!' shrieked that odious little voice again.

In denial, I thought, *in spades.*

Gasps and growls and howls of outrage. Followed by running feet.

Bugger it, they were *chasing me!*

Now this could have got really nasty because several of them would have clubs, truncheons and big sticks. One or two might even have knives. But the thing was, none of them were in that great a condition. They were younger than me, none older than twenty, but they all looked like they stayed away from gyms, swimming baths and even long walks. Greggs, Mackie Dee's and the kebab house were more likely haunts.

'Lyin' lezzer bitch!' yowled one chubby teenage fascist.

There was a crash of breaking glass, a dog started barking and somebody swore.

One of the Greyshirts must have tried lobbing a stone at me but his aim had been well wide of the mark and it had ended up taking out a front window. I'm not saying everyone in Thorns Road is a hard bastard but it's not a place where you want to go smashing people's windows randomly; the Greyshirts might soon have more distraction than they could handle. Still, I kept running; courtesy of all those large mixed kebabs and cheese'n'onion bakes, I was outpacing them. Better yet, half way between Lye and Merry Hill, Thorns Road goes uphill at quite a tick and I sensed at least half of the little fascist fatties gaspingly, coughingly giving up.

The mature thing to do would have been to carry on running until I was at the top of Quarry Bank. The mature thing to do would not have been to turn round and yell *'Charlotte Ronsard snogs my ginger fun fluff because it's fucking delicious!'*

But, you know, sometimes you can't help yourself.

Anyway, once I'd got that out of my system, I turned and carried on running. By the time I'd reached the top of the hill, I'd lost them.

All the same, they'd chucked a stone at me. And I was pretty sure about the clubs, truncheons and big sticks.

What had I said about 'hesitating to call myself a feminist'? Bugger that, when *Castrate Them All!!!* came out, I wanted a signed copy. And I might even offer to help sharpen the knives.

Around the corner was The Bull and Bladder, aka The Vine, a big brewpub where there'd be a good chance of bumping into Andy or possibly even Dougie, so I stuck my nose in. It was still very early in the evening and there was no one in that I knew, but Andy lived just round the corner and he was usually back from work by now so I dropped him a text.

I had a thirst on me and owed myself a few carbs. The only bitter the place did was their own, Batham's, a stickysweet honey-coloured goo which rotted your teeth worse than Ribeena and the mild was a bit too sweet as well, so I got myself a half of cider. These days I mostly drank cider in halves: doing so saved quite a lot of embarrassment. Andy rang me back.

'I've had a bit of bother with some Greyshirts,' I told him.

There was a worried-sounding pause.

'Come round mine' he said, eventually.

'Sure?'

'Yes. Just come. Now. Don't say any more. Not in public.'

I looked around me. The bar was harshly lit and hard-floored. People were talking loudly, some drunkenly, but there were no Greyshirts. And there was none of the finger-wagging sullenness you got from their sympathisers in places where beer was sold.

Was it getting to the stage when you had to watch what you said anywhere?

I finished the cider and went.

Andy lived on the second floor of a low-rise block of flats. I groped my way up a flight of steps, poorly lit and enclosed by concrete. He opened up before I had a chance to ring his doorbell.

We went into the kitchen and he put the kettle on. 'What happened?' he asked.

I told him. There was some quiet jazz on in the background. – European by the sound of it; Jan Garbarek, Arild Anderson maybe – Andy had a soft spot for that sort of stuff. Like the Batham's, it was a bit sweet for my taste.

'What were they like?' he asked, when I'd finished. I told him. I laughed a bit as I did so. He didn't.

'I think,' he said, finally, 'that you should wear a hat more. Your hair stands out too much.'

I didn't take that the wrong way. I knew Andy loved my hair.

'That's tough,' I said. 'I don't like covering myself up.'

'I know,' he sighed, 'but the Greyshirts were a nasty enough lot when Harry was running them. Now they've gone right downmarket: there's goons from the old BNP, the EDL and all that lot drifted into them. I don't think they've got anything against gingers yet – though they would have if they thought they were running short of buggers to persecute. Some of them had to swallow very hard over the blacks and Asians you get in the Greyshirts – at least Harry was no racist. But now they're looking for new sorts of victims. You just saw how much they're in

34

denial about Charlotte.'

'How do they manage that?' I asked, 'She's hardly ambiguous...'

'They manage it like the three bloody monkeys but they've got it in for gays – gays and bis – big time. I know it's been a while since you were with their boss lady but you've never denied it. So soz, love, you've crossed their radar. That's why you should wear a hat. Your hair stands out a mile and I don't know another ginge with so much of it.'

I smiled at him but he didn't smile back; he was frightened.

'I remember,' I said, 'it wasn't so long ago the Greyshirts were passing for a harmless neighbourhood watch group...'

'They were never that. You know they were never that. But it's not 2010 anymore, Lon. The next general election – and that's going to be sooner rather than later – is gonna put a Ronsardist government in – not a coalition with what's left of the Tories but a full-on Ronsardist government. Charlotte's going to be in Number 10 and *that* means...' (He paused and massaged his temples) '...you could be somebody they'd like to see the back of. If there's a fire at your place, it'd only need to look vaguely like an accident for nobody to want questions asked.'

He'd got up as he was speaking and now I felt something soft and warm land in my lap. It was a black woolly hat – a big one, like the ones rastas use to keep their dreads in. Way bigger than the little orange thing I'd left at home. I tried it on and looked around for a mirror. There wasn't one: Andy underrated his own looks.

'Trust me: you're beautiful,' he said and I got a smile out of him at last.

'It's bloody lucky for you, though,' he went on, 'that you've got a house in Glasgow. As soon as they name a date for the next election, get yourself north of the border sharpish; they've already put up a fence; it'll be minefields and machine gun towers before you know it.'

'Yeah... I guess it will be.' I laughed, involuntarily. 'I'm sorry, I just can't get over the idea that my ex – *my ex*, for God's sake, is going to landmine the Scottish Border! I've laundered her knickers – and her socks. I know what her farts smell like! Pretty bloody toxic, if you're curious. It just seems...' I shrugged.

'The wall's already going up, love. And it'll be the same with the Welsh, if the vote goes that way next month...'

I pulled my new hat over my eyes and I groaned. Goddess of goddesses, how I fucking *groaned*!

It was a very cosy hat, though, I told myself.

I was still wearing it when my phone went off on the way home. I'd decided to go the long way round, down Delph Road and Brettell Lane, then through Stourbridge. Plenty of friendly bolt-holes if I was targeted again. I answered.

'Hi Dad.'

'Good evening, Babalon. Have you been threatened at all this evening?'

Dad could be a prat in more ways than I'd ever want to go into, but his claims of clairvoyance had a hit rate high enough to strain anyone's faith in coincidence.

'Only by a bunch of kids.'

'Kids?' His voice had that insistent edge. He wasn't buying my attempt to play it down.

'Yeah. Teens. Greyshirt wannabes.'

Bugger it! I thought, *I didn't want to let that slip out!*

Of course, he was on it like a sodding ninja.

'Ronsardists, then?'

'No! No! Just a bunch of little prats trying to be Greyshirts...'

'I shall speak to Charlotte about this.'

'Da-ad!' I caught my voice sounding like that of a whining teen and I cursed myself.

'I always thought she treated you shabbily.'

'Dad, please!'

'Dumping you when it became politically convenient to do so...'

'Dad, that isn't how it happened!' It certainly wasn't; my thing with Charlotte had been back in '05, six years before she'd inherited her dad's role as Kingswinford's favourite fascist.

'And I will certainly not permit my own daughter to become the victim of homophobic abuse.'

'Dad – *really* – I'm alright...'

'I will go and see Charlotte tomorrow.'

And he bloody well would, too. I could see him practicing his patent 'Crowleyan' Hard Stare in the mirror all night. It was a good Hard Stare, I had to admit – enough to freak the shit out of most people. But it would not freak the shit out of someone whose dad had believed himself to be –

36

depending on what mood he was in – either the Devil himself or a Knight of the Round Table. People with dads like that are immune to any amount of Chaos Magick or Thelemic Freakoutery. Charlotte Ronsard would be quite unmoved – just pissed off.

'You should be proud of your bisexuality, Babalon.'

'I am, Dad, but...'

'As I am of mine.'

'Yes, Dad, but...'

'Bless you, Babalon.'

'Bless you, Dad.'

And he rang off.

Well: I'd gone down to a pretty resounding defeat there, hadn't I? Bugger it!

I began to internally flagellate myself with imaginations of Dad, showing up at Ronsardist HQ in Birmingham – they'd not long moved to a posh new place next to Snow Hill Station, all plate glass, shiny chrome bits and tooled-up security. There he'd be in his black coat and his black hat, straight-facedly assuring whatever hatchet-faced goon happened to be on the door that 'Ms Ronsard will be in no doubt of the necessity of speaking to me.' Well, it was the organisation's most public location so they wouldn't want to beat the crap out of him there and then – but duffings up happened to anyone who made life awkward for Charlotte. I could see Dad getting put on the list for a seeing-to – especially if he actually did get to talk to her. And he was an old chap now, though he was the last person to be told as much. They could wind up killing him even if they didn't particularly want to.

Unhappily, I jogged home.

The following day, not very much was achieved. I was torn between *Concrete Rectum* and, in a similar sort of vein, the memoirs of an Alan Garner fan who was also a proctologist: *The Bowel Service*. By about five, I'd had enough, so I got on my bike and pedalled over to Dad's new place in Romsley.

I let myself in. He wasn't about. Neither was his cat, Mithridates – large, fluffy, ginger and surprisingly good natured.

Now my place was a mess. Dad's place was a mess. Both of our places were the kind of bomb-sites even a couple of inveterate hoarders can't put together without a few years on the job. But his outdid mine. By a fair old bit. I sighed at the hefty pile of brown envelopes behind the front door. Opening a few – quite guiltlessly, because Dad would just see it as evidence of what a rebel he still was – I found final demands from gas, electric and water, as well as a court summons over unpaid council tax. Typical Dad. While I was waiting for the bugger to turn up, I made the necessary phone calls and lightened my current account by slightly under a thousand quid. At times like this, I was glad Angus and Cynthia had sorted me out the way they had. I stuffed the reminders, summonses and envelopes into my big brown hemp bag. No, I was not going to let Dad know the favour I'd done him: he wouldn't see it that way at all. Utility bills and all such demands were fine old excuses for acting the martyr and he'd be in a terrible sulk that, not for the first time, I'd deprived him of a chance to play Hamlet at the magistrates' court.

I did love Dad. He made me feel, compared to him, like something so boringly normal I could have come straight out of Kingswinford, and *I* didn't get to feel that way very often.

The purr of a taxi drawing up outside and I turned to the window. The streetlight here was pale and silvery. I could see Dad, paying the driver with something of a flourish (he paid for most things with at least a tiny bit of a flourish) and the driver was smiling: 'flourish', in this context, would include a fiver or so tip. He attempted to stride confidently up the path, having sensed my presence, as he always did. But the poor old sod's knees weren't all they'd once been and he'd clearly had a few so, while he wasn't quite 'waddling' or 'staggering', his locomotive dignity lacked a lot of the mythic grandeur to which it aspired.

'You've been on the piss,' I told him. 'In the Puke.' (Pub not really called 'The Puke' – though the yeast-thick stuff they served could be relied upon to have such results, especially on Dad's octogenarian insides). 'I hope you've stuck to the lager.'

'Very largely, my dear, very largely.' Which meant he'd also had a couple of bottles – at least – of Trappist looney juice, which would send his blood sugar into a potentially dangerous orbit and have him rushing to the Big White Telephone before too long; could a messy accident be averted in the meantime?

And indeed, his face suddenly turned Procul Harum. Knowing the drill by now, I turned him round and steered him to the downstairs bog, taking his hat and coat off as we went. He was thirty-odd centimetres taller than I, despite the stoop he'd acquired over the past five years, but steering him wasn't difficult: Mom had been able to do it easily. It seemed amazing now that, in the sixties and seventies, so many Kaotick disciples had been prepared to follow him off the edges of so many psychic cliffs. Still, he'd looked the part, back then – looked drop dead gorgeous, to tell the truth, and he exuded that weird sort of confidence that's so easy to fall for – so easy to confuse with infallibility.

I closed the bog door after him and went to the kitchen to get the kettle on as the ralphing started.

I made the tea the way Dave Calper taught: no prisoners. I could hear Dad splashing his face at the sink as I plonked a mug on the kitchen table, together with a pint of cold water from the tap.

He came out of the bog, still ashen, and sat down in the kitchen. 'Well,' I asked him, 'how did it go with Charlotte?'

He looked annoyed. He'd wanted to enlarge upon other matters. But he knew I was worried about him.

'She was charm itself,' he said, in a voice implying surprise that I thought she might have been anything else.

'*Really?*'

'Really. I was shown to her office as soon as she realised who I was. She is still in love with you, Babalon.'

No way was that going to be true. No – absolutely no way. There were quite a few of my exes who were still ga-ga about me: Ith, definitely, and her brother Paul would've been too, if his big strapping missus had left him any sex-drive to spare. But Charlotte? Nah, not Charlotte.

'She took details of the incident and will ensure there will be no recurrence.'

I felt a bit chilled at that – I didn't allow myself to wonder why.

I probed a little more but all I got was the Dad version: every detail tending to emphasize his own importance.

Eventually, we wandered into the front room and drank tea. Mithridates, who had come in through the catflap, plonked himself on my lap and purred, insanely loudly.

I thought I caught something funny out of the corner of my eye.

Mithridates, apparently seeing it too, leaped up on to Dad's desk and sat on a book, looking a bit belligerent.

What was it? Something to do with the book?

I went over and attempted to shift cat off book, curious to see what it was. Mithridates was most reluctant to be shifted, going all claws-out-and-fluffy-starfish on me when I finally hauled him off, before flouncing into the kitchen, protesting meowlingly.

'Oh,' I said, disappointed, once I got a clear look.

It was only Dad's copy of *The Tibetan Book of the Dead*, something I'd tried to get through several times over the years, without yet reaching the hundred page mark.

But for a moment, I'd thought there was something funny about the title.

Dad had gone quiet. I knew without looking that he'd have spotted that something spooky might be going on and he'd be watching me, keen to note anything he could characterise as otherworldly.

The title had changed – or had seemed to.

For an instant, it hadn't been *The Tibetan Book of the Dead*; it had been *The Tibetan Book of...* of what?

I turned my mind off but it wouldn't come. I wasn't sure, but I thought it might have been a name. I didn't know whose name. Or what name. But I knew it was a name I'd looked at recently – looked at but taken little notice of. And now forgotten completely. What was this all about? I seemed to be on the verge of remembering... something. I'd been screaming at someone to not do something. I caught the words *'Not his eye!'* in my mouth and coughed, painfully.

Had I dreamt this? No. Not dreamt.

Perplexed, I sat back down and, almost immediately, Mithridates was back in my lap, purring thunderously. Dad had remained quiet – as he sometimes did when he was thinking up a new spell or ritual.

'Lon,' he said, eventually.

Mithridates abruptly stopped purring, sensing my astonishment: Dad never called me 'Lon'. Any kind of shortening of the name he'd given me he felt as a transgression. 'Babz', the abbreviation I'd used now and then in my teens, he'd put up with, rightly sensing it was just a bit of fun. 'Lon', the shortening I'd hit on at eighteen, he'd been less happy about, understanding it would be more likely to stick around. For why would anyone wish to abbreviate so mythic a name as Babalon? It was the name of a being who would invoke demon brothers and inaugurate pleasure domes! Patiently, I'd countered that just-plain-'Lon' was the name of a being who would phantom the opera or turn into the werewolf. Or even get to tend the rabbits. Dad had looked really pained at that.

After a very strange pause, Dad spoke again:

'Do you know if Octavia Tolland is still alive?'

I was quiet for a moment. This was touching on things we both found painful.

'She changed her name, Dad,' I replied, 'to Shirley. Then she married Martin Icement. You know, the bloke who…'

'Yes, yes. I know. But what happened to… to Shirley?'

'Well, she was mixed up with Harry Ronsard when he was getting the Greyshirts started. When he got ill and handed it over to Charlotte, Shirley took it very badly. Martin – and Alice their daughter – had both just died but Shirley was making out that didn't really bother her. Lee was killed not long after. It must have all got a bit too much. She's been in a mental home ever since. In pretty much the same state as Harry: nobody can put a name to what's wrong with either of them, although shock must be a big part of it, in both cases. But they can hardly move and you can't get a word out of them. So she's still alive, yes, but probably not for much longer. The Ronsardists are pushing for some new legislation to have folk in her state put to sleep. I don't suppose they'll do it to Harry, of course, but Shirley…' my voice trailed off.

Dad's features screwed up. He inhaled sharply, swallowed, then said 'That could have happened to Ith.'

My head didn't know where this was all going – probably because it didn't want to. My guts were way quicker on the uptake and knotted up in terror.

Ith, now Dougie the drummer's other half and the mother of their sons, was a self-defence teacher and martial artist able to put her fist through a brick wall. Sixteen years ago, she had been my lover for six beautiful months. Thirty two years before that, as a child, she'd been brought up in the household of a group of outrageous occultists and ritual magicians – a group that had included my dad and her pa (it was always 'Pa', when Ith talked about her biological father: 'Dad', for her, meant her adoptive

41

father, Pastor Maitland).

Like us, our fathers had been lovers. In that group, everybody shagged everybody else. Pretty much. Not Ith – she'd only been eight or nine, so not Ith, obviously…

Oh.

Hang on, I could see where this might be going.

And I really *really* didn't like it.

Arthur Tolland had been in that group too. Shirley Icement's father, he'd also been a politician, a journalist and a notorious child-abuser.

But hang on…

'Dad, Ith told me the group split before Tolland had a chance to touch her. She was okay…'

'She was,' said Dad, 'but that wasn't the plan. That wasn't *my* plan…'

I felt horribly numb.

'I,' he admitted finally, 'brought him into the group. Tolland. And the other one – Mervyn. I brought them into the group and *I knew what they were!*'

My mind sprang to life and made all the connections. Convictions and traditions from any number of occult places fitted together like a bloody great jigsaw.

First thing: Ith hadn't just been the daughter of one of the group members; she'd been the sister of The Moonchild, of The Demon who Shone with The Warm Gold Light, and thus she was herself a semi-supernatural being – one of close to godlike significance. That's what Dad had believed. That's what Ith's pa had believed.

Second thing: Transcendental Illumination, the Knowledge and Conversation of the Holy Guardian Angel, the Obtaining of the Adept's One True Will, the Ascension to the Topmost Sphere of Paradiso, the Activation of the Eighth Circuit of the Brain…

And all the stuff that's really the same feverish attempt to put into words what is essentially – not just beyond words, but beyond the very Knowable…

How do you attain it?

All the sources agree: you attain it through shock or near-death experience.

So: if you've got yourself a potential divinity, all ready to start shining her light on to the Earth just as soon as she's achieved Illumination for herself, and you know that the pathway to such Illumination is through shock or near-death experience, what are you going to do?

You're going to place your little Goddess in the path of a couple of predatory kiddy-fiddlers because – boy-oh-boy – getting raped at nine meets anybody's definition of a shock or near death experience.

Knowledge and Conversation of the Holy Guardian Angel guaranteed!

On the other hand, it might just get the poor little sod banged up, a gibbering heap, in a mental asylum for the rest of her days, as had happened to Shirley Icement.

As might have happened to Ith. Who I knew I still loved.

'Oh,' I said. 'Oh you prat.'

'Yes,' said Dad.

'Oh you stupid fucking arsehole!'

'Yes.'

'Stupid fucking wanker!'

'Yes.'

I breathed in and out for a while longer. Then I wondered about Ith's dad:

'Did Alex know about this?'

'No. Of course not.'

I sighed. If it had been otherwise, I'd have needed to chuck every copy I had of Alex Chaplain's novels on to the bonfire: consign to the flames my favourite fictional character, Karnelia Diabolus, and her villainous uncle.

'When did you… when did you begin to see… what a fucking tosser you'd been?'

'Your mother had just died. It was thought you'd come to live with me. I was… terrified. I did not think myself remotely trustworthy when it came to taking care of anyone so young…'

Oh great. Dad's conscience had caught up with him just in time for him to get me made homeless. At fourteen. And pretty soon I'd shacked up with a house full of sweaty bikers (male, hairy and reeking of engine oil) in Giggetty Lane Wombourne. Where I'd probably have stayed until they tired of me constantly quoting Dion Fortune, if a certain friendly local book dealer hadn't offered to let me kip on his manky old easy chair

43

among all the piles of Barbara Cartland. Offered to let me kip there with a total lack of interest in compensatory sexual favours that had bewildered me completely.

'I don't know what Ith's going to do if I tell her,' I said.

'I told her sixteen years ago. She'll have assumed I told you long since, though she once said you'd kill me if I did. Still, I *should* have told you: I have been a coward.'

'You told her?'

'Yes. Have you not noticed, she has been strongly advising people not to trust me for many years?'

'Oh. Yeah.'

'And invariably referring to me as a stupid fuckwit?'

I nodded. It was true. I thought long and hard as I stared at this man who'd tried so absurdly to do things by the book. Because he had, you see. He had loved Ith so much he had believed her a goddess. And he had done his best to help her attain the godhood to which he believed she was entitled. Plough through everything Aleister Crowley or Langdon Tremayne ever wrote, you won't find a word to suggest that what Dad had intended might not have been absolutely in Ith's best interests – as well as a brilliant piece of occult science.

Which reminded me…

'Dad?' I asked, after a while.

'Yes?' It was the faintest of whispers.

'You know that talk on Crowley you're going to be doing in Malvern?'

'Yes…'

'Will there be a question and answer session at the end?'

'I… mean there to be…'

'Because, if I come to it, I'm going to be asking questions.'

'It is right that you should do.'

'They're going to be fucking hard questions, Dad.'

'It is right that they should be, my love'.

Mithridates purred a metal riff.

***

Warren Griefstick… When was I going to see him again?

Tricky enough, as we'd not swapped addresses, phone numbers or emails. Would I have to wander St Paul's churchyard until he turned up?

That'd be just like me, I guess: Babalon Kyle: the girl who hangs round graveyards, expecting to pull.

And of course, a few days later, I pulled. In the graveyard. Again.

Well, not exactly – but the person I was hoping for did quietly appear from behind a big tree. Mouth open, eyebrows raised – he'd not been expecting to bump into little Lon at all.

'You again,' he said.

'Me again,' I said.

I stepped over to him and put the flat of my hand on his chest (not as firm as I wanted; I was going to get him into a gym sharpish). In need of toning or not, though, he was certainly solid. Not a ghost.

His surprise had turned to puzzlement.

'Just checking,' I said.

'Oh?'

'That you're not a ghost.'

'Oh.'

'You can't be too careful.'

'Guess you can't. But I'm definitely not. A ghost.'

'I can tell that.' I prodded his chest and upper arms a bit. He didn't seem to mind.

'Though there's a fair few of 'em in the books I write: they tend to hang around stone circles and megaliths making moaney groaney noises like a downbeat dark ambient album and prophesying doom.'

'Oh, of course – your fantasy trilogy. Sold any more?'

'One on kindle last week. But I've decided to start a new one, so it won't be a trilogy very much longer.'

'That often happens.'

'Yeah. I thought *The Crusade of X'Vath!* – that's capital ex-apostrophe-capital vee-ay-tee-aitch-exclamation mark – I thought that had wrapped up all the loose ends. But I've been thinking about Greek tragedy, lately...'

'As you do.' *(Don't you just!)*

'As you do. And I remembered that the Greeks always used to follow their tragic trilogies with a funny play – so I'm going to do something along the same lines. It's going to be called *Bad Mullett of the Dark Lord.*'

My encouraging him in such a project would do nothing to enhance his social acceptability among normals. But sod normals.

'Tell me more,' I said.

'Well, in the new one, the Dark Lord of X'Vath – who's not taken on human form since way way back in the back story – he's released from captivity but, this time, the forces of good are ready for him and banish him through a gap in the space-time continuum. Problem is, four of our heroes are accidentally dragged through after him and they find themselves stranded with him in a new unknown plane of reality. Which is, of course, our plane of reality. There's Prince Virtue, Princess Chastity...'

'I dislike those two from the word go.'

'...plus Buggles the Rock Gnome and Donglebury, the crappest bard in the whole of the Kingdom of X'Vath – who's narrating.'

'Sounds more promising.'

'And, along with the Dark Lord, who's now taken on human form...'

'With a really bad haircut, I assume.'

'Exactly. Well, they all find themselves in Stourbridge.'

'*Stourbridge?*'

'Stourbridge. And what do you do if you're a bunch of refugees from a magical plane of existence who suddenly find themselves banished through the inter-dimensional portal to Stourbridge?'

'Go on. Tell me.'

'You form a proggie rock band, of course.'

'Ah! I see! *Ye-erst*, that does seem logical.'

'Exactly. All previous hostilities have to be set aside. A proggie rock band is what it has to be. With Prince Virtue on lead guitar, Princess Chastity on flute and keyboards, Buggles the Rock Gnome on bass, Donglebury the Bard on rhythm and...' he paused for effect '...*the Dark Lord on drums!*'

'With gatefold sleeves?'

'Definitely.'

'Roger Dean artwork?'

'Him or Hugh Syme.'

'And 180 gram virgin vinyl pressings?'

'As virgin as Princess Chastity herself.'

'Right! I think I'm getting where you're coming from...'

'And, of course, I'm going to have to put in a load of local colour. In fact, it's a bit weird me meeting you here because I was working on a chapter where they play support at a couple of gigs. One's when they're on before The Death of Wallenstein at the Maverick. I was going to ask you if it was okay?'

'Of course! Hey though... Now you mention it, we did have a support act when we played there who... Well, they did look a bit like the guys in your book... Must have been late 2004. One of them brought in a couple of swords...'

'A falchion and a spatha?'

'Yes! How did..? Is it going to be in the book?'

'It was.'

'He said it was a part of the act. But I remember... he gave them away to some bloke in the audience. We were all kind of freaked out by that. Especially since... this bloke looked a bit grim, to be honest. I didn't know who it was till much later...'

He didn't ask. I think I'd spooked him a bit. I looked up through the skeleton hands of the trees into the concrete murk of the January sky.

'It was Charlotte Ronsard's dad,' I said, 'Harry.'

'Good God! Isn't he supposed to have killed..?'

'No *"supposed"* about it.'

We wandered out of the church yard and took a couple of rights, heading down Avenue Road towards Rowley Regis station, with the railway cutting between us and the graves we'd just left.

'I'm not sure I feel up to putting that in my book,' he whispered.

'Change the names. Or at least, change Harry Ronsard's name.'

'Definitely. I quite like not getting my legs broken.'

'That'd be if you were lucky.'

'Phew. And I'd intended this one to be more light relief than anything else! It's the first one of mine Dad's ever liked...'

Anthony Griefstick: Martin's cousin...

'What's he like about it?'

'Well – he's relieved this one has a few laughs in it. He's always telling

47

me my stuff's way too… Hmm… *"Portentous"* is the word he uses. But I think there's something else about this one: he's been asking me about the idea of somebody – well, five somebodies – being stuck between two different worlds. It's really got under his skin. Funny, because he's never been much of a one for that sort of thing. He's always been into Arnold Bennett, Alan Sillitoe, that sort of stuff…'

'Oh dear!'

'No, I don't complain. They've been very patient with me, have Mum and Dad. Granny Kidderminster was always telling them I needed a boot up my bum… And what with Wendy doing so well…'

'Wendy?'

'My sister Wendy. She did biochemistry at Warwick. She works on vaccines. Saves lives, does my sis. She's moved up to Scotland, things being what they are, like most of the high-fliers. Me, I pay the rent working behind the till at Cradley Heath Tesco's…'

He didn't sound bitter. Or disappointed with himself. But there was more to tell.

We'd got to the end of Avenue Road so we crossed to the station, a one-floor thing about a century old that stands on a bridge across the tracks.

'I'm off to see *my* Dad, actually. He's doing a talk on Crowley in Malvern,' I said, looking in my purse for my bank card.

'Crowley? Now that *is* portentous!'

'Oh very definitely. Would you like to come and..?'

'Lon!'

I looked up. Warren Griefstick wasn't there. I'd heard his voice. I'd heard his voice shouting my name. But now I was alone on the platform. Alone – under a sky that swirled like the sound of a flute with a load of reverb. Something had taken him away from me. Something or someone. I didn't waste time on loss or fear – though the temptation was there. Instead, I began to feel angry.

4: Dave Calper

I'd not seen Lon look so drained before. Seems rotten to say it but, as she and Andy were the youngest in the band – by a long way – we old gits sometimes relied on the pair of them to get the energy levels up.

I stood and offered her my seat.

'I met him again,' she said.

'Oh,' I said.

'He vanished,' she said, 'on the platform at Rowley Regis. I was on the way to go and listen to Dad's talk in Malvern. I'd met Warren in Blackheath. I was trying to persuade him to come with me. But he just vanished. I thought I heard him shout my name... As if I was the one who'd vanished...'

Well, I could have said that the thought of one of David Kyle's Aleister Crowley lectures would be enough to make a lot of people vanish abruptly. Just possibly, that might have been all that was going on. I didn't think so, though.

Time to stick a mug of something merciless under Lon's nose. She stared at the conker-brown circle of liquid and sipped it. Then she knotted her face into that 'clever' expression she did when she was working something out.

'He's not a ghost,' she pronounced, firmly. 'I poked him in the chest, like this...' She mimed doing so. 'and he was completely solid. Could do with a few months in the gym to get him toned up but he's completely solid.'

'Did he mind? Getting poked?'

'No.'

'And then he vanished?'

'Yes. Vanished. One minute there; the next minute – *poof !*– gone.'

'Blackheath,' I said, 'can be a funny place.'

'It can. He reminded me about a gig we did, at the Maverick, back in

2004 or 5. Remember that weird lot who supported us?'

'What? D'you mean The Magic Kingdom? They were a strange bunch.'

'Warren seems to think they might have been characters who'd escaped from a book he's written.'

I hadn't seen that one coming. Not even slightly.

'Did you know,' I said. 'the bloke the lead guitarist gave those swords to..?'

'I know. It was Harry Ronsard. Charlotte's got 'em now. She was wearing 'em last week when she had that meeting with the PM.'

'At Number10?'

'Yes...'

We sat, stunned to think that until quite recently, it'd have seemed incredible that someone could swan into a meeting with the Prime Minister, a couple of offensive weapons dangling openly from her belt. But that sort of thing just didn't come as a surprise anymore. And the look on the PM's face had been... Well, let's call it 'deferential.' Everybody knew who was going to be behind the big black door the same time next year. And nobody wanted to look as if they were bothered whether there'd be any more general elections after that. Nobody who wanted to stay in one piece.

'Twice, then, he's just vanished into thin air...' I said.

'Well... not exactly... It might have just seemed like it...'

The sound of Lon Kyle attempting scepticism was weird enough to be funny – or would have been if she hadn't been going to pieces. I couldn't help myself – I put my arms around her, gave her a hug and found myself thinking that, if Starshine's kid had lived, I'd've loved it if she'd turned out like Lon. David Kyle, poncey, self-adoring twat, really didn't have a clue what a lucky bastard he was and, if I got to hear he'd been on the phone giving her a hard time about missing his bleeding lecture, I'd serve him his own bollocks on toast.

'I think...' she said, 'I think it might have something to do with the Sefirot.'

I sighed. The Sefirot: the symbolic spheres on the Tree of Life in Jewish mysticism: when people are in serious bother, you often find they get into that stuff.

'How d'you mean?'

'Well. You know the churchyard where I met him... You know it's right next to the railway line? The Birmingham to Worcester?'

'Ye-es.'

'Well... It's the stations between Snow Hill and Blakedown that I've been wondering about. I think they might somehow be analogous to the Sefirot.'

'Oh.'

Oh dear.

'And if I'm right... The power you could access there... I'm wondering if it could...' She sighed. 'I don't know...'

'Analogous how?' I asked, appalled and fascinated all at once. It wasn't that I thought she was going bonkers. Well, no more bonkers than me. But, unless you're Dante or somebody, all that Jewish mystical stuff is usually best left to the rabbis: people who start brooding over the Tree of Life have a habit of getting themselves into deep abysses.

'Well,' she said, 'if you start at the top – with that Great White Light that surpasses all understanding...'

'Surpasses all understanding? You're saying that's Birmingham Snow Hill?'

'Exactly.'

'Hmm...' I began to wonder if she might be on to something: Birmingham often struck me as a place that surpassed all understanding.

'Then there's Kether itself: the Infinite light of the Creator.'

'Jewellery Quarter? I see...'

'Then, moving down, there's Chokmah: Wisdom and Inspiration.'

'The Hawthorns? I can imagine there are quite a few West Brom fans who'd be with you on that one...'

'Oh definitely! Then comes Binah: the Divine Female that gives birth to reason and the emotions...'

'Well, I have been known to get emotional while waiting at Smethwick Galton Bridge, especially on the lower level...'

'You do get a lot of cancellations down there,' she said.

'Yeah. And it takes a fair amount of reasoning to work out which lift shafts go to which platforms if you're not used to it. So I guess there might be something to that one and all...'

51

'There might indeed! Then comes the big one! What comes between Binah and Chessed?'

'Well, that's The Abyss, so I... Wait a minute – of course!'

We spoke it as one: *'The disused Smethwick West Station!'*

Whole occult philosophies had been founded on parallels far less overwhelming than this. We gaped at each other.

'Then...' she said, hesitantly, 'then there's Chessed, kindness...'

'That'd be Langley Green. They do make a nice cup of tea at Oldbury Rep.'

'And then Geburah, discipline – particularly self-discipline...'

'Rowley Regis...'

'Then Tipareth – Beauty.'

'Old Hill? Yeah, that's a lovely place in the summer, when there's some leaves on the trees...'

'Then it gets weirder still. Cradley Heath would be Netzach, endurance and long suffering.'

'Cradley Heath. Yeah, what with the Chainwomen's Union and all that tradition – but it's suffering to some purpose. What about Lye?'

'Hod – Eternity. Lye was the last place in Europe to be Christianized – in the 1830s. And think about the way they were still living in those pre-Roman mud huts right up until the 1920s. Time does seem to get stretched out a bit in Lye. Yesod's the Sefirot of Dreams and visions, of course.'

'Stourbridge Junction.'

'Exactly, and given how many people in Stourbridge are going round off their tits on something or other...'

'Yeah. There's definitely a parallel there...'

'But, for me, the big problem is Malkuth.'

'The physical world? Yeah. I guess most people's problems do tend to revolve around that one.'

'I know. But it's not just that. What I mean is – which station is it?'

'How'd you mean?'

'Is it Stourbridge Town or is it Hagley?'

'Hmm...'

'I mean, once you get past Hagley and you're in Blakedown, then you've left the conurbation, so it's safe to assume that one represents some entirely different mode of being. But are we living in Stourbridge Town Malkuth – where the line stops dead at the bus station – or are we in Hagley Malkuth?'

'You talking about parallel universes here?'

'No! Erwin's poor old cat stands for something that goes on all the time in every place. This is something more specific. It feels to me as if something has been done – or is being done or will be done – to the physical world as a whole, at a particular point in time. Something that's going to split the world in two. So we're talking about two very different modes of existence, two very different Earths.'

'Represented by two very different railway stations?'

'Yes! And it certainly feels to me as if things have been... made that way.'

'Are you saying that... one of these Earths – one of these Malkuths, one of these Sefirotic railway stations... has got Warren Griefstick in it..?'

'Yes!'

'...And the other one hasn't?'

Suddenly, she was in tears. *'Yes!'* she sobbed, desperately.

I thought for a bit, then looked at her as she snuffled into a paper tissue.

'We're going to have to play a gig,' I said.

She blew her nose and nodded.

'It's going to have to be an illegal one,' I added. 'Because whatever its position on the Tree of Life relative to either version of Malkuth – Hagley or Stourbridge Town – the Abyss is something your Warren's going to have to get across if we're going to contact him.'

'He must have been doing that both times he met me,' Lon said. And given that the Guardian of the Abyss is Choronzon...' Her face cleared of tears like a Christmas Tree lighting up. 'And the last time we heard from *him*...'

'He was trapped in a pretentious, arty-farty packet of pork scratchings,' I concluded for her, 'on the back seat of a bus headed for the nightmare undersea city of R'lyeh. So his ability to guard anything is going to be... seriously compromised.'

'That's how Warren's been doing it!' she cried. 'That's why he disappears whenever he tries, or even intends to go somewhere else – like Malvern...'

'Yeah. It's the proximity of that stretch of railway – a stretch of railway that's such a powerful symbol of the Tree of Life! That's what's made it possible! When you look at it, it's so obvious...'

'So, what you're saying is we play a gig on the platform of Smethwick West station?'

'It's the only way I can see of dealing with this.'

'You're right. Neil's missus is going to go spare when we tell her.'

'True enough. And we've got to keep this well hush-hush. The coppers wouldn't be keen on it and now it doesn't look like Charlotte's keeping her goons on much of a lead...' my voice trailed off. Lon just nodded sadly and I went on: 'Largely acoustic, I reckon, maybe bring along a couple of car batteries to power the practice amps.'

'My Korg doesn't drink much juice. I will need it: I'll want to use a lot of Martin's tapes.'

'Good idea. We'll do it on a weeknight, if possible – after the trains have stopped.'

'There might be a few goods trains coming through all night.'

'Just a few, though; most of them turn off at Stourbridge Junction and go over the viaduct.

'Which platform do we use?'

'We-ell...' I said, 'the westbound has the shelter...'

'There's not much left of that – the roof's long gone! Remember, the place was shut down when I was eleven or twelve.'

'Bleeding heck, yeah! Time flies! Okay: we use the eastbound – that's got the pedestrian access ramp. Might be easier to get down that way. I reckon, if we put up a black windbreak, facing towards the tracks, and ditch the lightshow...'

'We should definitely ditch the lightshow.'

'Yeah. There'd be a chance the train drivers wouldn't notice us! The old bill might never show up!'

'Dave... Thanks.'

'No problem, love! This is the sort of stuff that brings an old hippy git back to life! D'you know how many times I went to the Stonehenge Festival?'

'No. Can you remember yourself?'

'Er... Now you mention it, probably not.'

'Which is the way it should be.'

So we were going to play a gig. And, in the days that followed, it got so that I was stressing myself out over it something chronic. Of course, this was partly because it mattered so much to Lon and I was scared to death we'd muck it up for her. And partly because there was always the chance of bother from the Goons in Grey. But after a bit, I realised there was something more to it. On a simple level, I just wasn't having enough sleep. And such sleep as I got was interrupted by awakenings that had me gasping for breath and finding I'd done my best to tear the bedsheets to ribbons while I'd been zizzing. What dreams had been doing this to me?

I resorted to the old occult magician's trick of keeping a dream diary. Each time I woke up, I'd rack my brains to remember what I'd been dreaming about and scribble down every detail I could claw back.

To my complete lack of surprise, I found I'd been dreaming about the Stourbridge Shuttle. Now this is a train service that runs for about three quarters of a mile from Stourbridge Junction to Stourbridge Town – the shortest branch railway line in Europe, apparently. If you turn up at the Junction, you want to go into the town centre and you've not left your car at the Junction Park'n'Ride, you cross over to Platform One and you get on the Shuttle.

Time was – but this was before I lived round here – time was when the line went to Stourbridge Town, then on, via the gasworks, over a level crossing to the canal basin by the Bonded Warehouse, to offload coal on to the barges. These days, it's a passenger service only and it stops at Town Station – stops dead: there's a sturdy set of buffers and a solid brick wall to make sure it doesn't go any further. On the other side of the wall, you've got the shiny new bus station.

Until a very few years ago, they ran the service with a single, normal-sized passenger carriage but that involved hauling a lot of empty space outside peak hours so, more recently, they've been using those smaller LPG-powered tramcars that get rammed solid when people are on the way to work.

In my dream, I'd been riding on one of those tramcars.

It had been after dark and I'd come in on one of the big express services on its way from Marylebone to Kidderminster. I'd got off at the Junction

55

– I guess I meant to change to a bus at Town, which would drop me just outside my place on Brettell Lane.

I had the idea that I shouldn't have got off at the Junction – that I should have carried on through Hagley, Blakedown, all the way to Kidderminster, then changed to another to take me to Worcester or Malvern or anywhere!

Because this little tramcar was reality – this little tramcar was the world. And the world – this version of it – was about to hit the buffers.

And as we got to Town Station, I dreamt there was a flickering in the air and then, with absolute suddenness, the whole of the night sky disappeared; it just wasn't there anymore. And where that night sky should have been, stretching from horizon to horizon above the world, was something like the mouth of an unthinkably vast machine of bloody red and steely grey. It was lined with scarlet metal fangs like a shark's, each one bigger than a planet. Row after row of the things. Between these fangs were an infinity of smaller things – things that filled webs and maps of crevices and channels. Things that crushed, things that ground, things that burned. Things that annihilated absolutely. And the whole world – the whole Solar System perhaps – was being drawn into it. And maybe I saw the Moon collide with one of those scarlet fangs and shatter. Maybe I didn't. But I only glimpsed it for a fraction of a second before everything was over. For that tiny stretch of time, it had been as if I'd been looking up at a vacuum cleaner from the point of view of a microbe.

I really should have stayed on the train to Kidderminster.

Awake, I reread what I'd written and trembled and sweated.

A thing like a machine that had eaten the world – or swatted it aside – or sucked it up without noticing it was there…

That was it! That was what had really spooked me! It hadn't noticed we were there! It was so vast, it hadn't noticed an entire solar system…

Maybe it had just wanted to clear the space so it could build a shiny new bus station.

So: just a dream then? Or was Lon's knack for premonitions proving contagious?

I had it a few more times. Each time I tried to drag a little more understanding out of the dark. I ended up convinced that the version of the world that was going to end – the Stourbridge Town Malkuth – was the one in which Warren Griefstick had died aged two weeks.

But what about the other version?

My mind drifted to a memory of one morning the previous summer. Dougie had rung me the night before and asked if I fancied a drive over the Shropshire Summits to start my Sunday off? Sounded reasonable. It'd have to be an early start because he was going to pick up his son, Luke, who'd been camping overnight as far from light pollution as he could so as to have a butchers at something distant and awesome through his new telescope.

Lon referred to Luke as 'The Voice of Reason' when she was feeling well-disposed to him and as 'Urizen' when she wasn't – which had been quite often when he'd been about eleven and was going through a bit of a Richard Dawkins phase.

Just before eight, we got to the rocky spot where he'd been camping and the gold and silver sunlight was just the sort that I'd have said surpassed all understanding. Except that to do so would have provoked Luke into explaining the properties of solar radiation and his explanations usually left my understanding not so much surpassed as pulverised.

The lad was waiting for us and bloody hell, he was getting a big bugger. Not quite as tall as his brother but taller than his parents by a fair bit. He'd got his tent and stuff packed up and ready to go; he was full of vim and enthusiasm and showing no signs of having had just a couple of hours' kip on a stony chilly hillside after a night's stargazing. Oh, to be fourteen! We helped him load his stuff into the back of the motor.

And on the way back, Luke talked astrophysics at us. Frequently consulting the notes he'd made overnight. Between us, I think we 'got' about one twentieth of what he said. We nodded and said 'Ooh' or 'Ah' whenever we understood a bit.

Then he surprised me by asking if I could keep an eye out for books about Buddhism? 'The legit stuff,' he said, 'not the California crap. I think I'd like to get something like that for Mom at Christmas. Seems like it'd be her cup of tea.'

I laughed. 'There's some branches of Buddhism,' I said, 'that'd be more your cup of tea than you'd think. But I do know what you mean. I'll keep a look out.' – Which I had done. With eventual success.

And now I thought back to that morning, I got the feeling that, if my dream had meant anything, Luke would turn out to know what to do about it – or he'd know someone who did.

They'd get us on the train to Kidderminster.

5: Lon Kyle

I've been sitting in front of this screen for the past hour and a half, straining to think of words to describe Sarah Haines' face when I told her what we were thinking of doing. Her complete inability to process anything about it shone through clearly and unforgettably.

'Surely...' she began, then faded out.

'Surely...' she tried again. 'Surely this is all completely illegal?'

'Oh yeah,' I assured her. 'Dave thinks of it as a kind of mini-Stonehenge.'

Sarah had been to the Stonehenge Fest a couple of times in the late Seventies, with Dave and Neil *(Jammy cow! They sent the goons in to shut it down the year after I was born!)*. The first time, she thought she didn't like it. The second time, she was sure she didn't like it: it was the toilet facilities, not the music that had been the deciding factor.

'I wouldn't mind you getting arrested so much but what if you get picked up by the Greyshirts?'

'We'll be very discreet.'

'But why does it have to be *there?*'

'It's a Kabbalistic rite. Dave and I have discovered that Smethwick West Station corresponds to the Abyss, the lost Sefirot of the Tree of Life.'

She looked at me, closed her eyes, opened them again and looked at me a bit more. Then she sighed.

'I thought it might be something like that,' she said. 'Is your dad mixed up in this as well?'

'Well he wasn't but I had to tell him. It'll be tricky for him to get over the fence without doing himself a mischief. But he won't sit this one out, no way.'

'No: I don't suppose he will. And how about Ith's dotty brother?'

'Ooh! I hadn't thought of him! Thanks for reminding me!'

The Spirit of Albion. Also known as Paul Maitland. Formerly Head of Science at Lawnswood School. Now widely published author on Druidism and early Christianity. Then again, I wasn't sure his wife, Sharon, would be at all happy for him to risk getting in a scrap with Charlotte's mob... Hmm... I'd always done my best to keep on the right side of Sharon, ever since Paul and I had our brief and unwise thing. So maybe not Paul.

When I went round to Ith and Dougie's, Dougie was ecstatic at the idea and even Ith seemed okay about it.

'I'll come along,' she said. 'The Greyshirts won't give you bother if I'm there. Harry used to think we were the next best thing to them...' (She was talking about Stourbridge and North Worcestershire Women's Self-Defence, formerly the Stourbridge Women's Self-Defence Unit, which she ran and which had a few members besides her who could punch through your front door with their fists). 'But keep the volume down. Dougie can use brushes and the rest of you practice amps. I'll not have the poor locals woken up on a work night by anybody's ritual. Explain to me what it's all in aid of.'

I hadn't wanted to, but I did.

We sat in her back room in Stourbridge. Outside, I could hear happy, wordless, not-particularly-in-tune singing from the greenhouse in the garden. Upstairs, I could sense an utterly silent yet terrifyingly intense concentration on matters involving the speed of light. On the mantelpiece, still, were two porcelain dragons, the copper and the blue.

'Hmm,' she said, when I'd finished, 'it all sounds a bit familiar.'

Ith was supposed – not by herself, though definitely by me, by Dad and by a fair proportion of other folk who bought most of their books from 'Atlantis' – to be under the protection of something called a 'Demon Brother.' Who might, possibly, be the ghost of her real, birth-strangled brother. Or might be something else, vastly more arcane. I'd learned not to talk to her about it.

'Is this "*Warren*",' she asked, 'your "Demon Boyfriend", then?'

'No,' I said. 'He's solid. I've touched him. He's as solid as you or me. He just has a way of... *disappearing* from this world. Disappearing off to another one. I don't know how or why. I want to find out.'

Ith's mouth twisted and pursed with concentration. This wasn't

60

anything she could put in front of her astrophysicist son upstairs: there wasn't a shred of objective, verifiable evidence. But I'd convinced her, somehow, that it was different to the occult mysticism of which her father and mine had been and were devotees and with which she'd had an absolute and permanent fallout. She was prepared to give it the benefit of the doubt.

'Okay,' she said, slowly, 'give it a go and see if anything seems to happen.'

'Something will happen.'

'I bet it'll seem that way to you,' she smiled, 'but I bet it won't to me.'

She was right there: she'd meditated her way to a scepticism that guarded her from any number of old sufferings.

Potentially obstructive other 'arfs reassured, we got ready.

Late January, dry and freezing, was nearly ready to hand it over to cold and slushy February when we snuck up to the weed-choked fence that barred the way to the overgrown remains of the station. It was just across the road from its big, chunky and brutalist replacement, Smethwick Galton Bridge. Beyond the fence was a pathway, also mostly overgrown, leading down the side of a wooded cutting to the eastbound platform.

It was Sunday, close to midnight. Both Daves, Dad and Calper, were getting too old for this sort of stuff. No use telling them that, though.

There were plenty of pained noises – tooth-clenched snarls from Dad, louder *'Oo bugger it'*s from Dave – as we helped them over the fence. We couldn't have done it without Ith and three or four of her sturdier girls from the Unit. True to form, Dad tried turning the charm on with one of these and, unpredictably to everyone but to him, to Ith and to me, he seemed to have a success. He still reckoned he had it, the randy old bugger, and this was a lass who could bend a steel bar an inch thick. Ith would be warning her off him at the end of the night.

With their help, we'd got things mostly ready – including three car batteries – and Neil, sitting on a black Marshall monolith far too big to be mistaken for a 'practice amp' was already tuning up. Ith shot him a dirty look that demanded the thing be turned right down. He complied – people did with Ith.

We were mostly dressed in camo or black, and went quiet when anything drove by. There was a dark polythene marquee to keep the rain off, and just enough low lights to work with. These lights gave everything a warm, drizzle-jewelled glow. Between the marquee and the tracks we'd set up a big black windbreak so, with luck, the driver of any goods train wouldn't register us if he was concentrating on the tracks. Relief when Andy and Dougie were able to take the two transit vans we'd used to a nearby parking space. They were back in under five minutes.

Now, at last, we'd made ourselves sufficiently inconspicuous.

Of course, it was a tiny audience: Dad, Ith and her mates.

'Seven people,' said Andy. 'We've had smaller crowds at the Fizzle.'

'Everybody ready?' croaked Dave, looking up from his tuning.

Dougie was tweaking his snare a bit but he'd soon got that sorted. He'd brought a small kit: snare, floor tom, hi-hat and a crash cymbal. He'd got to the stage where he could do quite a bit with just those and the intricate pulse he started on the tom assured us this was going to be a good one.

'Are we recording this?' Neil asked.

I nodded at the little DAT machine I had set up.

Dougie went back to the pulse.

Andy's eyes fixed on him, rigidly. Then he put down the flute he'd been holding and picked up the bigger bass flute. He made a long, sad noise on it.

I turned to my Korg and brought up a sample I'd not used much; it made me nervous. I'd got it from what was perhaps the last cassette tape recorded by Martin Icement. It was the noise that, through Martin's son, had given birth to the paintings on the walls of the house where Charlotte had grown up – the noise that had, with those paintings, turned her father into Satan and, in doing so, given birth to the Greyshirts. It was the sound of the wind in the branches of Cally Wood.

Neil's response was almost tentative. He wouldn't want to try explaining to the missus what was going on here. Dave was more reassuring: there was a solidity, a reliability about the pattern he established that meshed with Dougie's more complex pulse. It almost seemed to hold my hand. Which I almost seemed to need. And even when both of them joined Neil and Andy in their looser abstractions, I could still feel that pulse.

But the sound of that wind...

Across the tracks, around the end of the windbreak, I could just make out the concrete passenger shelter on what was left of the westbound platform. The roof had partly collapsed and it was a desolate sight by day. By night, you'd not have noticed it if you weren't looking. I was looking: the darkness within was the darkness I'd been seeking. It was a special, final dark – one anyone 'sane' would have fled from. But I wanted it. I wanted it because I knew I had to get through it. I had to get through it because I had to reach...

Time stopped.

Completely – it happened between one of Dougie's beats on the tom and the next. But it was an eternity. And something in the darkness in the collapsed shelter folded in on itself, then opened out. And I saw...

I saw a sitting room. In a flat, I thought, because it was on a first or a second floor. I knew, somehow, that it wasn't very far from here – somewhere to the south west. There were three adults and an infant – a tiny baby in a crib. Two of the adults were in their twenties perhaps, or thirties. It seemed they were a couple. She was slumped in a sofa, apparently unconscious. There was a black halo around her – an aura of terrible depression. The other woman was older: it was hard to work out how old, because her face was so set, so rigid, but her hair was grey and her eyes were grey and she was holding a heavy rolling pin. And there was something wrong with her face, something not quite symmetrical. But this asymmetry did not disguise her resemblance to the man, who stood there as if poised between action and inaction. And I knew him: Tony Griefstick –Warren's father. And I was watching all this from a funny vantage point – as if I was somehow painted on to the headboard of the crib, the crib that had the feel of an Aztec temple or a wicker man. Horribly, I got the sense of being a god to whom a sacrifice was about to be made. And I could scream all I liked that I wanted no such sacrifice: my devotee could not hear.

Suddenly I knew there were two ways this was going to turn out – two entirely contradictory but equally real versions: a Stourbridge Town Malkuth and a Hagley Malkuth. And the older woman with the rolling pin was Tony's mother. And the tiny baby was Warren who I'd met in the graveyard, the father of my boy, of my beautiful beautiful boy.

And Tony's mother, carrying that heavy rolling pin, was coming closer to the crib. What had been her name? I strained to visualise what I'd glimpsed, but largely ignored, on Dave's computer screen – the ancestry website…

Janice Griefstick, née Janice Croviss.

Janice Croviss.

And I knew I hated her.

I knew I existed to destroy her.

I knew I must find a way of doing it, even if she was already dead.

That bitch, that slag, that evil piece of shit was the thing that would deny the existence of my beautiful boy!

I was still playing the Korg. The guys were looking impressed. But frightened too. I wrenched some bitter lines from the keyboard and the wind in the branches became shrieks and snarls and they were mine.

And Dougie started getting louder on the floor tom, started hitting the crash more often. And I looked across the track again but the vision was gone. It had told me what it needed to. I knew who I had to kill. The guys were trying to bring me back, trying to get some structure into the thing – not just a riff or a bass line but something complex and melodic that would show me the way home. I couldn't hear it – couldn't hear it through the rush of all the Janice Croviss blood I needed to spill, couldn't hear it through all the Janice Croviss guts I needed to rip out. The Korg kept screaming for me.

And, through the dark, at the back of the concrete shelter, I thought I saw a word. I couldn't make out what it was. I had seen it before, when on the train in daylight, but I had forgotten...

A soft, low note on the bass flute. Something to hold on to.

I began to steer the Korg back into reality – back into the person I wanted myself to be.

The patterns on the tom and the bass slowed and simplified. My own gales and tempests were subsiding. Then there was only the flute and the guitar and the melody they found together was surprisingly simple, surprisingly sweet, as they brought us all home.

Ith's arms were around me. They weren't the arms of the woman who'd been my lover. They were impossibly strong and almost frighteningly dedicated to my protection.

'Lon...' It was Dave. He was wiping the sweat from his bass strings with a yellow duster.

64

'Lon...' his eyes looked as concerned as Ith's arms felt.

'You aren't meant to be a killer, Lon.' There. He'd heard it in my playing. Everybody had.

'I don't think...' Andy suggested, 'I don't think we should put this out anywhere. Not just yet.'

'Nah,' said Neil. 'Not just yet.'

I could feel Ith nod in agreement as she let me go. Inhaling, I realised how tightly she'd been holding me.

I felt a rush of fury: *I was Babalon Kyle – placed upon the Earth to rip that bitchslag Janice Croviss' guts out with my teeth! To taste the blood and the shit of her shredded entrails and to feel the splintered and ground-up fragments of her bones on my tongue!*

Then Ith's hand was on my shoulder and it felt like a green and yellow wire. For a moment, I was free of vengeance, though I knew it'd be charging me up again soon enough.

It took us a long time to get things disassembled: we were like a bunch of zombies and didn't notice the way the minutes and seconds were stretching out.

By the time both the vans were full, we were cutting it very close with the Monday morning commuter trains. They'd be starting to do their stuff between Worcester, Birmingham, Stratford and London – and there'd be a lot of them. One or two of the least groggy passengers might well be able to spot a psychically damaged krautrock band staggering around trying to lug their gear up the embankment.

In fact, at the very moment Neil finally closed the door of the second van, we heard the hissing of the rails and, round the bend from Langley Green, came the first of the morning.

'That was close,' Dave sighed.

Dad had ordered himself a taxi and I had to wait with him for what turned out about half an hour. Then Ith gave me a lift home.

'Sure you don't want to come round ours?' she asked.

'No... No thanks. I need to get my head down. I need to get my head sorted.'

'Drop round in the afternoon. I'm busy in the evening but I'd like to see you're okay.'

'Yeah. Sure.'

I got out of her car, waved at her with a weary smile and let myself in to mine as she drove off.

I had a bowl of cornflakes, made a pot of tea and sat down at my writing table; there were two or three new packages on it but I knew I ought not to look at them this side of a bloody good kip.

I couldn't go to sleep yet. What I'd felt at Smethwick West had got its claws into me and I'd need to try prying them loose before I could sleep.

I tried thinking about Ith's brother Paul. Should I have invited him?

Robed, staffed, long grey bearded. How far he'd come from the young, sharp-suited, clean-shaven Wordsley schoolteacher I'd seduced in the summer of '03. Never let it be said that a bit of 'ow's-yer-father with little Lonnie does nothing to expand your horizons. And he was the best anal I'd ever had -

'OH MOTHER, FOR GOD'S SAKE!'

Well.

That was surprising.
...thought I, as I picked myself up from the carpet and plonked myself back in my writing chair.
That was...
That was my beautiful boy!
I'd thought the words that would, one day, piss him off so much! It had had nothing to do with the moderately famous rock star on the bus in Lower Gornal. It had been a completely different shenanigan. But I'd thought the words that I was going to speak and I'd heard his reply!

I wasn't going to know he was there when I said them, was I? That would be creepy! No no! But I was going to be a bit drunk... Somebody's homemade rhubarb wine...

But my boy, my beautiful boy, he was going to be so pissed off! And that would only make me love him the more!

The sense of something having come from me but being so utterly different from me! Every parent of a teenager knows it. Many are destroyed by it. To me, it was like standing under a waterfall and feeling all that was petty and inconsequential washed away. And I was feeling it ten or twenty years before it happened.

Ecstatic, I necked the rest of the tea though it was still pretty scalding.

I got my laptop open and brought up a new document, then typed:

As an instrument for breaking down the veils that resist the expansion of the adept's True Will into New Modes of Consciousness and of True Knowledge, the clash of opposed sexual discourses cannot be bettered...

See, Dad? I'd cracked it! I'd found a way to Transcendental Illumination that didn't get anybody raped! I typed frenziedly until nearly midday. Apart from anything else, this was the best way of getting a clear sense of what I was actually up to. A mere desire to smash open the veil between two different versions of reality would not be enough...

In the meantime, editorial jobs I'd got waiting on the table sat there, as close to glowering as bundles of paper could get. Eventually, I had to take a look at them.

Two new ones had turned up: *The Compost Sagas* didn't sound very promising and *Hate: the Revengering* inspired little more anticipation.

I went and made another pot of tea.

And got back to my own stuff.

Five thousand words into what I was sure would be, amongst many other arcane things, the definitive account of the parallels between the West Midlands rail network and the Kabbalistic Tree of Life, I threw myself back in my chair, punched the air with both fists and experienced one of those spontaneous orgasms you get after a sustained bout of something creative. (What do you mean, *you don't*? Well then, you're not being ambitious enough in your subject matter. Go and have another listen to *The Adventures of Antidisestablishmentarianista Jones*. I hit the Big 'OH!' *six times* during the recording of that album and all I had to express it was a clunky old Yamaha DX7!)

I went and had a shower and changed my jeans and knickers. They needed it.

That done, I pedalled round to Ith and Dougie's.

Ith had a concerned look as she opened her front door. And, for a moment, it seemed to me she wasn't as pretty as she'd been back in the months we were together. Then, at forty-two, she'd been stunning – which I was happy to put down to my influence, of course. But that had been sixteen years ago and, since, there'd been a thinning of her lips, a tightening of the skin around her cheekbones – overall, her face had serioused up quite a bit.

But there was something between my eyes and my mind that was very good at compensating for this so that, within a minute or two, I was looking at she who'd been mine. This just confirmed I was still in love with her, which I'd never made the effort to try denying. Still in love with her in a way I knew I was no longer in love with Charlotte Ronsard.

She steered me into the back lounge, walking behind me with her hands resting lightly, protectively on my shoulders.

'I'll get the tea on,' she said.

Dougie was curled up in his usual chair, struggling with Proust. Upstairs, I could sense the silent and ferociously rational concentration on matters interstellar. In the same place, there was another consciousness, wondering and open-mouthed at the beauty of the colours in a gardening book. So things were going on pretty normally round at the Ith-Cayles'. In the kitchen, Ith made the tea.

And it occurred to me that between us, The Death of Wallenstein and our collective nearests and dearests got through a heck of a lot of tea: gallons of the stuff. Ith had been having a bit of an Earl Grey thing since last summer which was okay with me, though not always with Dougie so, as a result, they had two teapots – identical except for the metallic blue and iron grey finishes – now standing on the kitchen table.

Ith presented me with a big steaming mug. Earl Grey may have had associations of delicacy, but the way The Death of Wallenstein knocked it back could be as indelicate as we liked.

'So,' she said as she sat by me on the sofa, 'tell me what you think happened last night.'

I did so. It took a while.

'Hmm. Janice Croviss would have to be a very old woman now,' she said, 'if she's even alive. Old and probably in a lot of pain. Trying to punish her might just be putting her out of her misery.'

The part of me that could hear her nodded in agreement.

'By the way, Dad told me about Mervyn and Tolland,' I said. 'Told me what he was planning, I mean.'

Ith looked at me, not at all angrily – but puzzled.

'When did he do that?' she asked.

'Er… the week before last. I know he told you before.'

'Sixteen years ago!'

'He said. He knows he should have told me. He knows you assumed he had done. He was being cowardly; he admitted it.'

Ith exhaled furiously, then said 'Excuse me a sec,' through gritted teeth. She got up and went out into the back garden, where she usually practiced.

There was a much louder and more furious exhalation, together with a crunching crack.

Dougie looked up from his Proust.

'We're going to have to stock up on breezeblocks again,' he said, calmly.

Ith came back in, nursing the business edge of her right palm – which looked undamaged but must have been a bit sore.

'I won't say anything,' she said, and sipped at her tea.

'He knows you think he's a stupid fuckwit,' I said.

'I'm sure he does,' Ith replied; 'I've told him often enough.'

When it was time to go, she lightly rested a hand on my shoulder and took me back into the front.

I was getting my coat on when there was a heavy but precise and measured tread down the steps from above.

'The word graffitied on to the back of the shelter at Smethwick West,' said The Voice of Reason, 'is "Data".' He'd overheard what I'd been telling his mom.

'"Data?!"'

'Yes.'

'But that's... That's an anagram... That's an anagram of 'Da'at!''

'Da'at?'

'Da'at! The lost Sefirot! The primal information! The path of knowledge across... across The Abyss!'

The Voice of Reason paused a moment, then remarked: 'Amusing coincidence,' and I heard that heavy but precise and measured tread going back up the stairs.

'See? Just a coincidence,' Ith smiled, with caution.

She kissed me, briefly, on the lips and it was the first such kiss we'd allowed ourselves for some years.

'You take care now,' she smiled, as she opened the door.

Pedalling homeward, something else peculiar occurred to me: I wasn't sure how many typescripts to be edited were waiting on the work table. Four or five... I could remember the titles of four. I wasn't sure if there'd been a fifth. This was weird; I usually knew exactly what was on my 'to do' pile and I felt this uncertainty must have arisen from what had happened: the spell we'd cast at Smethwick West, at The Abyss, at Da'at – and the cry of teenage annoyance that spell had summoned from... from the world on the other side.

Perhaps, of all human emotions, only a teenage boy's irritation at his Extremely Embarrassing Mom is intense enough, precise enough, focussed enough to break down the veil between two possible worlds.

Perhaps that annoyance was just as important a contributor to what was happening as was the Imprisonment of Choronzon, sixteen years before.

I took my bike down the side passage, chained it to a drainpipe and put a polythene cover over it. Then I went upstairs.

I hesitated a moment before I put the light on.

I was frightened. Frightened in a way I'd never felt before because, somehow, I'd never felt I had so much to lose.

The switch clicked.

Five bundles of A4 paper.

And I knew immediately which was the one I'd not yet looked at.

I took my waterproof off and hung it up. Then I went and turned the heating on. Then there wasn't anything else to do – no excuse to put it off.

Somehow – *Somehow?! How the hell had I managed that?!* – I'd taken the thing out of its envelope and placed it back on the table without noticing anything about it. Anything at all.

It was a thing that seemed to have that knack of making itself unnoticed – until it wanted to be seen. There are people like that. My dad was one and Charlotte's had been another, though there are some folk on whom it never works.

Far rarer, though, to find the trick pulled by an inanimate object.

I really ought to read this thing…

No, I said to myself, it'll keep till the morning.

So I got undressed, set my alarm for 7.30 and went to bed.

I expected to lie awake until, defeated, I was forced to get up and look at it but, no, I was out like a light.

Perhaps the thing wanted me wide awake enough to give it my full attention.

The alarm went.

I got up quickly, showered, had coffee and toast and opened the curtains in the front.

The sky above was dull and grey but everything seemed lit up by the radiance of the mural painted on the side wall of the house opposite.

'Orpheus', I knew it to be called, but the mythical poet depicted looked awfully like the very real poet, Lewis Gladrell. *Tough shit, Satansfist, you sarcastic twat,* I thought. *You blew it there and he was always too good for you anyway.*

It was true: after a dodgy first collection, Gladrell had matured into a decent writer of narrative verse. He'd even been on Radio 4, the week before last, which was better than... Than what? I wasn't sure, yet I felt I ought to have been.

As for Satansfist... Well: I loved his work: I felt helpless with love when I looked at the photos of his murals in Charlotte's house. But I found it impossible to speak well of anyone who was perpetually addressing me as *'Marmalade Minge'*.

Something funny happened to me as I turned back from the window to my worktable.

The mural was fine – it was a wonderful piece of work, whatever I felt about the painter, but – but something felt odd about its being there...

Something odd... I hadn't decided... what.

I flopped down in my work chair and stared at the typescript. It was littler than the others – ought not to take too long to get through. Better make a start, then...

PART TWO:

EVIL
(JANICE CROVISS)

6: Frances Chessil

It was very quiet; I was surprised – I didn't remember schools sounding like this. Mrs Wildacres, the head, was talking in not much more than a whisper as she led me down the corridor. Somewhere close by, somebody was boiling a kettle – making a cup of tea.

It was just gone eight in the morning but it was still September, so it had been light for an hour or two. The corridors were narrow, the windows high and narrow. In the old days, this had been an ordinary junior school. 'High and narrow' would have summed up people's attitude to the kids, back when the place was built.

That way of doing things wouldn't work now – not with the lot that got sent here. 'The kids where God left bits out', the bloke at the agency had said. I'd tried not to look disgusted with him.

'Here we are,' said Mrs Wildacres. And here we were. It was a cramped room: you couldn't see out of the windows and the battleship-grey filing cabinets didn't leave much space for decoration. What space there was, though, Mrs Wildacres had filled with stuff. All of it was painted or made by the pupils so it was pretty clunky: the pictures that got framed and put on the wall here wouldn't have made the grade in any mainstream school.

A little 'un had wandered in and was staring up at one of them.

'Hello, Nigel,' breathed Mrs Wildacres. She'd know the name of every kid in the building: you could tell that within half a minute of meeting her.

'Ahwa,' *(Hello)* replied Nigel.

'Nigel's very proud we've put his pig on the wall. Aren't you Nigel?'

'Ah,' *(Yes).*

I stared at the supposed pig, trying to work out which bits were which. I managed to keep my brow from furrowing.

'Can you see where its head is, Miss Chessil?'

Hoping for the best, I pointed to a bit that had – I thought – an eye or two. Or maybe three.

77

'Yes! And can you see where its tail is?'

Slightly easier that: curly thing somewhere towards the opposite end from the 'head'.

'Yes! See Nigel? Miss Chessil can see where all the different parts are!'

And little Nigel's face lit up. He'd communicated with someone. A bit. Given the skills he had to work with, that couldn't happen very often.

'They're not really supposed to come in here,' said Mrs Wildacres after Nigel had 'run along', 'but someone like Nigel will be very lucky if he can grasp that sort of thing by the time he leaves us. Here's your desk. Make yourself a cup of tea. There's milk in the fridge next door and a kettle. I think we're getting a bit low on sugar. I'll be back to put something in your *In* tray in five or ten.'

And off she went. She was indeed back in five minutes with a big bundle of stuff to do. There'd be no chance of a second cup of tea until lunch.

When the bell for that rang, Mrs Wildacres stuck her head round the door and asked if I could 'find Tony Griefstick for me? He's easy to spot: he's the only male teacher here who hasn't got a beard.'

The place was small enough that it didn't take much doing. Tony Griefstick was talking to three nine year-olds who were looking a bit lost. Nigel was one of them.

'I'll be with her in a sec'; I just need to drop this lot off with Miss Hughes. Thanks.' He gave me a terse but genuine smile.

Something about him caught my attention – possibly the seriousness with which he was taking the little ones' perceived problems. There wasn't anything patronising about the way he related to them.

He was a bloke of average height, a bit thin, with a short haircut. It was getting towards the end of the 1970s and short haircuts for men were on the way back in, but his was more the sort that had died out ten years before than the sort that was coming back. It was a haircut you'd have if you needed to put a lot of effort into keeping Mum and Dad happy. But that didn't seem quite right either: mummy's boys never stray so far from mummy. This was North London and Tony Griefstick, who was making no effort to disguise his accent, came from the West Midlands.

I decided we'd have to have a chat. I didn't know how long I was going to be here, but it'd be nice to talk to someone from near home.

I say 'near', but that didn't mean we were from the same place exactly. I was a Kidderminster girl and my accent wasn't one that leapt down Londoners' earholes as if intending to mug them. Tony Griefstick came from somewhere a bit to the north-east of me – Cradley Heath or Halesowen maybe – and the way he talked would sound a lot more sinister round here. This didn't seem to bother him and I liked that.

That night, I finally made it to the swimming baths and did forty lengths. Phew. I laughed at myself a bit: I hadn't fallen for Tony Griefstick but he did seem interesting and I wanted to look okay when he was around. Living and working in London, there's less time to spend taking care of yourself: it's easy to let it all go and wind up in a right state. If I could use the vague beginnings of possibly fancying some bloke to prod myself into doing some healthy stuff, all well and good.

I'd forgotten how much I hated the stink of chlorine, though.

It wasn't until the middle of the following week that we got to sit down together for lunch. I mean, sit down in the staff room, rather than in the cramped school hall, where our attention had to be focussed on the little 'uns even when trying to digest the extremely tough battered scotch eggs that were the least disgusting things on the menu two days out of five.

'Kidderminster?' he said. 'Thought it might be there.'

'Yourself?'

'Blackheath – just up the road from Rowley Regis train station'

'I know it. I mean, I've been through it. Never got off there.'

'Few do.'

We smiled at each other: the provincial English knack of self-deprecation – beating the Londoners to the punch.

'Still got family back there?' he asked.

'Mum and Dad,' I said. 'They're okay. Mum can come across as a bit fierce. It's in the family: Granddad was a union man. Mum hasn't got a kind word for Mrs Thatcher.'

'Well I'm with her on that.'

'Dad's just a big softie, though. How about you?'

I felt something like a drop in temperature. It wasn't that I'd annoyed him or put him off – but I'd asked a question that was hard for him to answer.

'Just Mom,' he said. 'I was only a year or so old when my dad died, so I don't remember him at all. Mom works at Birmingham Crown Court. She's one of them who types things up. I think… she has to listen to some pretty nasty stuff, one way or another…'

His voice trailed off. He didn't actually say *'So she's got to be a bit of a hard number,'* but the words hung between us, unspoken, unmistakeable.

About two days after that conversation, I was in a phone box talking to Mum, when she got the idea that I'd *'found myself a feller.'*

'Mu-um!'

'Pffhh! It's obvious!'

'Not to me, it isn't!'

I didn't press her about how she could tell. Something in my voice must have given it away – God knows what. To her credit, she asked for no details, just insisted I acknowledge that she had not been 'born yesterday'.

'You weren't born yesterday, Mum.'

Which didn't alter the fact that, as far as I was concerned, I was still single.

But when Tony asked if I'd like to come with him to see *Othello*, it was easy enough to say yes.

The Aldwych was one of those cosy-shabby Victorian theatres you get in the West-End of London. Walking into one for the first time comes as a shock to us provincials: we're never expecting something so obviously falling to bits. Tony told me the theatre company was planning to move somewhere much swankier – a big cave of white concrete.

'They want to prove to you that the future's finally showed up,' he said. We both laughed.

We weren't laughing by the interval.

The best Tony could manage was a quiet 'Enjoying it?' – and that seemed to cost him a bit of effort.

'Well...' I replied, about to make an attempt at something dismissive but deciding at the last moment to be honest, 'up to a point, yes, but I wish it didn't look so daft.'

'You mean the makeup?' he asked.

'I mean the makeup, yes. Donald Sinden really surprised me; I'd only ever seen him in *Two's Company;* never thought he'd be so good in this sort of stuff – but however well he says the lines, it doesn't work if he looks like one of the Black and White Minstrels.'

He laughed. Encouraged, I went on:

'I've always thought the Black and White Minstrels were creepy. Don't you?'

'Totally.'

'I mean, couldn't they find any decent black actors for this? What about that bloke from *Rising Damp?*'

He went and got us both an ice cream. A choc ice for me; I forget what he had.

At the end of the show, both clutching programmes, we emerged into the night.

'I didn't think...' I said. Then I dried up.

'Didn't think what?'

'Didn't think it was going to be like that. I mean, I knew Iago was going to be the baddy but...' I dried up again. This time he just looked at me, curiously.

'Well... nobody's that evil, are they?' I concluded, feebly.

He became very quiet. And he was frowning – not angrily, but with concentration. My question, a throwaway remark as far as I was concerned, meant something to him.

'Oh,' I said, trying to put some brightness in my voice, 'I know there's people like Hitler, but they're only rare, aren't they? And they're mentally ill: they've got something wrong with them.'

'I wasn't thinking of Hitler so much. I guess it was true of him: it's not so much they've got something wrong with them. It's that they've got something missing: the bit that gives you the power... to imagine somebody else's pain. Sometimes it's not there in somebody. Other times... it gets destroyed. People like Iago can't really tell a story – or they can't tell a story and believe in it. They can pretend to, but not really.

To feel sorry for someone or to want to help them, you have to be able to imagine their story. People like him can't do that. So other people's pain... they don't get it. They can't get it.'

'You ever known somebody like that?'

He frowned again, as if he really wasn't sure.

Then he looked at his watch and discovered that Shakespeare plays are a lot longer than most other things you go to see at the theatre. 'Here, come on, we don't want to miss the tube.'

On the way home, we found out that we were living around the corner from each other, both in cramped bedsits, in a part of Islington that was not the scariest, but still pretty scary.

We started to see each other. Usually, to begin with, it was just a couple of drinks in a pub close to our places. After a month or two, we started going back to mine after for a coffee. It was just that for quite a while – a coffee. We didn't go any further until we'd known each other nearly six months. By then, I wasn't working at Tony's special school any more. Perhaps we wound up in bed partly because we realised there might be a danger of us drifting apart: if you've made a friend in London, you really don't want to drift apart. I don't remember which of us first raised the possibility but neither of us were very assertive about it. Nor were we very assertive once we were actually between the sheets. Something in the way Tony went about things almost made me think he was scared of damaging me. A lot of my girlfriends back home wouldn't have put up with this: they'd have had him down as useless and dumped him on the spot. I sensed he had his reasons and, though it seemed daft, at the same time I sort of liked it: it was a sign he cared about me. Whatever, when we eventually got down to things we were so low-volume that we never gave the neighbours any reason to suspect we were up to anything at all – which was just as well because the wall on one side of my place was a single sheet of hardboard.

Not long after, of course, we moved in together – into another Islington flat only very slightly bigger and with only very slightly thicker walls. It was a part of North London that was going to get gentrified a few years later. Sometime around 2010, just for a laugh, I had a look at the website of a local estate agent and spotted a flat in our old place to let. Was it two or three zeroes that had been added to the rent we'd paid? It really was that mad.

But, when we were there, all that was in the future. Islington was a place of fags, football and as much cheap lager as you could get down your neck. Even I took the long way home to avoid walking past a couple of pubs, though I thought of myself as a thick-skinned Londoner by now. There was one in particular where there was always a bit of aggro and I had sense enough to know that some of the nutters you got staggering out were just too unpredictable. I'd never had anything against pubs back home: Dad loved his pint of Banks's Mild and no amount of the stuff ever turned him into the kind of idiot you got round here. But city pubs – some city pubs – were different to small-town pubs and I knew I had to steer clear of a few of them if I was on my own.

Once in the flat, though, we felt safe. There was never a peep out of the neighbours on the one side and on the other there was an old chap who only ever disturbed us with the volume of his telly. He was pretty deaf, so we never made a thing about it. I remember those years – there were two or three of them – as happy times. Tony stayed at the school and I carried on temping. We went out to the theatre a bit, and to the cinema less often, but not too many other places – even back then, you couldn't afford to live it up in London if you actually *lived* in London. Tony got us a quiet little stereo on which we played classical music and a bit of folk. And we began to fit together like a pair of old shoes.

But still, I admired him. I didn't think he was any kind of saint: you don't think that when you get to wash somebody's smelly socks, but the way he cared about the kids he had to look after – my God, he took that job seriously!

He'd make, one day, a brilliant dad for somebody.

For nearly a year, there was next to no mention of his mother. He went down to a phone box nearby, maybe once a month, maybe not even that often, and had a quick chat with her. It was a quick chat too: I don't think he was ever gone for longer than ten minutes. And he had nothing to tell me about such chats – nothing that amounted to anything. He'd just mumble he *thought work had been getting her down a bit* or that *things were going on same as usual*. It wasn't so much that he was being secretive; he just couldn't work out what to say. To me, that seemed strange: I went down to the same phone box and, with Mum on the other end, I could be stuck in it for half an hour – what with her always being so keen to hear about life in the 'Big City'. More than that, after a while, I could sense when it was getting time for one of his chats with his mother: I could sense his nervousness, though he couldn't.

Then, one evening, he seemed to realise that we'd been together long enough that not having talked about his family was pretty weird. The idea struck him very suddenly because he was making the tea when he just froze absolutely. He scowled and, by now, I could spot that it was a scowl directed at himself.

'You know,' he said, finally, 'I really need to talk to you about... back home.'

At last. I'd known this was coming. I assumed grim stuff was on the way.

I didn't press him and waited until the two mugs of tea-milk-no-sugar and the two plates of macaroni cheese on toasted Hovis were in front of us on the tiny red Formica worktop.

'So,' I said, between scrunches, 'back home.'

'Yeah,' he replied, 'Back home. Backhomebackhomebackhome. I don't know. I can't see why it's so much bother talking about it. I'm being a real idiot here, sorry.'

'Well,' I said, 'start at the start.'

He did.

'I said, didn't I, that I can't remember my dad?'

'You did.'

'Well, he died back in 1951. I remember going to look at his grave, the once. But Mom didn't like me doing that.'

'So it was just you and her?'

'Mostly it was. She never remarried. Thinking about it, the idea of her getting married again seems... way weirder than it ought to. But... I don't know. We never had any close friends. Neither of us. There were a couple of cousins, Kevin and Celia – they were Mom's cousins by her uncle Ted, but I don't think we saw them after Auntie Frieda died...'

'Auntie Frieda?'

'Auntie Frieda. Mom's twin.'

'She had a sister.'

'Yes. Auntie Frieda died back in '68. Saw Kevin and Celia at the funeral, along with Great Auntie Doreen. Then we lost touch. Oh! Wait a minute! We saw them one more time, at Grandma Doris' funeral, a couple of years later. And Uncle Fred – Frieda's husband – and their son Martin was there too. But we lost touch with all of them after that. Pity, in a way: Martin came across as really cool. I didn't think so at the time. He was starting to grow his hair and come on like a hippy. I thought all that was a load of crap, to be quite honest. I hated anything to do with all that Peace'n'Love stuff. I was really peed off that I hadn't been able to get into the army and I thought he was trying to wind me up.'

'*You?* In the army?' The thing I liked most about Tony was his gentleness. The idea of him hoiking an Armalite around Belfast was too unlikely to be frightening.

'Oh, yes,' he insisted, neither amused nor insulted. 'I spent most of my teens in the cadets. Thought it would sort me out...'

'Sort you out?'

'Yeah.'

'How did you need sorting out?'

He frowned at that.

'You know,' he said, 'it's not that easy to put into words. But I definitely used to think I did. One way or another. Something I needed to do, needed to be – but that I wasn't. And I felt going in the army might make it happen. Anyway, I got knocked over when I was seventeen and bust my pelvis. Haven't you noticed I walk with a limp?'

'It must be very slight: I haven't seen it.'

'Oh, it's there, if you look. But it did for my military hopes. Couldn't walk for a year. No way I'd have made it through basic training.'

'Well. It saved you from Northern Ireland.'

'Guess so. I didn't see it that way at the time; I couldn't.'

We finished off our tea. Then we sat quietly. I noticed how dark it was getting and stood to put the light on, frowning to think how long it had taken us to have this conversation, though nothing about it had upset me.

Tony washed up, then plonked himself on the bed. He smiled up at me. 'Cheer up,' he said, and I felt myself do so – a bit.

'It did give me a lot of reading time, though,' he said as I sat next to him, 'which is how I eventually wound up doing the English degree.'

85

'Which suits you better,' I smiled. 'You're a bloke who took his bird out to see *Othello* on our first date. A squaddie wouldn't have thought of that.'

He laughed.

'A few would,' he said, 'but not many. Thing is, though... The thing is, I do get that it's weird I've not talked much about Mom and I've been acting, I suppose, as if there's some big secret but... Hey! Why am I crying?'

Because he was. He rubbed the moisture off his cheeks and stared at it glistening on his fingertips.

'Is there something you're trying to remember?' I asked him, softly.

'Well,' he ventured, 'yeah. There's some bad stuff: Granddad Jethro. He wasn't my real granddad. Grandma Doris married him after my real granddad died in the war. Jethro had... a drink problem. I don't think we used to call them "alcoholics" back then. But he was one. A bad one. He could get very violent. Mum and Auntie Frieda must have copped it pretty badly, quite often. He had a go at me, the once.'

'How did that happen?'

'Well,' he said...

7:   Anthony Griefstick

When I was born, there were a load more factories in Blackheath – the air used to clang with foundry hammers. The way I remember it, the skies were grey all the time – no, really, *all the time.* That's crazy, I suppose: there must have been some sunny days. It's just that I can't remember them.

A lot of people had big back gardens or allotments where they grew rhubarb and cauliflowers and beans. We'd just got the yard with the bathhouse. But Mom had a dark brown bakelite wireless that I think had been Great Auntie Doreen's but she hadn't wanted it once she went deaf. It had a big round gold-grilled speaker and you'd have the BBC Home Service on it. Just the Home Service: Mom didn't like the Light Programme: she thought some of the music they had on it was... a bit suspect.

And nobody used to say anything.

Yeah, that was the problem: not the foundries, not the rhubarb, not the BBC Home Service. It was that nobody used to say anything.

Again, though, this is going to be my memory more than anything else: somebody must have spoken. A bit, at least.

There's no doubt, though: everybody I can remember was a bloody sight quieter than they should have been. You'd have thought Mom and Auntie Frieda, being twins, would have had loads to natter about. But you never caught them at it. It was as if each of them already knew everything that the other one might say and so they didn't have to bother. And if you didn't have to bother – better to stay quiet. Perhaps they didn't want to risk giving their position away to some unspecified enemy – Granddad Jethro, most likely.

I don't think Dad having died made much difference to Mom. She never talked about him and, by the time I was old enough to notice, there was nothing of his left around the place. I couldn't tell you if he had any hobbies or what he used to drink or anything. And it wasn't even like

Mom didn't want to answer such questions – it was more than that. She wasn't afraid of the answers: in her mind, there was no possibility of the questions being asked in the first place. And she passed on that sense of impossibility to me without having any idea she was doing so.

So much for Dad. I didn't see anything strange about it at the time. Now and again though, I used to think I could... sort of... remember myself remembering him and I'd drive myself mad trying to look around the corner of my mind... look around the corner and see him. No joy; but then, this was Blackheath: *'No Joy'* was the town motto.

One funny thing: some days, Mom and Auntie Frieda used to go off somewhere together and leave me with Grandma and Granddad Jethro. I followed them once, when Jethro had nodded off half way down a bottle of Johnnie Walker. I must have been about seven. They went to Saint Paul's Churchyard. They were standing by a grave when they spotted me. It was the only time Mom ever gave me the kind of clouting I was always half expecting off her. She hit me so hard I threw up. On the way down, I bonked my head on a grave. I was staggering all over the place, trying to get home. *'Concussion'*, they'd probably call it today. *'Acting silly'* and *'showing off'* is what Mom called it then. Proper old Blackheath is Mom.

I never found out what I was supposed to have done wrong. Mom never has gone in for explanations. Whatever it was, it was none of my business. I think... though I'm not really sure, I think it might have been the same grave where Auntie Frieda got buried, later on. But I never went near the place again to find out. Except for Frieda's funeral, obviously. And I made sure my eyes were pointing in any direction but at the gravestone, all through the burial. I wasn't that keen to know who else was buried there and I didn't want another clobbering.

Anyway: Jethro. Dudley bloke. Worked in one of the foundries, where all he was ever supposed to do was *'lomp it wi' 'ommer.'* That's Hard Black Country for *'Hit – it – with – a – hammer'*. Not many folk left speak that way today. By the year 2000, they'll have gone, I reckon. Apart from a few in Gornal.

It's not too surprising that Grandma Doris wound up with someone like Jethro. All Grandad Bob ever was to me was a photo but I get the feeling he was a nice bloke. He had some sort of fallout with his brother, Uncle

Ted. I don't think it amounted to much but they died estranged. And in those days, a single mother with two daughters was sure to think she needed a new man.

Don't get the wrong impression: I've got a degree, sure, but all my family were either steelworks, mine or foundry. And most of 'em seem to have been... well, mostly okay. Thing is though, I reckon Jethro was a bit too clever for it. You used to get people like that. Too clever for the work they were given. And some of 'em got resentful. That's when the trouble would start. They'd turn nasty. A lot of 'em would take to the booze. Jethro always had liked his beer, apparently, but by the time I knew him, he was into that Banks's Old Ale stuff: it's wine strength – ten or eleven per cent alcohol. Anyway, it was either that – and he'd get through bottles and bottles – or the whisky. He could knock back a bottle of Johnnie Walker Red in an hour and a half. Like I say, he'd perhaps had the makings of a clever bloke. But it had all gone wrong. By the time Grandma Doris saw how wrong, it was too late. She was stuck with him.

I'd've been about thirteen when he had a go at me. Maybe fourteen. I remember, that TV show, *Doctor Who* had just started. We were six episodes or so in. I wanted to watch it but Jethro suddenly got the idea I was too old for it. He said something about me needing to watch something 'proper and sensible'. As Mom never allowed the telly at ours to be switched on, round theirs was my only chance to get a look at anything. So I played my face a bit. It never took much to set Jethro off, though, so he lobbed the frying pan at me – one of those big old fashioned frying pans – like a Le Creuset, only without the enamel. Rusty looking thing – cast iron. Wallop.

I blacked out for a bit, of course. When I came to, Grandma Doris was looking daggers at Jethro.

After a fair old while deciding who was most to blame, they got next door to drive me over the hospital. Nobody was going to trust Jethro behind the wheel of anything – although I don't think he was actually that far gone at the time – not by his standards.

Anyway: that was the night I had a little taste of what Mom and Auntie Frieda had had to put up with off Jethro. Only they'd had to stick it for two years or so before they found themselves Dad and Uncle Fred.

89

Amazing Jethro lasted as long as he did. He went within six months of Grandma Doris, maybe January, February '71. Alcohol poisoning, of course, and I think he knew exactly what he was doing. They found two hundred empty Johnnie Walker bottles in the house after he went. It was a running joke all over Blackheath for months.

I've said that Mom and Auntie Frieda hardly ever talked but that didn't mean they weren't close. The sense you used to get of their absolute togetherness, sealed off and apart from the rest of the world, could be suffocating for any bugger unfortunate enough to be in a room with the pair of them – as poor old Uncle Fred often was.

Against everybody else, there was a barrier. I'm not sure what Mom had been like with Dad, of course and, apart from that one clobbering, I always had the sense that she felt it was her duty to make sure I never had any reason to speak ill of her. I guess she can't have been much different towards Dad. But still, I was somehow outside that special circle that cut off her and Auntie Frieda. Like the rest of the world, I was somebody who didn't count, somebody they could never trust. And I tell you what: I never once got the feeling that this was how she wanted to feel; ever since I've been a tiny tot, I've always known she's had no choice: it's what she *is*.

When Auntie Frieda died, things seemed to go downhill – to me, if not to Mom. When it happened, I was sure the loss would be the worst thing she'd ever known and was half expecting her... maybe not to make a big show of grief but at least to say something about how it made her feel. Instead, she grew more numbly and deadly silent than ever.

Uncle Fred and Martin went their own way. I heard – I can't remember from where – that Martin had turned to drink. Then, four or five years back, Mom told me he'd married some posh bird. That was it. I'd thought Mom might keep in touch with them and it spooked me a bit when she showed no interest in doing so. Maybe I asked her, just the once, quite soon after Frieda's funeral, if we ought to go round and see them? This in spite of the fact that I found Martin a berk. Yes, I must have done that – because I can remember the look she gave me and it was enough for me to know that I shouldn't ask again. I still sometimes wonder how they're doing.

I stopped doing the cadets when I had the accident but I found other ways of keeping out the house. Mostly, I'd be doing homework in the school library – that could take me until five o'clock. Then I'd get home and have the table laid for dinner. Mom would get back from work at about six thirty or seven and do the cooking. We'd eat noiselessly and by the time we'd finished, it was past eight. Around the time Auntie Frieda died, I got into the habit of offering to do the washing up. Mom, with a single irritated shake of her head, had the habit of turning down my offer.

So I'd go upstairs and read a bit and, if there was any extra homework, I'd do that. About half-past nine, I'd usually go to the loo. Mom's place is one of the last in our street to still have an outside bathhouse with a single tap and a lavatory. This was getting old-fashioned ten years ago – especially the fact that we had no hot water as such. When either of us wanted a bath, we had to boil a couple of saucepans on the kitchen hob, cart them out into the draughty, red brick bathhouse, then stick the contents in the tin bath which we topped up with cold from the tap.

Draughty the place might have been, but I still took my time in the loo. I'd often take a torch and a book with me because, although there was a light above the tap – bare-bulbed and about seven or eight watts – the lavatory cubicle was unlit. I took my time, I'm afraid, because of what I had to look forward to at the end: Mom, as you may well have guessed, was the sort of person who always insisted on Izal Medicated. Ever experienced Izal Medicated? Lucky you. It's getting pretty rare these days. Izal Medicated is not like other toilet papers: one side is shiny and, if you don't crumple it, it isn't much good at wiping anything off anything; if crumpled though, it changes into a sheet full of sharp edges, some sharp enough to give you a nasty scratch. The unshiny side, called the 'rough' side, is less painful – maybe – but still has the texture of fine sandpaper. Like a lot of Blackheath people of her generation and older, Mom firmly believes that the bog is not a place where anybody ought to be going in order to enjoy themselves.

I think you can understand quite a bit about Mom, if you appreciate that only one toilet paper was ever thinkable in her house and that was Izal Medicated.

Before long, though, she would be getting the kettle on for the end-of-the-evening pot of Brooke Bond Dividend. So, eventually, I'd have no choice but to grope blindly for the first vicious oblong of Izal.

I said we listened to the Home Service on the radio – and I'm sure Mom must have stayed with it when, shortly after I'd gone away to uni, it turned into Radio Four. Like I said, the telly never got switched on. One Saturday, when I'd been about to start grammar school, I'd noticed Mom was out and tried it. Of course, it hadn't worked. Five years later, after I'd done my 'O' levels, I'd tried it again. Still hadn't worked. This was no mystery to me: Mom didn't want it to be noticed that she didn't have a telly; everybody else in the street had one, apart from Mrs Hengest at Number Twenty Nine and she was ancient. Mom set a lot of store by looking normal. But she hated telly. You could tell this on the very rare occasions when we went round anyone elses's and they happened to have it switched on: she'd watch it out of the corner of her eye, paying no attention to whatever the programme was but furiously suspicious of the thing itself. I think she felt it might be watching her back and was scared of what it would see. Sometimes I almost thought I understood this feeling and I was so sorry for her it broke my heart but I didn't let her know that: Mom could be pretty sharp with anyone who she thought was feeling sorry for her.

I'll give her her due, though: she worked her guts out for me after I'd had my accident. Kept up the job and, at the same time, made sure I was looked after – either herself or she'd get Mrs Pollitt next door to come in and do what was necessary. Auntie Frieda wanted to help but, by then, she was fading fast: it just wasn't going to happen. I think there was even some question of Martin, Frieda's son coming round but, no, Mom and Frieda silently agreed that Martin was and always would be useless for anything.

When I went away to uni, I got into a conversation with someone in halls and learned that a lot of people actually kept some stuff of theirs back at their parents'. Like, it had neither been brought with them nor thrown away. I was astonished. This had never occurred to Mom as a remote possibility. Again, to be fair, it had never occurred to me either. But I thought back to the day before leaving Blackheath, to when Mom had been over what was about to cease to be my room – been over it very carefully in the cool September afternoon sunshine – and checked that everything had either gone in the bin or been packed up ready to go. And I'd joined her in that examination.

When she'd finished, she'd given a short click of her tongue and I'd felt, with no feeling of satisfaction or relief but with a sort of accepting numbness, that I'd passed the test. There'd be no real need for us to see each other again.

At the time, this seemed just normal but, later, thinking back on it while I was at uni, it seemed… well… frankly a bit peculiar.

8: Frances Chessil

The walls of our place's backyard were yellow brick – sickly-looking stuff. The paving was the same brick but painted white – I'm not sure why they'd done that, because it showed up all the mucky footprints and bike tracks that had ever crossed it. The gate had to be locked shut behind you and the heavy, windowless back door had two deadlocks as well as a Yale so it always took a while to get in. I looked up and the sky was a funny mixture of heavy grey cloud with metallic blue showing through the gaps. *'Changeable',* you might have called it.

The sun sneaked round the corner of a cloud and stabbed my eye just before I went inside. I weaved my way through the back room, where the landlord kept all manner of crap in big cardboard boxes, and clunked my way up the stairs to our flat.

I stuck the radio on and it was something about Northern Ireland. A bomb had gone off. Four people had died.

That was what I was listening to when Tony came in.

He heard a bit, winced and looked at me. 'D'you really want to listen to that?' he asked in a quiet, pained voice.

'Not really,' I replied and flicked the set into silence.

He flopped down beside me on the bed and I looked at him. He didn't look back. We stayed that way for what seemed a long time. The sun found a way through a gap between the houses as it got near setting and it lit up his face. It didn't stay lit for long but it was long enough for me to see that he was worried so I asked him what it was all about?

'They're talking about closing us down,' he said, flatly.

I made all the obvious objections to this idea; it sounded so destructively stupid. Tony just nodded and agreed: no, it wasn't that they weren't busy enough; yes, it was crazy because there was nowhere else to send these kids; no, the staff would not be offered similar positions at other places. This would be a close-down, not a merger.

'Never mind us – never mind the staff,' he said. 'They're talking as if the kids themselves don't exist. Close the place down and – *poof!* – they're going to disappear. I don't see where these people get their ideas from. They keep on telling us to see things "objectively": *objectively*, the funds aren't available to pay for the place; so *objectively* it needs to be closed. But what's going to happen to these kids once it's gone? Aren't they objective enough for you? They don't seem to have an idea about that, "objective" or otherwise. Let alone how much it's going to cost when the poor little sods screw up, as a lot of them will.'

He spoke very quietly. The walls in this bedsit were thicker than the hardboard of my old place but they were still thin.

'If it all gets closed,' I said, 'we might have to move out of London. We'd have to go wherever the jobs were.'

'Yeah,' he said, 'I suppose we would.'

But he'd shuddered as he'd said it – almost spasmed. And I could smell the fear on him. It was infectious.

'Do you like living in London *that* much?' I asked.

It was a reasonable question. He had his teaching. I'd got myself a degree in Fine Art which had failed to get me a job, and an RSA in typing, which had succeeded. We had the combined income of a teacher and a typist. That would have done alright back in Kidderminster, but not in London. I knew, though, that that wasn't really the problem.

'We wouldn't have to go back to Blackheath or Kidderminster,' I said. 'Or anywhere in the Midlands. We could move where we liked.'

The relief poured off him and the springs in the bed creaked a little as his body relaxed.

The sun finally disappeared behind the tall houses and everything got shadowy.

'What d'you want to eat?' I asked, keen to lighten the mood a bit, as I think he was.

It wound up being beans on toast, an apple apiece and Nescaf. Nicer than it sounds because we put a bit of Worcester Sauce on the beans and we'd splashed out on a jar of that posh Blend 37 stuff earlier in the week.

'Time, I suppose,' he sighed between munches, 'to start looking at the *Times Educational* again...' He took a swig of coffee.

I put my hand in his hair and tousled it. It had got a tiny bit longer since we'd been together. Not much – but just a tiny bit.

'I'm glad I've never seen you with a crew cut,' I smiled.

He laughed.

'I think I'd like to meet your mom and dad,' he said.

'It is about time,' I said. 'We've been together for a while.'

We were eating on the edge of the bed and getting toast crumbs on it. Now it wasn't the end of the world to go to sleep on toast crumbs, to have to rub them off each others' skin first thing the following morning, but we decided without really talking about it, that we wanted to make the effort and sleep in a crumbless bed, so we took the sheet off and remade the whole thing. Then I closed the curtains and we got the washing up done. Two plates, two knives, two forks, two mugs and a saucepan. Not much of it. We both had a sense that, for him if not for me, tomorrow was going to be a hard slog, so we weren't out of bed very long. I held on to him, trying to be reassuring. He was asleep very quickly but I had trouble. I could sense something bad coming – maybe it was just Tony losing his job but, as I thought it through and realised that, no, that didn't necessarily mean a disaster, the bad feeling didn't lessen. It'd make things easier moving out of the capital. It'd make things cheaper. *But...*

I went over this in my head for a couple of days. Overall, I had to admit, London hadn't particularly worked out for either of us. And I didn't think – I still don't think – it works out all that well for hardly anybody. It'd have been okay if we'd had more money – a lot more money. We'd both met a few people while at college who were working down here and loving it but we were losing touch with them; they were on the kind of salaries that meant they could take advantage of the place. The theatres, the galleries, the restaurants and all the other things that made London special would have been more accessible if we'd actually had a home somewhere else. The cash we'd have needed to regularly go anywhere interesting mostly got Hoovered up by the rent.

And, as I came out of Highbury and Islington Tube a couple of nights later, I looked around me and thought, *Bloody Hell, this place really is no better looking than the Horsefair!*

It was time to move on.

So we made arrangements to go and see Mum and Dad, a couple of weekends later.

Tony booked the tickets and he chose a route that would take us from Paddington to a change at Worcester.

'Wouldn't it be better to go up to Birmingham and change there?' I asked.

'Nah. Whatever the timetable says, Birmingham New Street is always a nightmare. Delays, cancellations, you name it. A lot more reliable to go through Worcester.'

It was the first time I'd ever sensed that he wasn't being completely honest with me.

Okay, he wasn't lying. But going via Worcester avoided Rowley Regis; he was being even more careful than I'd expected to keep away from his old home.

It turned out to be a nice train ride, though. We got to Paddington at about eight on a Saturday morning. British Rail coffee was less tasty than Blend 37 – much less tasty. But the views from the train windows were the sort of thing Americans come to the UK to see. The sort of thing Turner and Constable painted. Slough, Reading, Oxford and all the quiet little towns that form everybody's idea of what England is, each rose up from the trackside to say hello and, slowly, then quickly, sank back into the gently hilly stretches of field and woodland. I'd never been to any one of them. I was just passing through, this once.

And, for a while, I was so wrapped up in the prettiness of what I could see from the window that I didn't notice what was happening to Tony. It was a slow cooling and stiffening that might have started as we got on the train but by the time we went through Pershore and Evesham, I couldn't ignore it: he was, all at once, withdrawing into himself and ceasing to be himself: he was turning into a protective shell with nothing inside.

I felt I was losing him and, quietly panicking, I tried to work out where I was getting the idea from? He wasn't looking at me as much as perhaps he usually did – and he wasn't looking out of the window either. His gaze was fixed on to the carriage wall. Sometimes he'd look up at the ceiling. And when I touched his arm through his clothes, the muscles were knotted and taut. I didn't know whether it was fear, anger, despair or some unholy mix of the three.

We were getting too close to his mother. I knew it but didn't want to say it.

It didn't seem very long before the train pulled into Worcester Foregate Street but, when we got off, we were aching. There was a lovely little wood-walled café on the platform. It was like the 1930s hadn't gone away. Tony seemed to snap out of the state he was in: when I put my arm over his shoulders, the sick tension I'd felt wasn't there – at least, not so much. He seemed at home here and I felt at home too. We had a big pot of tea and slices of fruitcake with butter.

'I could stand living out here,' I said.

He was just polishing off his fruitcake and starting to smile when the stiffness came over him again. His eyes – perhaps – had flickered over to the opposite platform, for a second, no more. Then he took a swig of tea.

'You okay?' I asked.

He pursed his lips, then sighed. 'Thought I saw someone over the way,' he said. 'Probably wasn't her.'

'Who was it?' I asked. 'Didn't seem like it was anyone nice.'

He sighed again. 'Just Mrs Pollitt,' he said. 'Mom's next-door neighbour. Bit of a busybody, a nosey parker, but harmless, basically.'

'Oh,' I said.

The train towards Birmingham got in about half an hour later. It was a smaller, scruffier thing than the one from Paddington to Worcester and I half-feared it'd conk out on its way to Kidderminster. But it got us there early in the afternoon and we started walking downhill towards the centre of town.

'You'll like Mum and Dad,' I said brightly, as we turned into our road. It seemed odd to me then that I'd not mentioned this before: it was certainly true. 'They tend to... well, to *get* people...'

'Sounds about right,' he said. 'Sounds sort of like you...'

I rang the doorbell, though I'd got a key, and waited for someone to open up. Inside, I could hear Dad yelling that he'd get it and his awkward, lumbering shadow darkened behind the frosted glass. Then the door was open, he was all smiles and loud '*Hello!*'s and, suddenly, I was sure it was going to be alright.

The house smelled as I remembered it: furniture polish and home-made cake. By Sunday afternoon, we were going to have got through quite a lot of cake. There was a big chocolate Swiss roll on the dining room table, together with a cream-jam sponge and a shoal of little Eccles cakes oozing sugary dried fruit. And there was tea. There was always lots of tea.

Dad, over-eager, took our coats and attempted to hang them on the coat-stand in the hall. He got the balance wrong so that the thing toppled over and conked him on the head. He found this funny, but Tony was full of concern. Coats stashed, it was time to sit at the table and deal with some of the cake.

Tony's account of the end of his current job set Mum off, of course. Her opinion of Mrs Thatcher and of any similar politician was quite as negative as her dad's had been but, unlike Granddad, she didn't turn the air bright blue when she gave them. Very genteel, was Mum.

I don't think we put the telly on all evening – or the following morning. Mum and Dad took Tony to their hearts. Mum even let him help her with the Sunday dinner. It was a surprise when Dad, showing me the bean sticks he'd put up in the back garden, said:

'You've found yourself a good bloke but...'

He paused. I must have given him a very funny look.

'Have you met the family?'

'There's only his mom. Everybody else...'

'Dead?'

I nodded. 'Apart from a couple of cousins – second cousins, I think...'

'Ah,' said Dad. 'Thought it might be something like that. There's bad stuff gone on in his family.'

'There has. He's told me.'

'He has? Good. Well, he's done a good job of walking away from it but still, it does show. He's a bit too nervous of things. I don't blame him for moving down London. Good place to lose yourself. Have you met his mum?'

'No. I don't think he has either – not since we've been together. He hardly even phones her.'

'Ah. If it's like that, things aren't going to have been sorted out. You take care, lovey. And don't go pestering him to take you to meet his mum. Might not be a good idea.'

The beans were growing quite well around the sticks – they'd reached past the level of Dad's knees (He wasn't much taller than I was). Dad had a good sense of what it was that made things grow and flourish. And the spring sun shone on the greens and browns of the leaves and the sticks and the pink of his shiny bald head and lit it all up.

An hour or so later, it was time to go.

9: Anthony Griefstick

We were back in London and both back at work. I had five or six kids in front of me; they were trying to get through their 'Topliners' and finding it very hard going. Poor sods. And they could sense the place was in trouble: kids can pick up on that sort of thing and low-ability kids are often quicker to do so than others. I could usually keep the interest of these sorts of teenagers; I guess I was just patient enough, but today they were restless. And so was I.

One of the little 'uns was asking to go to the loo. He was fairly harmless so I let him: I knew which ones in the group would use such a trip as an opportunity to set off the fire alarm. 'Five minutes tops, or I'll send Mrs Wildacres to drag you back.' (Mrs Wildacres was one of the sweetest-natured people I'd ever met but she did a fantastic job of not letting the kids know that).

I'd been sending off application forms and they always took an age to get done, so it was eating into my sleeping time. And there'd been a couple of disappointments; I'd gone all the way to Plymouth and back, middle of last week, only to find there was an internal candidate primed and ready. At the same time, there'd been more serious interest from a place in Worcester.

I didn't really have a problem with the idea of moving anywhere close to Kidderminster. My insides grumbled that it was nearer Blackheath than I wanted to be but, as I kept telling myself – again and again and *a-bloody-gain* – it was all well outside the stamping grounds of Mom or of anyone she knew: my hallucinating I'd seen Mrs Pollitt on the platform of Worcester Foregate Street Station had been just that – a hallucination. A very brief, very slight hallucination.

And it wasn't the idea of seeing Mom again that, in itself, had me worried. It was just that I knew with an instinct I trusted absolutely, that Frances and Mom would be a bad combination. I'd not told Mom I was with anyone. Our conversations were brief – neither of us liked phones

– and it had been easy to make no mention of Frances whatsoever. I supposed that, one way or another, Mom would be quietly and disapprovingly certain that I had a girlfriend. But she had no intention of us talking about it. All I needed to do was to provide a rundown of how I was fixed for cash, what my accommodation was like and what were my job prospects. That was all. And most of the time, she needed to tell me nothing in return. That was just how it was.

But if we were living closer, mightn't she decide to venture out as far as Kidderminster? No – that wasn't going to happen: apart from her journeys to and from work, Mom rarely left Blackheath. She was like a lot of Blackheath people of her generation: she felt that anywhere outside the home town was suspect. But you never knew: she might decide it was right to summon me back to the old place and it was just possible, assuming I'd owned up to Frances' being, that Mom might also think it right for me to drag my wife-girlfriend-whatever along on such a trip. It would not end well.

With all this going on in the back of my head, keeping any focus on the lesson was more of a slog than usual.

'Feeling alright?' Mrs Wildacres asked when she came into the staffroom at lunchtime and saw me drooping with discontent. She sat next to me.

I gave her a potted summary of my worries.

'Hmm,' she said. 'You know you've never mentioned your mother. She doesn't sound at all a happy person.'

'No. No, she isn't.'

'I'd leave it to her to decide if she wants to see Frances or not.'

'Hmm...' *Sounds sensible.*

'And it might be a good idea if you got married. Pretty quickly, I'd say.'

I sighed. 'That won't make any difference.'

'Oh, I think you'll find it will. To someone of her generation.'

'Yeah, I know how... how it is. But Mom's not like that. That sort of thing wouldn't cross her mind.'

Mrs Wildacres, bless her, looked at me a bit doubtfully.

'Mom's never bothered about respectability,' I tried to explain. 'She's worried about being seen as normal, not respectable. That's not what's wrong. I wish I could put it into words...'

'Well, you just leave her to take her time. Let her feel she's not losing control of things.'

She looked a bit worried as she got up. She wasn't a woman who usually failed to see to the bottom of anything but she could tell that, whatever the problem was, it went down a fair old way.

As I headed home – on foot; I lived close enough not to need the tube – I wondered if it was true to say that Mom resented me and, if she resented me, did she resent the whole world besides, for not being Auntie Frieda? Auntie Frieda, it seemed, had been the one person she needed. But Auntie Frieda was twelve years dead.

Maybe there was something in that. But it didn't explain everything, because while Mom had been better when Auntie Frieda was alive, the pair of them had still been pretty hostile towards everybody else. There was something I was missing.

I nipped into a newsagents' and bought *The Times Educational Supplement*. Once back at the flat, I went through the jobs and there were a couple that looked promising, in Hereford and Bridgnorth. I'd have to check how easy it would be to commute, but I rang them up to get the application forms the following morning.

One of them turned out a good one: Hereford. Within three weeks, I'd had the offer. September start. During that time, Frances got hold of some secretarial work in Birmingham. So that settled it: it being a fairly easy drive to Hereford and Frances far keener to get close to her mum and dad than she openly admitted, to Kidderminster we went. All I needed to do was pull my bloody self together and stop hallucinating Mrs Pollitts all over the place. Easy.

We got hold of a two bedroom flat above a chippy on the Bewdley Road. A bit smelly to most nostrils but, hey, we'd just left London: the worst air quality Worcestershire could come up with was going to seem pretty fresh to us. And – Jesus! – two bedrooms? Two *whole* bedrooms? I'd forgotten what it was like to have so much domestic space. The first night, we bought some take-outs from the pub over the road – my first taste of Banks's Mild for a long time – and danced around the place to the radio, getting slightly drunk. We were a bit noisier about the way we made love that night. A bit noisier than we'd ever been in London. The following morning – not hung over because Banks's Mild really isn't that strong – we both worried about what next door might have made of us. But there was no problem – they never said anything. I think the walls were too thick.

It was a week or so before I got my first surprise.

I'd started looking through the local ads for a motor and, after a day or two, I spotted a recently MOT'd second-hand Ford Cortina. In Stourbridge, so not far away.

First thing the following Saturday, I was driving again.

I remembered the shops in Stourbridge had used to be quite good so, looking at my watch, I saw there was still an hour before I had to be home. I made a stop in town and went for a look around one of the shopping centres.

'Hello,' said a voice outside Woolworths, 'Are you Tony Griefstick?'

10: Frances Chessil

'I met Kevin Croviss in Stourbridge,' said Tony, hesitantly, as he got in. 'My cousin – Kevin Croviss.'

'Croviss?'

'Yeah. That was Mom's maiden name.'

Cro-viss. Tony's mom's maiden name. He'd never mentioned it before. It had a leaden, unfriendly sound.

Tony hesitated a bit before he asked me a question.

'Is it odd if your mom never tells you that she and your auntie used to have a little sister?'

My first reaction was to say that it was more than 'odd': it was just about the bloody weirdest thing I'd ever heard. I bit that answer back and thought about a different reply.

'It seems odd to me,' I said at last. 'It's not something Mum or Dad could have kept secret. I mean, I know about Uncle Des in Australia and about Mum's little brother who died of the polio. But I suppose it depends: if she was only a tiny tot when she passed away, your mom might not have wanted to upset you.'

'No. No. She lived to be ten years old. It's funny because… because Kevin says she was the only person Mom and Auntie Frieda could ever really talk to. I mean, if it was like that, you'd have thought… you'd have thought…'

There were so many '*you'd have thought*'s that he couldn't get them out. I saw his hand was starting to shake and I led him to the lumpy old settee in the living room. We sat together and my arms went round him.

The following Friday, we went out for a couple of beers with Dad at his favourite pub. We got back around eleven. You reached our flat by climbing a rattley old metal stairway that led from the back yard up to the kitchen. The landlord had assured us that it was as safe as houses.

'Okay then, marry me,' Tony said, suddenly.

'Hmm...' I said as I scrabbled around in my handbag for my keys. 'Err...' I said as I twisted the key round in the stiff lock. 'Alright,' I said as I finally closed the door behind us.

We ran a bath and got clean and made love at the same time. It was doable – though there were points when I was wondering where exactly the soap had got to?

The following day, I was doing some temping at an office in Deritend. I don't know if anybody else noticed but I felt, as my fingers clattered back and forth across the keyboard, as if I was twinkling like a Christmas tree.

***

It was a week or so after we'd got married – a very low-key registry office do with Mum and Dad and a few old friends of mine in attendance – that I first met Kevin:

'This is Kevin,' Tony said, half-apologetically, it seemed, as the pair of them stepped into the kitchen.

'Hello, Kevin,' I said.

'Hello, Frances,' said Kevin.

He was a man in his late forties, quite handsome in a careworn and serious sort of way – the way you find in a lot of older Black Country men if they've not put on weight. I could see quite a resemblance to Tony so I liked him.

It was a Monday evening at the end of September – brightly sunlit still – and the weekend had been perfect.

'Sorry to bring bad news,' said Kevin to Tony, 'but your mom's had a nasty fall. Bust her leg.'

There was a silence. Then Tony asked: 'Was it that rug on the landing?' Kevin sighed and nodded.

We invited him into the living room and heard the story.

'A rug on a polished floor?' I asked.

'Yes,' replied Kevin.

'That's a disaster waiting to happen! Any fool could have seen it coming.'

'Oh yes,' said Kevin.

'Mom's more than capable of seeing it coming,' said Tony. 'But she couldn't do anything about it. Doing anything about it would have meant...' He groped for the words.

'Not polishing the landing floor,' Kevin concluded for him.

'Yeah, or perhaps not having a rug. And she wouldn't have been able to do either. They'd have seemed...' his voice trailed off again.

'Slovenly,' Kevin helped him out once more.

'Yeah – slovenly. And slovenliness is a no-no for Mom. Nobody – well, nobody who's ever set foot on her landing...'

'That's not going to be that many people,' Kevin broke in.

'No. Not many at all. But none of them will have thought about trying to talk Mom out of putting a rug on it. Not for one second.'

I sighed.

'However lethal the arrangement,' Tony concluded.

'How did you hear about it?' I asked.

'Mrs Pollitt gave me a ring, just after it happened,' Kevin said. 'I knew her from way back and my name's still in the phone book. She'd not heard you were living so close: Janice hadn't mentioned it at all. Typical Janice. You might want to tell her you've got married. Though I don't suppose it'll make much difference.'

'Suppose I'd better go and see her,' said Tony, softly.

'She's in Burton Road Hospital,' said Kevin. 'I'll drive you over if you like.'

11: Anthony Griefstick

Mom's leg was bust and the look on her face had blamed the whole world for it. The whole world – but me in particular.

As Kevin and I walked out into the dusk, I glanced at my watch; we'd been sitting there for forty-five minutes. I waited until we were both back inside Kevin's Granada before I said anything.

'You're not going to believe this but I'd never noticed that Mom had ever got burned. Not until tonight.' The instant I made that confession, the relief felt like oxygen.

Kevin did up his seat belt. 'I am going to believe that,' he said. 'Janice wouldn't want it to be noticed, so you wouldn't notice it. Janice can do that. Frieda was the same. Jenny was too – but in a different way.'

'But the burns are all over her!'

'Just her left side but, yeah, I know what you mean. Still, you wouldn't notice them if she didn't want you to.'

'How... What happened?'

'Jethro got pissed. As usual. A lot of the time, when he got pissed, he used to take it out on Janice and Frieda. I think they'd sort of got used to it. But that one time, he started having a go at Jenny. Janice and Frieda... well... what they'd put up with for themselves, they weren't going to put up with for Jenny. So they turned on him. One of them took his left eye out.'

'*That's* how he got his eye patch?!'

'Yeah.'

'Serves the bastard right. How old were they then?'

'Oh... this must have been, what, just after the war, so Janice and Frieda would have been not quite seventeen. Jenny maybe nine... Your mom may look frail enough now – she looked frail back then – but it turned out she and Frieda could be proper vicious when they needed to. Jethro was screaming fit to bost, of course and he smashed an oil lamp over 'em. Don't know what they were wearing but it went up like a torch. All your mom's left side got burned and all Frieda's right.'

We were both silent. The car was stuck in traffic in the middle of Dudley.

'He'd have done it again if we hadn't...' He dried up. Then he went on: 'Me and a few mates went round to see him when he got out of hospital. We... did him over. Pretty badly... Warned him to watch his step – and to not let on his eye hadn't been an accident...'

I was silent. The middle of Dudley was still gridlocked and we were going nowhere fast.

'Didn't do much good, though, as it turned out,' he finished. His voice was cracking.

'How d'you mean?'

'Well, inside six months, Jenny had gone down with the whooping cough. She didn't see the next spring. Christ, what a bloody Christmas that was!'

I was silent again. Then I said: 'I'm glad somebody at least tried.'

'Thanks,' he said, and sniffed loudly. 'Thanks.'

The traffic loosened up a bit and we made it as far as the Lamp Tavern. On a clear day, the view from here reached almost out to Wales, over the Shropshire and Worcestershire hills. But now, it was dark. We drove on.

'Y'know, it was weird, the way Janice and Frieda got burned on opposite sides, so they were still like a mirror to each other. Some people who didn't know, thought the scars were – what is it? – psychosomatic, you know, brought on by losing Jenny. Might as well have been.'

We drove through Brierley Hill, then down the hill to Amblecote and turned left into Stourbridge. Then on towards Kidderminster.

When we pulled up in the car park at the back of ours, I invited Kevin in for a cup of tea.

He looked at me, thought for a second and shook his head. 'You need to talk to your missus about all this stuff,' he said. 'It's come as a shock to you...'

'Well...'

'No. It has. And you need to talk to her about it. I'll be round the day after tomorrow. You take care till then.'

'Shouldn't we be going round Mom's to make sure everything's alright there?'

'We can do that at the weekend. Mrs Pollitt's got the keys. She's a bit of an old cow but she'll look after things. Go and talk to Frances.'

So I did.

I clattered my way up the stairs. Before I was half way up she had the kitchen door open. She looked terrified.

'How is she?' she asked, hugging me and dragging me inside.

'Well – not great. Her eyes are open but I'm not sure she can see anything. She doesn't react to anything you say.'

Frances frowned. 'How old is she again?'

'How... Er... She must be fifty-one.'

'She's too young to be losing her marbles then, surely?'

'You'd have thought so. Some people do lose it younger but... Nah. I don't think that's what's going on. It feels like she's... I don't know... locked up in something. She can't talk to anybody. Not hardly. And she's not moving a muscle.'

'Have the doctors said anything about this?'

'Not to me. But they've certainly got her pegged as a bit of a funny-ossity.'

I sat at the kitchen table and Frances was about to put the kettle on.

'Would you rather go out for a drink?' she asked, pausing before she lit the gas.

I thought for a bit.

'Okay.'

She drove us out to Bewdley, over the bridge and up the hill to an ancient-looking pub called the Hop Pole. It was a bit rough and spit'n'sawdust-y, but unthreatening and the beer they sold – it was called 'Marston's' and I'd never heard of it – was delicious. I allowed myself two pints. Frances stuck to the lemonade.

She talked about work, about how crap the train service was from Birmingham New Street and about how her dad was planning to put up a new garden shed: would I help? Of course I said 'yes.'

Then we started for home. 'So, have you found out much more about Auntie Jenny?' she asked.

'Not much. It seems like Mom and Auntie Frieda both loved her. Seems like she was the only person they ever did love.' I kicked myself internally for sounding so sodding self-pitying: I hated that sort of thing. 'No, what I mean is, well... they got themselves scarred, once. Uncle Jethro was having a go at Auntie Jenny and they got in his way. He set them on fire. They both got badly burned. Mom still shows the scars. Jenny died a few months later; I think that must have really done their heads in. It was the whooping cough.'

'Oh God, you used to have loads of kids go from that.'

'I know.'

Frances took her left hand off the steering wheel and clasped my right. Clasped it very tightly, as if I needed it. Which I did.

'And your mom's never mentioned her to you?'

'No', I said. 'She's never had that much to say for herself. And right now, she's not talking at all. I think the doctors reckon it might be from the shock of the fall. Except...' I paused, unable to say the words without remembering them: 'Just as we were leaving, she did speak. She said...' I paused again, realising that, though I now remembered them and understood what they literally meant, I had no idea what their real significance might be: 'She said, *I'm ashamed of you.*'

***

Just as he'd promised, Kevin came round to see us two days later. We sat him down on the sofa with a strong cup of tea and swapped stories.

'When I was a little kid, I never used to see very much of your mom and her sisters,' he began.

'Did they live very far?' asked Frances.

'Not really – just the other end of Long Lane but, in those days, in Blackheath, that was the other end of the world. There'd been some kind of falling out between Dad and Uncle Bob; I never found out properly what it was; it all happened before I came along.

'By 1940, the pair of them were both off abroad. As far as I could tell, Mom and Auntie Doris took no notice of the fallout; once the bombings started, Mom asked the four of them to spend the evenings with us in the Anderson Shelter.

'Now this shelter was up the top end of the garden, next to the rhubarb patch, as far as you could get from the house. It was a big "U" of corrugated metal, ten foot long, five foot across and painted olive green. Olive green paint was cheaper back then – I suppose they were having to make so much of it for the camo. Dad had built a brick wall in the one end that was half-buried in the compost heap, and he'd fitted heavy wooden doors to the other. He'd got this all done just before they posted him off we didn't know where (It turned out, when he got back, to have been North Africa and he brought a nasty bit of shrapnel with him that the doctors never took out until 1968).

'Funnily enough, after it was all over, he knocked the brick wall down and shifted the whole thing so it stood right next to the house. There, as a coal bunker, it stayed until the pair of them passed away. That was in the early nineties. Then we sold it for a fiver to a neighbour who turned it into a tool shed for his quarter-acre at Winson Green Allotments. You can still see it there, with one or two others very similar, just the other side of the railway tracks from the Metro stop.

'It would have been cosy enough in there with just the seven of us but somebody had the bright idea of fetching Granddad up from Olive Lane so, to add to our terrors of getting TNT'd, we had to put up with the old chap's constant moaning about his rheumatism, his sciatica and – his favourite cause for complaint – his piles.

'Bloody hell, what we didn't know about Granddad's piles by the time the Luftwaffe finally gave it a rest in '43 would not have taken much telling.

'Dad had done the old 'uns a favour just before he'd headed off: he'd got hold of a long electric cable. We could plug it into the chunky Bakelite socket in the kitchen and run it through the window, then up the garden path to the shelter, so we could have the radio on. I say 'the old 'uns' because even then, when I was only seven or eight, and ten to fifteen years before Elvis, it was getting so I'd had quite enough of The Henry Hall Orchestra.'

I remembered hearing from Auntie Frieda that Kevin had got to be a teddy boy in the late fifties. She and Mom had been disgusted. But it made sense that all that smoochy wartime big band stuff was never going to have been his cup of tea.

'It didn't matter,' he went on. That dial used to light up with a warm electric glow and those BBC voices – the sort you don't hear so much today – used to light us up with the same sort of warm glow. Wasn't so convincing, though, when the sky turned to Krupp steel and we had the sound of Birmingham going up – only five miles or so away. Things would turn silent as soon as the first bombs went off. Grandad even stopped moaning about his piles. The little light from the radio and the bigger light from the hurricane lamp looked fragile. All of us felt so small – so bloody small. And I think the grownups felt smallest of all of us.

'Sometimes, Mom put me in charge of Celia, my little sister. She was a noisy bugger usually, but the sound of the Jerry planes above shut even her up. She'd make up for it straight after, though! The first rising note of the all-clear had her squealing her guts out.

'Until Jenny stepped in. How old was she? Younger than me. Five, maybe. I never took much notice of her until I first heard her singing. Don't remember what it was – something by Gracie Fields, probably. As I said, I never cared for that sort of stuff but it did the trick with Celia. The tears dried up, the squealing stopped and – *poof!* – she was zizzing away as if Hitler didn't exist.

'And now I think back on it, perhaps there was something about that voice of Jenny's. Mesmeric, you might have called it, or hypnotic. It made you think that everything was going to be alright.

'She was a pretty little thing, too. If she'd lived, she'd have grown up to be a stunner. I'm biased, I know, but I can imagine her as one of those models in the swinging sixties, like Twiggy or Jean Shrimpton. It wasn't just the looks: there was a calm about her – something weirdly wise that seemed to come from deeper than what ought to be in a tiny tot.

'Jenny Croviss. We all loved her for what she could do.

'It was a different story with your mom and your Auntie Frieda. They were about eleven when the bombs first started. And, even then, you got the feeling they didn't quite belong in this world – that just being here scared them to death. It didn't help being stuck in an Anderson shelter with the bombs coming down, but, when the all-clear sounded, the rest of us always looked relieved; they never did.

'It got to be a ritual, the eight of us scrunched in that upturned metal "U" (or even ten, sometimes, now I think of it, depending on whether Great Aunties Violet and Flossie had come over from the Cakemore Road). However loud the bombs, however explicit the update on the state of the piles, we got so that we just put up with it, bar the occasional incident of Auntie Flossie telling Granddad he should go and see Doctor Adden about some pile ointment if they were that much of a bother. Granddad would look hurt.

'A ritual, then – for all of us except the twins.

'I sometimes thought they welcomed the bombing. It gave them something to pin their fears to. A big *"something"*, of course, but better that than being afraid of... they didn't know what. Every time they came out of that shelter (sometimes so late that the sun was getting up), every time they poked their faces out into the air, or came into our back kitchen with that bright electric light – 'cause of course, until 1958, Auntie Doris only had gas…'

'What?!' Frances exploded with incredulity.

'It's a Blackheath thing,' I explained. 'Another Blackheath thing.'

'Too true,' said Kevin. 'Anyway, every time they knew they'd got through one more night, they looked like they'd got a little thinner, a little paler, a little more like they'd wanted the bombs to get them. A little more like they'd longed for a death-by-bombing to save them from something worse.

'I remember: one time, early morning, we got back into the kitchen and your mom asked where the toilet was? It was rare enough she and Frieda did even that separately but, that time, Frieda had stubbed her toe on something and was in tears, little Jenny singing softly, consolingly to her.

'My mom reminded your mom that it was at the back of the scullery: your mom had gone there often enough that she shouldn't have needed telling.

'Frieda's cries got more persistent; we didn't really notice that your mom had completely ignored Mom's directions and started going upstairs. I could just make out her soft clump-clumping on the stairs over Frieda's racket, but I don't think anyone else did. God knows why she thought it was up there because the bog at their place was in the washhouse over the yard. Once she'd got to the top of the stairs, she was silent and there was only Frieda's snivels – reluctantly quietening down – and Granddad's pile-inspired groans. Mom had gone back up the shelter to get the radio, though everything had been off-air for hours.

'Which was when your mom screamed.

'It wasn't like one of Celia's screams. There was something too unhealthy about it. Auntie Doris was up the stairs like a shot. I followed, curious.

'Your mom was in the front bedroom, on her knees, rigid and staring.

'In front of her was an old mirror. It was a dreadful bit of Victorian tat with a flaking gold-painted frame, spotted and giving a nasty, pee-coloured reflection. The thing had come down to dad from someone in his family, years before, and Mom, growing sick of having it in the front parlour, had carted it upstairs and leant it against the foot of the big bed.

'Auntie Doris didn't say anything. She just took your mom in her arms and held her. The kid started to shake, though her eyes stayed as unblinking as a corpse's. God, that look! I had nightmares about it!

'After a couple of minutes, she spoke, in a cracked whisper.

'"There was a' old woman," she said. "A' 'orrible old woman. A' evil *evil* old woman..."

'I'd never heard so many words come out of her at a stretch.

'"Is everything alright up there?" Mom called up to Auntie Doris.

'"*Yes*" Auntie Doris called back. Then, quietly to your mom: "There's no old woman. There's only you..."

'I stared into the mirror myself for a moment. There was something about it that put me off – more than just the ugliness of the frame. I could believe your mom had seen something in it. I was glad when Mom chucked the bloody thing out a fortnight later.

'Meantime, Frieda had started crying louder again downstairs – and even Jenny couldn't calm her down. Bit by bit, your mom joined in and their wailings made that dawn a miserable one.

'*A' evil* evil *old woman...*

'*What could she have been dreaming of?* I wondered. I didn't allow myself to think: *What did she see in that thing?*

'Slowly, we went back downstairs and came into the kitchen – just as Grandad was getting on to the subject of his rheumatism.'

Kevin ended his story with a terse, humourless laugh.

'I never wondered what it was Mom had against mirrors,' I said. 'She never had one in the house and I never wondered why…'

'You don't.' said Frances, softly, 'When it's what you've always known, you don't wonder. You don't wonder about anything.'

12: Frances Chessil

A still grey Saturday afternoon when I got a call from Tony. I could hear loud traffic through the receiver, almost drowning him out – so he was in a phone box, not at his mom's.

She'd been out of hospital a while now. Dutifully, regularly, Tony had been going round to see her. Bit by bit, it seemed, she was on the mend. But it was hard to be sure because, though the news had tended to be either 'good' or 'as good as could be expected', Tony never spoke as if he thought any of this was going to turn out well. So I was not expecting what he was about to say.

'Mom wants to know... er...' He hesitated. He was very nervous.

'Mom wants to know if... er... if... er... you'd like to come round. Come round here, I mean. You... come round here.'

I felt cold.

It had done him so much good – being in London, being over here in Kidderminster – being anywhere apart from being back in bloody Blackheath. Ever since her accident though, ever since he'd been visiting his mom, I'd been watching the life get sucked out of my husband.

He was still a kind man, still concerned for me, concerned for my folks and concerned for the kids he was teaching. A new shed had gone up in Mum and Dad's back garden, as he'd promised them. But there was something gone from him and, whatever had caused it, it took shape in a conviction, not wholly conscious, that, whatever he did to try and help things, it would all, in the end, be so much rubbish to go on the bonfire.

'You've talked... talked about me, then?' The thought frightened me and I tried to hide my fear with a laugh. But no laugh emerged – not even a little one. And the sweat between the plastic of the phone and my skin – the skin of my ears and the skin of my palms – was weirdly cold. Without wanting to, I was pressing the receiver against me with painful force.

'I've told her we've got married.'

This was the first time he had admitted it.

'Was she angry?'

'Didn't show it. She just said "Oh".'

I'd not expected any blazing rows; no – that hadn't been it at all – but I had expected her to find some way of hurting Tony for doing something so... something so... I didn't quite know what.

Which was crazy because, of course, I had no reason to think she'd be nasty at all. I'd still never actually clapped eyes on the woman.

And all the things Tony had told me about her – which had been corroborated by Kevin – all those things made her sound just plain pitiable. Her dad dying, her sisters dying, 'Uncle Jethro'. Jesus Christ! If anyone deserved a bit of a break, a bit of a second chance, it was Janice Griefstick, born Janice Croviss.

I began to feel ashamed of the causeless aversion I felt for her.

I tried to sound hopeful. 'That... that sounds good. For her, I mean...'

'It is... for her.'

'Right. Shall I come round now?'

'*No!*' Tony's response was sudden and terrified. He inhaled and stammered – tried to stutter excuses:

'Sorry. Sorry. No. No, I mean, she's still a bit... you know... a bit... a bit...'

'Frail?'

'Yes! Yes!' The gratitude I heard in his voice – the gratitude for my giving him the word it had been impossible to find by himself – the gratitude was almost daft. 'Look, just let me have a word...' he gabbled, 'You know? Have a word with her. Okay? Please? Please.'

'Of course, love. There's no rush. Just let her name her own time. We want to make this easy for her.'

'Yes! Yes! Make it easy... for her.'

'Calm down, Tony.'

'I'm sorry. I'm sorry. I'm okay.'

If I'd known him in any other context than marriage, this would have seemed incredible. I'd seen him once or twice with some of the kids he dealt with day-to-day. Quite a few were big fifth years, due to leave at Easter if they'd got jobs. Not the easiest bunch to keep in line.

Tony had been fine with them.

So how come a single fifty-two-year-old woman had pulled his heart's plug? Had done *this* to him?

'Nothing to be sorry for, Tony. Are you with her now?'

'No... No... I'm using the phone box in the centre of town.'

'Well. You decide when it would be good for me to come. No rush. Maybe next weekend.' At his end, a particularly big truck thundered past; I assumed my words must have got lost in its racket so I repeated: 'Maybe next weekend.'

'Yeah. That sounds about right.'

'Okay then. Well, you take care.'

'I will. I'll be back with you in an hour or two. Mrs Pollitt's going to drop round in the evening to make sure everything's alright.'

'Good. Good.'

I didn't have a lot to do that afternoon. The place had been painted, I'd done the shopping in the morning and the two of us never made much mess. So I drove round Mum and Dad's for a cup of tea.

'She *spoke?*' Dad cried in mock astonishment when I told them.

'Don't be naughty, Reg,' Mum scolded.

'It is a bit of a turn up, though,' Dad said, 'you've got to admit.'

Mum's lips twisted. She was finding it hard to argue. 'Well,' she said eventually, 'it is good to hear she's starting to get better.'

I just nodded. And sipped tea. And tried to think of something meaningful to say. Neither Mum nor Dad were going to be satisfied with waffle.

'It's been pretty tough for Tony, of course,' I said, 'and I know I need to expect it to have been.'

'There's a big "but" on the way,' said Dad.

'There is. I just wish I knew what it was exactly. But, the way Tony tells it, when she was in hospital, she only started talking when...'

I paused. Dad drank his tea. Mum patted my hand.

'...when she realised it was looking weird to the nurses. Somebody had a psychiatrist come in to take a look at her. Then she started talking. She didn't want them to think she was doolally.'

'Is that how Tony tells it? I mean, are those his exact words?' Mum looked thoughtful.

'No. But it doesn't take much working out from what he has said...'

'Ah.'

'And I think it's her being so quiet that's taken it out of Tony. Though, by the sound of it, she's always been that way.'

'Well. You've got to feel sorry for her, but it's not the rest of the world's fault that she lost her family. And it's especially not your fault. You mustn't let her go thinking it is.' (Implied threat: *if you don't remind her isn't your fault, I'LL be round to remind her as much.* Mum wasn't usually overprotective: she'd let me move down London on my own, for God's sake. But, like me, she was a bit spooked by the spectre of Janice Griefstick. And I could see her having a right old ding-dong with the woman if she went round in the mood she was in now. This was something I wanted to avoid.)

It was upsetting to admit it but, only six months before, I'd have said Mum was worrying about nothing. The state Tony was in, though – the state his own mother had got him into... You'd almost have thought this was what she wanted.

No, that was crazy. She didn't want to be the way she was...

But then, I thought, *neither does any parasite...*

I finished my tea, gave both of them a kiss and headed back.

Tony had got in before me. He'd flopped down on the sofa without taking his coat off and fallen asleep. His breathing seemed laboured and his skin was very pale.

I sat beside him, whispered *'Love ya!'* quietly enough not to waken him and ran my hand through his hair. He was a ginge, like Mum had been, though his hair was curlier than hers, getting almost frizzy now it was longer. Still he did not wake.

It was starting to rain. I went over to the stereo and flicked through our very small album collection. I chose something I thought would be quiet enough not to wake Tony but, when I put it on, it was louder, more insistent than I'd thought. I turned it down. He remained asleep.

Minutes went by and I put my head on his chest. His breathing changed from 'laboured' to something closer to 'snoring.' I smiled.

A while later, he dragged himself up from the sofa, groaning 'Ooh, me back!' and went to put the kettle on. His skin looked brighter, pinker than it had.

'You okay to come with me to Mom's, next Saturday morning?' he called from the kitchen. The question seemed to have cost him no effort at all.

'Of course,' I said and the brightness in my voice wasn't faked: I was genuinely pleased and – I had to admit – surprised that he'd asked me with such apparent casualness. 'What time?'

'Be there for eleven,' he said, 'so let's get going about ten fifteen. You can have a look around Blackheath Market while we're there. It's a bit of an institution.'

I joined him in the kitchen and put my arms around him from behind.

'I'm glad things are getting sorted,' I said, my face buried in his back.

'Well,' he sighed, 'it looks like they are.'

The week went by quickly. Mum and Dad said nothing more about Tony's mom. Saturday was bright and windy, high stacks of fluffy cloud strolling across the blue sky like self-important white elephants, trees just beginning to bud, thrashing their twigs around merrily. All very cheerful like an English winter's end ought to be.

But Blackheath didn't do 'cheerful'. Never had done. You drove into the place and you could tell. The long, narrow streets of terraced redbrick with grey slate roofs, the little, uninviting Banks's pubs, the factories, some still pluming out the smoke mid-morning Saturday... You wanted 'cheerful', you should go to Birmingham, you should go to Dudley, you should even go to Tipton, because they all had a bloody sight more 'cheerful' than Blackheath.

Tony parked the car opposite his Mom's and we got out. I'd done myself up a bit – put perfume on, which was rare for me. Tony looked as he normally looked. We joined hands and crossed the road together.

The front door had opened before we reached the kerb. A woman of about sixty stood there. She gave us a frown that looked genuine, followed immediately by a smile that didn't.

'Hello, Mrs Pollitt,' said Tony.

'She's just nodded off,' announced Mrs Pollitt in an affectedly loud whisper.

'Oh, we'll be very quiet,' I replied in a whisper quieter than hers.

'Shh!' she said.

Oh dear. I could see I wasn't going to get on at all well with Mrs Pollitt. The smile I gave her bravely attempted to look benevolent but I doubt it was successful. I didn't suppose I needed to worry. She didn't strike me as someone particularly concerned with how people felt about her.

We went in. Dried flowers, furniture polish – and, of course, floor polish. There was a hallway with stairs which went half way up, then took a sharp turn leftwards out of sight. There was a door into the dining room on the left and another, straight ahead, into the kitchen.

This kitchen was where the business of the house had always taken place: one glance into the dining room ('front parlour', I was sure Tony's mom must call it) confirmed the sense that an awful lot of polish and dusting went on, but little or no actual living happened in there. It was like an exhibit behind glass in a museum. In the front parlour, according to the stern, dark wood of the furniture and the clean, cold fireplace, Neville Chamberlain was still Prime Minister and any suggestion to the contrary was about as acceptable as *Lady Chatterly's Lover*.

There were only the two rooms on the ground floor. We followed Mrs Pollitt into the kitchen.

Tony's mom sat on an easy chair of grey upholstery and amber-coloured wood. There was a white cotton antimacassar beneath her head, with a lacy edge and a few pink flowers embroidered in one corner. Her hair was grey and her dress of turquoise cotton. And, yes, you could still see the scars. They weren't overwhelming but there should have been no mistaking their silvery unevenness on her face and her hand. How had their unmentionableness been transformed into invisibility in Tony's mind? How had she done it?

And she was still. I could hardly see breathing. What was she again? Fifty-two? She looked much older and it only made it worse that, despite the scarring, the symmetry and assertiveness of her features showed clearly enough that, once, she must have had, not necessarily a beautiful face, but certainly a face that could have been – ought to have been – very likeable.

The chair, and the little coffee table beside it, didn't really belong in the kitchen. Tony's Mom clearly felt it necessary that space be made for them. A small single bed had also been got hold of and crammed in somehow. – All this just to spare the sacrosanct 'Front Parlour' – which was quite a bit roomier.

We didn't say a word and our steps on the old orange quarry tiles were as silent as if the kitchen had been carpeted.

'Hm-mhhh?'

Tony's Mom made a waking noise. Mrs Pollitt shot us a look of furious accusation. Tony took no notice: he'd clearly grown very used to Mrs Pollitt.

'Hello Mom,' said Tony.

'Why have you come round?' she asked. Her tone wasn't as negative as her words; it didn't sound like an accusation, simply a request for information.

'It's Saturday, Mom,' said Tony.

A flicker of a frown creased the brow of Janice Griefstick.

'Saturday?'

'Saturday. I'm off work.' A long pause then, because she gave no sign of having understood him: 'I'm off work so I can come round to see you.'

His mom's frown deepened. 'I know you don't work on Saturday,' she said. 'What do you think I am – puddled?'

'Of course not. Anyway. We came round because you asked... you asked to meet Frances.' He indicated me. She did not respond to his gesture. He gave a tiny, desperate little laugh: he knew well enough how to deal with his mother, but had no idea how to manage relations between her and the rest of the world. 'Mrs Griefstick, meet Mrs Griefstick,' he attempted. Not successfully: still his mom failed entirely to take note of my presence.

Instead, she started talking about the rooms upstairs. And how they needed cleaning.

'I did them last week, Mom. Don't you remember?'

It seemed she did not. Which was fair enough in a way, because I'd have bet my bottom dollar that, had she been able to get upstairs and check them out, she'd have found his efforts pathetically inadequate.

And, for about an hour and a half, I found myself ignored.

I wasn't insulted – that was the funny thing. I knew damned well that she'd taken in the fact of my being there – that she'd even managed to process the idea that I was her daughter-in-law. But there was something more than simple contempt in her imposition of invisibility on me: I knew, and it chilled me, that she felt herself commanded, with a supernatural absoluteness, that my existence must not be acknowledged, that to do so would be corrupt.

Tony, after a bit, gestured with a little nod that I should sit on a slightly rickety wooden chair, just out of his mom's field of vision. I did so, though from Mrs Pollitt's expression, you'd have thought I'd weed on the Crown Jewels.

Tony, after a bit longer, promised to nip upstairs again and check that everything was up to scratch. No good. His mom now started on the subject of Mrs Pollitt and how all this just wasn't fair on her. Mrs Pollitt's expression remained fixed but she still somehow managed to radiate a harsh sort of delight.

It wasn't fair, Tony's mom lamented, that Mrs Pollitt be expected to do everything. It wasn't her job to make sure that upstairs didn't look like a pigsty. It ought never to have been allowed to get in that state, she said, but that was what it was: a pigsty. An absolute pigsty! It made Tony's mom ill to think about it. It made her positively ill. And when she thought about how it used to be. When she thought about how proud it used to make her feel! Why, she was ashamed. Ashamed! And what was worse...

Quietly, without looking at her, I stood, stepped around Tony and nipped into the hall, then upstairs.

There were two bedrooms – no bathroom. The whole place was, of course, immaculate. Tony's efforts had played a part in this but, credit to Mrs Pollitt, she'd done a good job too; if I'd thought she had been doing it out of anything close to benevolence, I'd have felt gratitude.

The carpet and the wardrobes and the bed linen were as dark and pre-war as everything downstairs but the light shone in brightly through the lace curtains. There was something odd, though...

It took me a moment or two to notice: no pictures. No mirrors of course, but no pictures either. Not a print, painting or photograph: the walls were plain dark wallpaper, unpunctuated by any friendly image.

Well it might have been spotless but just – I said to myself – just to reassure Tony's mom, I'd give the place a run over with the vacuum that I found in what had used to be Tony's bedroom. It was quite a new, light

124

one, which surprised me: I'd have expected some lumbering World War One tank of a contraption that I'd struggle to shift. I was certain Tony's mom would have possessed such an appliance: in truth I bet she'd had one, hung on to it as long as possible and only parted with it when it was completely knackered and falling to bits. The piece of lightweight modern decadence that I now steered around the carpet must have seemed a right letdown: using it was... just not painful enough to be Morally Right.

I'd been Hoovering for thirty seconds when Mrs Pollitt's frantic furious footsteps came detonating up the stairs. She stopped in the doorway of the bedroom and gawped at me, aghast.

I took no notice.

It took her a while to realise that I was taking no notice, and a little while longer for it to sink in that I wasn't going to take any notice.

'What..?' she began, then inhaled, sharply. 'What..?'

I glanced up at her and smiled, then got back to work. I finished the Hoovering in the bedroom and looked under the bed. Spotless.

Then I turned back the bedclothes and had a sniff at the linen.

I looked up at Mrs Pollitt and smiled again – which seemed to annoy her all the more.

'All clean and fresh, Mrs Pollitt. I must say, you've done a wonderful job, keeping it all so nice.' I smiled once more, all sugar-coated cyanide.

'What do you think you're playing at?!' she finally hissed.

'Just a quick bit of Hoovering. I know you've done it, but just to reassure Janice.'

I started the Hoover again and did the little bit of carpet at the stair head and the first couple of steps. Then, stepping around the rug on the polished floor, which was indeed a death-trap, I went into the other bedroom.

My use of Tony's mom's first name had been a further trespass – my worst yet. Mrs Pollitt was out for blood.

'You're doing it all wrong!' she hissed.

'No I'm not,' I said with yet another cyanide smile. 'Look, I won't be a couple of minutes, Mrs Pollitt. Why don't you go back down and put the kettle on?'

Her eyes narrowed and her lips contracted. She said nothing but turned and scuttled down the stairs in a way that was unmistakeably 'making a tactical retreat' but definitely *not* 'beaten'.

There had been no way in which I could have made a friend of Mrs Pollitt. Not ever.

I took my time finishing off the Hoovering and a little while looking around for surfaces that had not been dusted or polished. There were none; perhaps anticipating my arrival, or the arrival of someone like me, Mrs Pollitt had made sure it was all one big immaculate accusation. Or defence. Or whatever.

When I got back downstairs, the atmosphere had turned sullen. Tony's mom sat there silent, still not sparing me a glance. Tony was talking to her – possibly about me. Mrs Pollitt, similarly, was most careful not to look in my direction. She just looked sourly at Tony, as if she really could not believe the bloody nerve of the bloke.

Tony, though, was a proper trouper. He just carried on describing how we'd lived back in Islington, how the job had ended. His brief, barbed reference to Mrs Thatcher drew a terse *'Well I voted for her!'* from Mrs Pollitt. Ignoring this – ignoring Mrs Pollitt completely – Tony plodded on, bringing, or trying to bring his mom up to speed on how things were with us now. I listened – sort of. That's to say, I listened not to the words he spoke, but I listened very carefully to the spaces he left between some of those words – the opportunities he gave her to say *'Oh, that's very nice, I'd like to come over and take a look myself,'* or *'Well, maybe we can go over there together sometime soon.'* or anything like that. All those opportunities were declined with a silence thick and resentful like rancid syrup.

After about ten minutes, I realised I needed the loo. I mouthed an inquiry in Tony's direction and he pointed at the back door.

Then I remembered what he had told me. About the bathhouse. And the single cold tap. And the Izal-bloody-Medicated.

And it turned out it was all true.

Bewildered, I went back in the kitchen.

It was mid-afternoon by the time we got away and, by then, I think even Tony was getting close to losing it.

'No need to come to the door with us, Mrs Pollitt. We can see ourselves out,' he said, determinedly brisk. Then, to his mother: 'I'll be round on Tuesday night so don't try to do get any cleaning done: I'll be seeing to it. See you then. Ta-ra.'

Then, we were out. And outside, it was beginning to cloud over.

We waited until we were both back in the car before speaking.

'I thought she was easing up,' said Tony, 'but she's never been as bad as this. I'm sorry.'

I put my hand on his shoulder.

'Is it Mrs Pollitt?' I asked.

'Nah. Mrs Pollitt's just a glove puppet. It's all coming from Mom.'

'Are you going to come back on Tuesday?'

'Bloody right, I am!' He was momentarily angry. 'I don't know what Mom's trying to do to herself but I'm not going to…' His voice trailed off. *Not going to let it happen?* But what could he do about it?

A son who wanted to save his mother from herself. Never an easy thing for any child to do. But for the child of Janice Griefstick…

But the problem wasn't Janice Griefstick. I was beginning to doubt that, on one level, she'd ever really registered that she'd got married, that she'd become a mum (and bloody hell, there had to be something mightily wrong with a woman who'd *not noticed* the act of childbirth). The problem went back to a time before she'd been Janice Griefstick. The problem was all about Janice Croviss.

Except the problem wasn't Janice Croviss either. Or not just Janice Croviss. It wasn't even the loss of her father and the appearance of the evil sod of a stepdad. Or not those things alone. It was something about her sisters, the three of them together, and their being separated. It was all about Janice Croviss and Frieda Croviss and Jenny Croviss. It was all about the Croviss Girls.

On the way towards Halesowen, we nearly hit a pink Fiat Panda at an island. We got honked at by more than one car. Tony pulled in and sat there, trembling.

'D'you think I should drive?' I asked.

'Yeah. Yeah. Stupid. Shouldn't be letting things…' His voice trailed off.

'Things like this will get to you. Come on; let's swap over.'

We did so and I gave him a kiss before I turned the keys in the ignition. I thought about asking him if he was sure about Tuesday but I didn't: he'd got the idea fixed in his mind.

13: Anthony Griefstick

Frances said I should 'go and have a lie down' as soon as we'd got back. There was an insistence in her voice that wasn't exactly veiled; the suggestion was ready to transform itself into an order. For a moment, I almost became the one who was resentful. What reason did she have..? Then I remembered: I'd nearly crashed the car. Yes, that was reason enough...

I looked, bitterly amused, at the seedling of resentment that had sprouted up in me. Resentment of Frances. Resentment of her thinking it was her place to try and stop the pair of us getting killed at Shell Corner (there were more romantic places to die). Pure Mom, that; if I let myself, I could wind up just like Mom. If I let that little seedling of resentment grow...

That little seedling... I looked at it a bit more carefully. By Christ, it was an evil thing. Tiny, but evil. Feed it on the death of your dad, on an abusive step-father and the deaths of two sisters... What might it have grown into? What fruit might it have borne? I began to feel afraid of Mom. Because I could understand her. And I began to feel even more afraid of the way I'd lived with her until I was eighteen, never noticing the shadow cast by... *(What?)* Never realising how afraid I ought to be.

Frances came in.

'Want to talk about it?' she asked. Good for her. Not '*Everything alright?*' because of course it bloody wasn't.

I thought for a moment. 'Haven't worked out what I think about things,' I said. 'Don't really know what to say yet.'

'Want a cup of tea?'

I smiled and raised myself on to my elbows.

'Yeah. Yeah. That'd be great.'

She smiled, patted my hand and went.

I exhaled and stared at the ceiling – brilliant white and newly painted. The cotton of the pillow was comfortingly cool against my neck. I heard

Frances clump down the stairs, put the kettle on and take out one of the very few pop or rock albums we'd got – The Moody Blues.

She came back up with two big mugs. I propped myself on my elbows and took one. We lay together with the hot china in our hands, heads against the bedroom wallpaper, and sipped carefully as the Moodies waltzed their way through 'Dawn Is a Feeling.'

'Love this song,' said Frances.

'Really unfashionable,' said I.

'Bum to fashionable,' said Frances.

And we finished our tea and it brought me back to life.

'I think,' she said, 'if you go round your mom's on Tuesday, you should ask Kevin to go with you.'

'He's a busy bloke,' I said. 'Got his own family.'

'I know,' she said, 'but if he's not *too* busy. He knows your mom. He'll understand.'

And he did.

I rang him that evening. He said okay before I'd even told him about crashing the car. When I did tell him, his lack of surprise was unnerving.

'Ah,' he said. 'Yeah. I know. Stuff like that.'

'Stuff like what?'

He hesitated. 'Wish I could tell you. Funny stuff. Funny peculiar stuff. Happens around your mom. Used to happen around her sisters too. You remember your Auntie Frieda was just the same...'

Yes. I remembered.

'Used to get it even more around your Auntie Jenny,' he went on. 'Though with her, it was always nice stuff – stuff to make you laugh.'

Different to Mom and Auntie Frieda then. Very different.

'I'll come with you on Tuesday, not to fret,' he said. 'Try not to get in too much of a state about it between now and then.'

'Cheers, Kev. See you Tues.'

'See you then. Tararabit.'

Relieved, I put the phone down and smiled up at Frances. She smiled back.

'He's going with you?' she asked.

'Yeah.'

Her arms went around me and we hugged.

'I need,' I said, 'to find out a bit more about my mom. And her family.'

I felt Frances nod, gently, against my shoulder.

'Won't be much good asking her though, will it?' she said.

I sighed. 'No,' I said.

'And Mrs Pollitt won't be any more help.'

'She won't,' I said. 'She definitely won't.'

'And if either of them find out you've been asking...'

'It'll be a sodding Greek tragedy. Shrieking furies, Clytemnestra's ghost, the lot.'

'D'you suppose Kevin knows much more?'

'Doubt it,' I said. 'Well, not anything that's very important. But I'll ask him.'

Frances went down to change the record over. 'Tuesday Afternoon' came on. She came back up and we made love. Then we got the dinner ready. Each thing we did together was like a stone added to a wall between us and... and whatever it was that had got Mom. Yes, here was another way of looking at it – perhaps a more rational one: something had 'got' Mom. Maybe, between them, all those deaths and sodding Jethro had bitten so many chunks out of her personality... That felt more like it. A personality with bits bitten out of it. Leaving a lot of pain and a lot of sharp edges for others to cut themselves on.

I'd got used to those edges. I'd made it my life's work to skirt them without getting snagged or pierced. I'd been a loner at school because the skills that made you functional around Mom had the opposite effect around anyone else. But Frances... I was starting to realise how good she was at coping with the very strange family life – well, not exactly 'family life' – which I'd unthinkingly dragged her into. A lot of other women would have been telling me to sever all connection with 'the old bat' or our marriage wouldn't last any longer. Frances seemed the model of patience. But she wasn't blind to the risks of having too much to do with Mom. She was being very very careful.

And that care showed on her face as I set off for Kevin's on Tuesday.

Kevin had three kids and the two lads were a pair of little headbangers. I narrowly missed treading on a couple of well-used *Star Wars* toys in the hall. His missus, a flustered little woman with a big smile, was all apologies but I told her not to worry. We weren't able to hang around as it was already dark, but it didn't take very long to get to Mom's.

I opened the door. Mrs Pollitt emerged from the kitchen, looking ready to start making issues out of things, but the sight of Kevin took the wind out of her sails. We put on the charm for all we were worth, though she wasn't the least bit softened. As we then did for Mom, with a similar lack of result.

I went upstairs and Hoovered. It didn't need it, but I did it and carefully too. Kevin went into the inner sanctum, the front room, and polished. It definitely didn't need it, but he bloody well polished. While we were at this, Mrs Pollitt left.

'You've upset Mrs Pollitt,' Mom accused in a low voice, as we came back into the kitchen.

'Oh, I'm sorry. How?' I asked, trying to sound just the right degree of concerned.

'Well,' Mom said, then seemed to dry up. Then, after a pause: 'You don't seem to realise how much she puts herself out.'

'Oh, I do,' I said, feeling that, just this once, a bit of insistent contradiction was necessary – though it made me very uncomfortable. 'We're very grateful for all she's done. That's why I'm going to be dropping round a bit more often – to take some of the burden off her.'

Kevin gave me a worried look as I said that.

'Don't talk rubbish,' Mom grumbled.

'How is that rubbish?'

'Don't try it on with that sort of stuff.'

'What sort of stuff d'you mean? I'm just going to help out a bit. Until you're back on your feet a bit more...' I was in danger of starting to gabble, to act defensive. That would be a mistake – it would set her off all the more and she might turn really nasty. So I made myself shut up.

There was a very grim sort of silence. She stared at me, and at Kevin, at the level of our hearts. She did not, to begin with, meet our eyes.

When she eventually raised her gaze, it was a very peculiar thing – very empty.

'You'd better go,' she said.

'Okay, but I'll be back same time next week,' I said. 'It'd be wrong not to.' I kicked myself for saying that. Her eyes flashed furiously.

'Don't give me any of that *"right"* and *"wrong"* stuff,' she said, coolly matter-of-fact. 'You don't know the meaning of the words.'

'Wait and see,' I said.

She made a contemptuous noise as Kevin and I headed out.

'D'you really think you ought to make a habit of coming round here?' asked Kevin as we crossed the road to the car.

'Yes I do. I mean, I can see what she's going to be like...'

'She could get worse. She's spent a long time wanting to take it all out on the rest of the world. Now you're back in this neck of the woods, "The Rest of the World" means you. You and Frances. You need to watch it.'

'Ah,' I said as the car started, 'but I'm not "in this neck of the woods." Kidderminster isn't Blackheath – not to someone of Mom's generation.'

Kevin thought about that. 'I see your point there. But... keep a distance if you can.'

I began to wonder if there was anyone else I could possibly go to for help. It didn't seem fair to be bothering Kevin so much and I wasn't planning on asking him to help out the following week. But he was at least family. Anyone else...

And again, I could see myself acting like Mom: I needed help here – genuinely. But I wasn't asking for it. Just as Mom would have thought even the most desperately needed help, if it didn't come from Mrs Pollitt or Auntie Frieda or Auntie Jenny, was forbidden. To ask for it was criminal – abominable.

'It's not normal, you know,' said Kevin, in the car.

He didn't need to explain what he meant.

'We both used to think it was,' I answered. 'Mom and me. We used to think it was normal. If we thought at all.'

'Frieda was the same. Since Jenny died, all the pair of them have ever done is mind their own business.'

'It seems that way,' I said, going round the big island in the middle of Blackheath. 'And yet she doesn't seem worried about having Mrs Pollitt's help.'

'Hmm... That's always been more like a business arrangement than any kind of friendship.'

'Mom doesn't do "friendship".'

133

'Too right. Still, Mrs Pollitt acts like she's getting something out of it. Wish I could work out what.'

'So do I. She's not somebody who I'd have thought would do anything out of the goodness of her heart.'

We changed the subject. Kevin, it turned out, worked for the gas board. It was a dull, pen-pushing sort of job but it had always been reliable. 'Might not go on that way,' he said, 'if they do what some people are saying.'

'Hey?'

'Flog it off to the private sector.'

'*What?*'

'That's the word around the camp fire. Sounds crackers to me but, you know, anything's possible...'

The same sort of thing that had cost me my job down in London. These were worrying times.

'D'you know anyone else who'd remember Mom, back when she was a kid?' I asked, the previous subject dragging me back.

'Apart from me, no. I bet there are some in her street, though,' said Kevin. 'But be careful. You don't want to have her or Mrs Pollitt thinking you're poking your nose into things.'

'No. I don't,' I said.

And there we left it.

Kevin asked me in when we got round his place. It was past nine, and his mother-in-law, a big fat jolly woman, was doing her best to tire out the nippers by dancing with them to a Duran Duran tape. 'Do you like Duran Duran, Tony?' she asked me.

'Er... Well, I haven't heard them much.'

'Ooh, I think they're lovely!' she said, and sang along with the chorus, hand in hand with the little 'uns as they circled around.

This was a woman ten years older than my mom – at least. Yet the idea of Mom being prepared to put up with Duran Duran – no, make that the Beatles – no, make that Frankie Vaughan – was bonkers.

For the next few weeks, things settled into a pattern. This suited Mom fine, I guess: she was a one for patterns. I'd be round there every Tuesday night. Sometimes Kevin would come along; sometimes he wouldn't. Sometimes Mrs Pollitt was there to monitor us, gloweringly. Sometimes she wasn't. We'd dust, Hoover, polish and keep as cheerful as we could. After the first couple of times, Mom stopped complaining so much. I even wondered, once, if she was growing to like our visits, though perhaps not consciously. You'd have expected her to: she didn't seem to see anybody else. But no, I told myself, feeling a twinge of real fear; that'd be a dangerous assumption to make. My being there made her angry. My staying away would have made her angry. I made her angry... by existing. I wasn't insulted or hurt by this. I knew the rest of the world made her just as angry. Except for Mrs Pollitt. Everything and everybody made her angry because...

I was driving home from a Tuesday night when I finally understood and I teared up.

Everything and everybody – including me – made Mom angry because none of us were Auntie Frieda, because (more importantly) none of us were Auntie Jenny. It should have been obvious to me as soon as Kevin had told me of Jenny's existence, but it was such a huge part of Mum's being that I'd been too close to see it.

Auntie Jenny had been Mom and Auntie Frieda's way of relating to the world. Their means of feeling anything positive about it, of feeling anything at all about it. And she had been stolen from them. It had taken its time, but that alone had killed Auntie Frieda.

And that alone had turned Mom into someone – into something – I could trust even less than she trusted me.

I got home, clanked my way up the stairs and let myself into the kitchen. 'Frances?'

'In here!' she called, brightly, from the lounge.

I plonked myself on the sofa next to her and our arms went around each other. She looked almost luminous and happy beyond words.

Of course, that was the night she told me she was pregnant.

14: Frances Chessil

Pregnancy breezed in along with the spring and Mum began to make the sort of quiet, effective fuss that I'd expected. She was always round, always helpful, and always brilliant at finding ways of making it not obvious that she was being helpful. The flat stayed tidy – exactly as tidy as Tony and I always kept it, not a bit tidier. I loved her for that.

Tony was still around his mom's every Tuesday night – that had become 'Mom Night'. Apart from that, he hardly mentioned her. He'd changed his mind about going round more often: he was being canny with himself, rationing the time he spent there, knowing that spending more would do her no good and himself a lot of harm. His focus was back on us.

From what I heard, his mom seemed to be doing alright. She was beginning to act fifty-two, not seventy-two. Up on her feet unassisted and pottering round the house. Even going out and, apparently, there wasn't a day Blackheath Market was open when she wasn't round there. Haggling a hard bargain, I was sure.

She still wasn't saying much but, he told me, little of what she did say now was particularly hostile. Tony was full of quiet, blissful relief at this but he still didn't tell her I was pregnant.

Shortly after, though, Janice Griefstick must have found out that somebody else in the family had given birth: Martin Icement's wife, Shirley, had had a daughter a year or more back.

To start with, neither Tony nor I had any idea what had caused the sudden relapse in his mom's mood; he came back from hers the one Tuesday night and I could see from the state he was in that everything had changed. He was as grey as a corpse and his hands trembled as I shoved a cup of tea into them.

'Tony... what..?'

'Thanks,' he whispered, necking more of the tea at once than he should have: it was hot – he must have scalded himself.

'What happened?'

'Happened?'

'Yeah, *happened*. You look half-dead, Tony. Come and have a lie-down.'

His brow creased and he blinked. 'Nothing happened. I just... I just Hoovered a bit.'

'Hoovered? You look like you've lost half your blood.'

'Oh well... then... perhaps I should... should...'

'Should have a lie down, Tony. Come on.'

I plucked his sleeve and he followed me, dragging his feet like a shell-shocked soldier. He finished his tea and I guided him upstairs, where he collapsed on to the bed. I dragged his legs up on to it and helped him turn himself round. With a bit of a struggle, I got his shoes off.

He was out cold and I knew there'd be little point trying to rouse him. I went back into the kitchen, sat down and sipped my own tea – Christ, it was still scalding! One thing was for sure: I wasn't letting him go back there next week! His mom could grizzle all she bloody well liked.

Maybe...

Hmm... Maybe if I went round there myself and did the Hoovering again? That'd shake her up a bit and maybe make her mind her Ps and Qs.

I smiled to myself. The more I dwelt on it, the more it seemed like a good idea. If she wanted anything more to do with Tony – if she wanted anything to do with the grandchild she'd soon be having – she'd better not give him another dose of... whatever she'd given him tonight.

I washed up the tea things, had a bath and undressed. On the bed, Tony still lay, breathing shallowly. I dragged his clothes off him – apart from the shirt, which I could not shift – and got under the sheets next to him.

Half way through the night, he woke up.

'Ey?' he said.

'You passed out,' I told him.

He sat up, took his shirt off and scrabbled after his pyjamas.

'What happened at your mom's?'

He exhaled, heavily.

'Tell me in the morning, if you like.'

'No... no. Nothing happened. It was just... I don't know... something had put her in a bad mood. A hell of a bad mood.'

There was a pause.

'Let me go over there next week,' I said.

'Sure you want to? I mean...'

'I'm not that far gone, yet. And it won't do *me* any harm.' I wasn't yet quite ready to use the plural pronoun in respect of me and the child-to-be.

So I went round the following Tuesday.

To find that Tony's mom had had the lock changed.

I put the key she'd lent him in, twisted it, and hit resistance.

Hmm... I might have expected this.

I rang the doorbell. Tony's mom opened it.

'Oh,' she said, with no evident emotion.

'Tony's not too well. I'll do the Hoovering this week. You've changed the lock.'

'Yes. There's some funny people about.'

'Hmm. I'm sure. Got a spare key for us?'

'No. There's only the one. With Mrs Pollitt.'

That almost sounded reasonable: Mrs Pollitt was, after all, her next door neighbour. If it hadn't been possible to have *two* spares made, I'd have swallowed it.

'We'll have to get another one done,' I said. 'I could nip over on Saturday and go round to the locksmith's.'

She shot me the predictable look of withering contempt. I deflected it with my blandest smile. That annoyed her even more: her brows screwed themselves up into a frown that looked quite painful.

'That won't be necessary,' she whispered.

I smiled again, still bland.

Now with anyone else, I'd've expected a cup of tea. Absolutely anyone else. Not here, though. Not a flaming chance. But that gave me a bit of an advantage, because it brought her uncomfortably close to a state of obvious strangeness. There was one thing I was sure of about Janice Croviss: she insisted on being spoken of – on being *thought* of – as completely normal. Of course she was the weirdest person I'd ever met and, beneath all the cold and scrupulous propriety, she did know this. So she was – necessarily – worried sick that me or anyone else might, at some time or other, point out to her – point out to her very very politely,

138

because that'd hurt all the more – her own extreme peculiarity. Now that she was physically better and thinking straight, unless she felt herself threatened, she wasn't going to be too obnoxious. She didn't want to provoke the likes of me into telling her that she was in any way odd.

I went upstairs and Hoovered the carpet. Then I came down and grabbed the polish and some dusters. I'd thought I'd remembered where they were kept but I'd asked Tony in order to be sure. Janice Croviss sat back down in the kitchen and picked up a copy of *Woman's Weekly*. She raised it like a shield. I went back upstairs.

I found myself reluctant to put too much strain into doing the polishing: okay, it was early days but I wasn't going to take any chances at all. Not when the signs were that Tony and I would eventually have to cut all ties with this woman. But both of us felt that, when that day came, we'd need to know that we'd been fair – completely fair. I mustn't give her the tiniest cause for complaint. So I took my time. Every niche and cranny was purged of dust and muck. I left upstairs pristine – I out-Pollitted Mrs Pollitt.

Down I came – bringing the Hoover with me. I turned it on and did the 'front parlour', lifting up the tablecloth to make sure I got every smidgen of dust from under the big, dark wood dining table – on which I bet no one had dined in thirty years.

I finished the Hoovering and dusted. Then I put everything away and went into the kitchen.

'There's nothing for you in here,' said Tony's mom, tonelessly, from behind her *Woman's Weekly*. 'Nothing.' She looked up, her face expressionless: 'Mrs Pollitt's been in and done it.'

Mrs Pollitt again. Ah.

'What about the bathhouse?' I asked.

She twitched; she'd not thought of that.

I crossed the yard and looked inside. Triumph! The place was in a bit of a state. It had only been a few weeks since I'd last seen it but the walls had gone mouldy. They'd have been prone to that all along, of course: they'd never have had any damp-proofing. Tony's mom must have felt she was scrubbing up her virtue itself when she got the brush and the household bleach to them – you could still smell it a bit. But she'd forgotten to send Mrs Pollitt over here while she'd been ill, and now green-black evil had claimed the walls.

I went back into the kitchen. For once, Janice Croviss looked defeated: head lolling, arms hanging limp and silent.

I looked in the cupboard. There was the bottle of bleach, there was the white enamelled bucket and there... Hmm. I held it up: not very impressive.

'We're going to need a bigger scrubbing brush,' I said.

Too late to get one now: the shops were shut, so I promised to have one with me the following week.

That was the only time, out of company, that I ever got a word of politeness from Janice Croviss: a whispered, dusty little 'Thank you' that seemed amazed by its own existence. Janice Croviss had surely waited a long time to feel able to say it. I almost took her hand. But that'd have been going too far.

Tony was concerned.

'You sure you ought to be clambering over the sink getting the mould off?' he asked when I got home and told him.

'I'll be okay. I'm still not that far gone...'

'I think I should come with you,' he suggested.

'NO!'

I'd never heard myself shout like that before. Never heard myself so angry, so frightened. I tried to explain, stammered and stumbled over my words, then tried again.

'I think she might... I don't know... She was bad enough to start with but at the end... There was something... Something seemed to be happening to her as if...'

I gave up. There was only one way of putting it that made any sense but it seemed so inadequate:

'As if she's getting back on track. Getting back on track in the head, I mean. Something had knocked her off course but...'

A brief silence. Tony put his arms around me.

'But I think she needs... She needs a bit... She needs a bit more...'

'She needs a bit more time,' he said. 'I know.'

We gave her a week.

In that time, we had another visit from Kevin.

'Frieda's Martin's a dad,' he told us. 'A girl. Alice.'

'What's Martin's surname again?' I asked.

'Icement.'

'Alice Icement.' Nice. It sounded like a faerie name. A name for a little girl who'd grow up in some faerie place and put all kinds of well-meaning spells on people. On all sorts of people.

'Was that what put her in a funny mood the other day?' I wondered.

'Very likely,' said Kevin. 'They'd waited nearly two years before they let her know. The nipper's a right little chatterbox already.'

Yes. Well, not being told for two years would have peed off most grannies, I supposed. At which moment, the crazy idea of dinner or tea at Janice's flashed into my head.

'Could you give the Icements a ring and ask them to come round?' I asked. 'Come round Janice's, I mean?'

Tony spluttered over his tea at that.

'Well Martin and Shirley, yes,' said Kevin, 'but poor old Fred's not really able to get about since he had the operation...'

'Pity about that. But I was going over there Tuesday,' I said, 'in the evening to scrub the bathhouse. It might be nicer if we all dropped in...'

...And did what any family would do. And maybe dragged Janice Croviss into normality.

'Should you be thinking about scrubbing the bathhouse?' asked Kevin, 'I mean, in your...'

'Oh don't you start! I've had all that off him–' tipping my head at Tony. 'My Nannanan had Grandma at a shop-stewards' meeting after a *full day* in the carpet factory. I think I'll be able to scrub a bathhouse.

'Okay, okay, just as long as you're sure.'

I was sure. I was surer still the following day when, in preparation for Tuesday next, I bought a big scrubbing brush – eight inches by three and with the stiffest bristles I'd ever seen.

I was less sure when Mum announced that she and Dad would like to meet 'Mrs Griefstick' too, now she was getting a bit better. And why not make it Tuesday next?

The scope for things going wrong was too obvious to mention, too frightening to ignore.

'Er... Mum... Could it possibly..?'

'Possibly what?' her voice crackled down the phone line.

'Possibly wait until..?'

'Until when?'

'Until the week after..? Maybe..?'

'Whatever for?'

'Well, her nephew's coming on Tuesday as well, with his wife and their two-year-old...'

I'd said the wrong thing. Toddlers were irresistible to Mum.

'Ooh! We must come then! What's the name, your little cousin?'

'Er... Alice.'

'A girl! Oh, I shall have to bring her something...'

Mum would make sure 'something' meant something useful. Not pretty, necessarily, or expensive, but helpful. The Icements would have cause to be thankful.

Next Tuesday came. It had been quietly decided that my scrubbing the bathhouse could wait a bit: there'd be too much else going on. The evening was a warm, golden one with clouds like big yellow monuments from another planet. Kevin had to cry off at the last minute when his younger lad sprained his ankle from sliding down the bannister. We turned up at Tony's Mom's, to find the Icements at the door seconds before us.

What a peculiar pair they were. Shirley Icement was an immaculate dresser. There was something oddly familiar about her face: it was sculpted-looking with high, prominent cheekbones and pale grey eyes. I'd heard she was a teacher; those eyes could have kept any number of teenagers nervous and silent – for just as long as she wanted them to be. A teacher – yes. She must have been a bloody good teacher.

So what was she doing married to Martin?

I'd never seen a bloke so nondescript; he seemed to be willing himself out of existence with every breath. He met no one's eyes, spoke in monosyllables but, a lot of the time, you could see his lips moving as if he were engaged in a constant internal monologue. I thought I caught the words *great laugh* at one point. And yet I could see the resemblance to Tony's Mom, even to Tony himself, a bit. *Tony could have turned out like this*, I told myself.

So Shirley Icement might have looked purposeful and self-sufficient but, away from her job, there must have been a bloody great crack in all that. Nobody with perfect self-confidence would have married a man whose only function could ever be to offer no resistance, to merely nod in mute agreement. She might have got her stroppy fifth-year bottom set fooled, but she wasn't fooling me. Little Alice stood next to her, cradling a doll, with a tiny bright smile for us. I thought she was sweet enough to charm the Devil.

Mum and Dad had squeezed out of the back seat of the car and were getting themselves ready for the front door to open. Mum brushed a lot of imaginary fluff off Dad's woolly and looked him up and down, judging him adequate with a terse, bossy little nod.

Then she noticed Shirley Icement.

Whatever was familiar to me in the woman's face, it was obviously familiar to Mum as well. I noted Mum's brow creasing a little. And of course, Mrs Icement noticed that she'd been noticed. There was a wrinkle of displeasure around those cold beautiful eyes. Mum and I both saw that *'I know your face ever so well'* would be the wrong thing – very much the wrong thing – to say to Shirley Icement. So we were careful to look at her as infrequently as possible for the whole of the evening.

The front door opened.

Janice Croviss amazed me. She was wearing the most charming smile you could imagine – her professional face.

And her posture was similarly professional: efficient. I could tell Shirley Icement noted this efficiency and, I supposed, approved of it. Her expression as we went in suggested as much. But I wondered how deep the approval went. Given her choice of husband, would she really want him closely related to someone like Janice? Someone who was anything but the kind of hopeless case with whom she seemed comfortable?

We were shown into the front parlour – The front parlour! Janice Croviss was breaking out The Big Guns tonight! Again, Shirley Icement looked dryly approving; Martin Icement looked oblivious. He plonked himself down at the table like a sack of spuds. Janice gave him a bit of a dirty look – which she hooded almost instantly. Shirley gave him an even briefer look, full of terse disapproval – but of no surprise. Janice then gave her a nod of encouragement and she sat next to Martin. There was a high stool for Alice – Janice must have borrowed it from somewhere – but it wasn't quite high enough and Alice's bright little eyes peered Kilroy-like over the table edge, across the vast white cloth.

We sat opposite. I looked from Martin to Tony and back again. The sense of amazement was growing in me – that Tony had managed to turn out different to Martin! For what had happened with Martin was absolutely clear: Janice and Frieda Croviss had been two for a pair and, however they'd wound up the way they had, they'd needed their menfolk to be harmless. But it was a need that could never be met: no man could ever be unthreatening enough. So both of them had ground away at their husbands and at their sons, trying to smooth out all the rough edges. Martin was the result. Tony, somehow, was not. How had he managed that? Where had he found the self-discipline?

Mum and Dad squeezed themselves into two chairs with their backs to the front window.

Tony's mom went to get the tea.

She returned with a plate of sandwiches. White bread, crusts cut off.

'Do help yourselves,' she said, with her professional smile.

So I helped myself to one. I took a bite out of it.

Cucumber. Not cheese and cucumber. Not salmon and cucumber. Just cucumber. I had not thought it possible, in 1981, that anybody was still eating cucumber sandwiches. It went, I supposed, with the Izal Medicated.

Mum had turned the charm on so, when Janice returned with an ornate white teapot, she smiled and said: 'Leave mine to stew a bit, please.'

Again, a very brief, very slight flash of disapproval crossed the face of Janice Croviss. Even tea, if it got a bit too strong, seemed to carry the taint of excess and of threatening masculinity.

Predictably, the stuff she poured for the rest of us was what I could hear, as if telepathically, Mum thinking of as "pee-wee tea". Pale beige and utterly tasteless. I drank mine politely, as did Tony.

'I think your little great-niece is an angel, Mrs Griefstick,' said Mum, with another smile. Which was the right thing to say, because it got them all on to the subject of small children. Which Janice either was interested in or did a very good job of pretending to be interested in. Much was said, affectionately, about what a 'little terror' I'd been. Shirley looked

144

apprehensive; Martin looked blank. Janice had quite a bit to say, much less affectionately, about Tony and Martin. She found a lot of points of comparison, mostly with Martin coming out in a better light.

That was – until it came to 'the dreadful business with that "band" thing.

'Frieda wouldn't have stood for it,' Janice explained. 'Frieda wouldn't have stood for it at all. But she'd just died. And within two years – just two years – he was with these horrible people. Horrible horrible people – and he was getting just as bad as them. Hair growing – over his *ears*.'

I glanced at Martin just long enough to see that long hair would have suited him.

'And telling people he was making music,' Janice insisted. 'He can't play anything! Never could! He was just acting silly with a tape recorder – weren't you?'

Martin nodded and gave a wan smile.

'I don't...' he began, then hesitated. 'I don't remember much about those days.'

'I should think not,' his aunt declared. 'I should think not.'

'*Hammahammahamma...*' sang Alice.

Mum tried to get Tony to say a bit about the kids he taught. Alice kept interrupting with her '*Hammahammahamma!*' until Martin, suddenly understanding, ventured a hesitant little laugh.

'She's trying to sing that Kate Bush song!' he explained, '"Hammer Horror!"'

'I wouldn't know,' said his aunt, coldly and giving him a filthy look.

'*Hammahammahamma...*' Alice wasn't giving up. It was like she was defending herself against something. Defending herself – and maybe defending her dad at the same time. I could see a nasty light dawning in the eyes of both Janice Croviss and Shirley Icement. Everything was poised to End in Tears.

'She's a bit restless, I think,' I broke in. 'Shall we take her for a toddle around the block?'

I smiled at Shirley. She looked blank. Then, sensing that this was the best way to avoid a scene and not liking scenes at all, she nodded.

So little Alice Icement, Frieda Croviss' granddaughter, went for a toddle with her mother (neither 'mom' nor 'mum' seemed quite right for

145

Shirley) and with her Auntie Frances, leaving Martin, Tony and my folks with Janice.

Oddly enough, it was quite a pleasant toddle – for the most part.

A nice evening and the sunlight on the redbrick of all those Blackheath terraces made them look like somewhere you'd want to live – the place had lost its *Coronation Street* gloom.

We wound up wandering into St Paul's Churchyard – dragged by Alice's pretty, tiny little hands.

'Do you know any nursery rhymes, Alice?' I asked her.

She made a noise of uncertainty.

'Do you know "Round and Round the Garden"?'

There was a sudden tension in Shirley. I ought to have taken more notice of it, but I was too swept up by how charming Alice was.

> *'Round and round the garden,*
> *Like a teddy bear*
> *One step, two step –'*

'*PLEASE!*' Shirley's cry was sudden and shocking. 'Please don't...'

And her voice had changed. Until now, it had sounded ordinary – perhaps even local. In pain it had transformed – become unmistakeably '*pahblek skoohwihl*'. And I knew I was hearing her real voice.

She was suffering: I could hear that too. And though I found her a funny coot, I could tell she had grounds for her suffering. However much wealth she'd grown up cushioned by – and those pained vowels told me there'd been a lot of it – she'd found some very sharp edges buried among the cash. Edges that had cut.

So I changed tack, quickly.

'Let's stick to Kate Bush then,' I said, 'Let's stick to "Hammer Horror".'

Shirley's smile of gratitude was genuine.

'*Hammahammahamma...*' sang Alice.

'I love the video to this song,' I said. 'Have you seen it?'

'I'm not sure.'

'It's got all those old troupers from the Hammer Horror films miming doing the backing vocals – you know: Christopher Lee and Peter Cushing and Kenneth More. Hilarious.'

'Oh... I don't really... listen to much music.'

'Really? I thought you and Martin..?'

'Oh, he'd finished with all that rubbish years before we met. We just bumped into each other in a pub in Kingswinford. He'd gone down there to get "blind steaming drunk" as he put it. But his mates had had a fall out and it wasn't happening. So we wound up...'

Very odd. Didn't sound to me like adequate grounds to have kicked off the process of falling in love – if 'love' was what it had been. And I sensed it must have taken some mighty peculiar circumstances to have got Shirley into a Kingswinford pub in the first place. This whole family was carting round too much fear. And apart from Tony, they'd all failed to find places to put that fear. It was always getting in the way. If only they'd been into Hammer Horror, they could have hung their terrors up on the convenient imaginary fangs and claws of Dracula, of Frankenstein or of Diabolus.

We went on wandering around the churchyard, Alice treating us to her high-pitched little Kate Bush tribute. We had '*Hammahammahamma...*' and '*WahwahwahwahwahWOH!*' and '*Eekliff!*' – enough to wake the dead: I hoped they thought it was as funny as I did.

We got back. Mum had taken charge of things. Janice Croviss was as relaxed as I'd ever seen her. Dad was just getting back from the loo, a shocked expression on his face. '*Izal Medicated,*' he mouthed silently in Mum's direction when Janice wasn't looking.

The evening ended with a few thin slices of sickly Battenberg sponge cake – that little Alice scoffed eagerly – and a few more cups of peewee tea.

Martin said nothing; Dad and Tony said not much more. It was that kind of a gathering. But I could tell Mum had done a good job: she'd bought a sketch pad, some pencils and some crayons for Alice, which had gone down well. When it was time to get off, me and Tony were both relieved that so little had gone wrong. Compared to what we'd expected.

'Phew,' said Tony, as we got into the car. 'Thank you very much Granny Kidderminster!'

It was the first time he'd given Mum that title and she loved it.

***

The morning sickness and the funny eating habits were getting started: I wasn't yet craving the time-honoured classic of pickled gherkins dipped in strawberry yogurt but I was making some pretty strange foodie choices: fried fish and bananas anyone? Apple pie and chicken gravy?

Mum and Dad thought that last one was hilarious. Dad wondered aloud if it was a taste I'd got from too many Chinese or Indian takeaways while I was down in London? Mum, alive to the least sniff of 'racism', slapped him down for that.

Tony didn't find it so funny – certainly not when he found me chucking up in the toilet the following morning.

'Are you sure the apple pie and chicken gravy was such a good idea?' he asked.

'Yes,' I snapped, full of buggeratious obstinacy, then turned back to the toilet bowl.

'O-kay...' he conceded, dubiously.

After a few more minutes chucking, I straightened and went to wash my face. Tony had had to head out before I'd finished.

Soon, I'd need to pack the temping in for a bit. I was determined that it would only be 'for a bit'. I'd decided that there was nothing worse for a kid of, say, two years or more, than to have a mum whose only work was housework: how'd you like to get brought up by someone who spent all day every day boring herself to death? Mum had seen my point, but said it'd probably turn out more complicated than that.

Still, it was Janice Croviss that worried me. I'd begun to think of her as that: 'Janice Croviss'. Not calling her 'Janice Griefstick' put a bit of space between her and Tony. And I wasn't keen on sharing a surname with her either.

But it wasn't an entirely hostile gesture; if I'd wanted to be hostile, I'd have used the name 'Janice Sidaway': according to Kevin, much against their will, the three sisters had, for a short while, carried it. I might have been afraid of Janice Croviss – too afraid to bless her with the name Griefstick – but I wasn't going to curse her with the name Sidaway.

Spring turned to summer. Tony finally told his mom about my condition, one Tuesday evening when I was at home chowing down on sardines and custard.

'What did she say?' I asked when he got back.

'Not much,' he replied. 'Just that she had wondered – oh, and she did ask how long you were going to stay at work?'

Whit Week saw me getting home on a Tuesday to find Tony sitting on the sofa, staring straight ahead of him as if in a trance. In front of him was a cup of perfectly good coffee – Blend 37 – left to go stone cold. I knew he'd have spent most of the day over at his mom's, to get enough done so that, when my needs and the little 'un's needs got too much, he could leave her be with something like a clear conscience.

'Hello..?' I whispered, dreading something Janice-ish.

Tony almost jumped. He stared around him, then focussed on me and on breathing in deeply.

'Er... Sorry. It was... it was Mom.'

'Is she alright?'

'Er... Well, kind of. She just started asking me stuff. All sorts of things. And it was... mostly about you... How you're getting on? Pregnancy stuff. She asked me to find a pen and paper. Started noting bits and bobs down. You know. Advice...'

What a turnaround! It was as if Janice Croviss had only just now twigged that she was soon to be a granny – I wondered what could be at the back of it?

'Could I... Could I have a look at what she wrote?' I asked.

Tony picked a little notepad out of his jeans back pocket. It trembled as he handed it to me.

Janice Croviss' handwriting was neat, professional and elegant. Very old fashioned – nobody wrote like that anymore. It was the kind of handwriting you'd expect to see in the credits of a TV Jane Austen. Odd to be getting it from someone whose home didn't appear to contain any books apart from appliance instruction manuals.

Her style was terse, as I'd have expected. Everything was laid out in bullet points and if a word didn't absolutely need to be there – it wasn't. But, over fifteen or twenty pages, she'd put together quite a good little booklet of 'must remembers' for any first-time mum. Many of the details matched, uncannily accurately, the advice my own mum had offered. You'd almost have thought the pair of them weren't the complete opposites they seemed.

I was as bewildered as Tony. Up to now, Janice Croviss had shown Tony and me little but aversion or frosty acceptance. Why this interest in our welfare or, at least, in the welfare of Warren or Wendy? (I'd a name ready for either possibility.) If she'd so clearly got nothing out of being a mother, why take any interest in being a gran?

Still, it seemed to represent something positive and, despite its chilly matter-of-fact-ness, I thought it must be kindly meant, so I read it

'I want you to thank your mom for this, Tony,' I said. 'Please tell her that I said so. Please tell her that I'm grateful.'

'I will... I will, only... Only I don't know, I think there's... there's...'

'You think there's more to this than meets the eye. I do too. Don't know why. But still, I want you to say "thank you" and I want you to tell her I've said "thank you" too. Don't make a big deal of it: that's not going to work with her, is it?'

'No. Definitely not.'

'But do thank her. It might... it might be really useful to her if someone does that...'

'Don't get your hopes up too much, Frances.'

'I won't. But if we can help her, we should.'

We gave each other one of those warm but terribly careful-don't-squash-the-little-'un hugs that parents-to-be start doing weeks before they really need to.

The day after, at work, I threw up into a waste paper basket. I was told that, yes, it was probably time I went off on maternity leave and that, no, nobody would think the worse of me.

I staggered off home early under a heavy Birmingham July sky. All the shops were full of Royal Wedding malarkey, starlings racketed about overhead and the trains at New Street were delayed. I'd walked out of work at three but I didn't get home until past six. Oh well.

Mum was there, smiling but full of sympathy, and got us a pot of tea, which wasn't going to be much like Janice Croviss'.

'Get a drop of that down you,' she said and I did.

I put a bit of sugar in it. I'd gone off sugar when I'd moved away to uni but now, pregnancy being what it was, I needed the stuff again.

I stirred it and sipped. Better.

'Have a look at this,' I said and passed her the little notebook, open at the first page of Janice's instructions.

She took it and read a bit. Her eyebrows raised.

'Lovely writing,' she said. 'What had they used to call it? *"Copperplate."'*

'It's Janice Croviss',' I said.

'Thought it might be. Looks all sound advice. You'd think the idea of being a grandmother...'

'Was melting her a bit?'

'Yes. You'd think. Mind you, I wouldn't rely on it. She was trying her best when we went round to tea but by and large, people like her can't change. Not in my experience. From what you said, that flipping Jethro did a right job on her.'

'I know. Be nice if she could, though. Change. Come back. From that.'

'Yes – it'd be nice if she could.'

And, for a moment, I felt almost hopeful.

'I had a friend who had a dad like her stepdad,' Mum concluded. 'Only she didn't take it out on anyone else. It stayed inside her, stewing away. In the end, she gassed herself. Buggers, people like that Jethro.'

I got up and stared out of the window. I could see some of the old factory roofs, looking pretty and golden in the sunlight. Factories where they'd made carpets and made 'people like that Jethro'. I sighed.

There was a clatter on the stairs. Dad had turned up. He had some big brown paper parcels that were awkward to carry; he made a right sight. It turned out he had got hold of some baby stuff cheap in Worcester. I said it was 'a bit early' but the prices had been a giveaway and neither Mum nor Dad could say no to a bargain: if you'd lived through the 1930s, as they had, you couldn't be expected to.

So we got a crib set up in the spare bedroom and there it was to sit, quietly, for weeks, gathering dust. Still: one less expense to worry about. It was painted sunlight yellow, with the image of a laughing teddy bear Letraset-ed to the headboard. A peculiar thing, that teddy bear: – goofy-

151

toothed, ginger-haired and the ginger hair was very frizzy. But the artist had given it nice eyes: kind-looking, blue... blue like Wedgewood china. All chirpy and confident without being snooty.

August came and the hot weather. It put me in a mood and I'd get in a right strop at the drop of a hat. Tony was taken by surprise, sometimes. More than once, Mum took him to one side and explained the allowances he needed to make. Sometimes, I disgusted myself and, half a minute after snapping at him, I'd be all over him, tearfully begging forgiveness – which bewildered him even more. Poor old Tony!

Then came the big surprise. It was a Wednesday afternoon and Tony was off doing the shopping. I'd been doing a few gentle exercises in the lounge when I heard somebody coming up the stairs from the yard. The steps were measured, precise and light.

As I went into the kitchen, there was a light little tap at the glass of the door.

Tony's Mom stood at the stairhead.

She smiled – without seeming too professional about it, either.

I opened the door and smiled back, stood aside and let her in. She stepped over the threshold graciously and looked around. Faked or genuine, her expression showed approval: we kept the place nice and tidy.

'Would you like to come into the lounge?' I asked.

'Thank you,' she said.

She sat on the sofa, frowning at the big turquoise oblong before her.

'My exercise mat,' I explained.

'Oh,' she said, and frowned a bit.

'Gentle exercises,' I said, trying to be reassuring. 'The doctor gave me a lot of advice.'

That little frown would not be shifted.

'Tea or coffee?' I attempted, thinking to change tack until I found a way of changing her expression.

'Tea, please,' she said, and managed a neat little smile. I went to get the kettle on.

She really was looking better than I'd ever seen her. In fact, for a woman in her fifties and despite the still-visible burns, she was looking very good. Okay, she was no Shirley Icement but her features were animated, now, by something that almost looked well-meaning.

I went back into the lounge. She had stood and was looking around the room.

What *was* that look on her face?

I nipped back into the kitchen to pour the kettle, then re-emerged with teapot and crockery.

We sipped tea – hers poured a while before mine – and I said something about her having worked at the court for so long... How long had it been, exactly?

'I started there in 1945,' she said, 'just after the war. Didn't do much but the washing up to begin with. I had a little time off when we had Tony.'

I wondered, silently, if the 'we' meant herself and her husband, Maurice, or herself and her sister. I wondered if she knew herself.

'Of course,' she said, cool and matter-of-fact, 'Maurice died the following year so I had to have some more time off to get things sorted...'

How inconsiderate it had been of Maurice!

'The same thing happened when Frieda died,' she went on, and her voice did shake a bit there. 'Fred was useless. I almost feel sorry for that son of his. That Martin. If only Frieda hadn't died, he'd never have turned out the way he did. None of that hideous horrible racket. She'd have put a stop to it.'

Tony had convinced me that it wasn't the 'horrible racket' Martin had been into that had pickled his brain cells, but the four-year drinking bout he'd got into afterwards. But I wasn't going to argue with Janice. I was genuinely curious to work out how she saw things and I just made the quickest little comments to encourage her.

'Where,' she asked, finishing her tea, 'will sh- will the little one be sleeping?'

I took her up to the second floor and showed her. She looked around the clean bright room and made tiny, clucking noises of approval. She looked long and hard at the crib, seeming to have mixed feelings about it. I don't know, perhaps it was the teddy bear. But, as she came downstairs, she nodded silently to herself. So far, our childcare provisions had passed the test.

But I still couldn't quite place the look on her face.

We had a drop more tea, then she made to go.

'Sure you want to? Tony'll be back before long.'

'Oh, that's alright. I'll see him again next Tuesday. And I'd rather avoid the rush-hour.'

Two minutes later, she was going down the staircase to the yard, her neat, precise footsteps making a clatter against the metal.

It wasn't till she'd gone that I twigged what I'd been looking at in her face: hope. It had been missing from her until now. Six months before, I couldn't have imagined it being there; nor, I'm sure, could Tony. Least of all could Janice herself...

15: Anthony Griefstick

Summer got warmer, then cooler, and I went back to work. Frances stayed home and kept on throwing up. Everything seemed okay. Sort of okay.

The kids at school were – strange to tell – a big help. With September, we got a new bunch of Second Years, aged twelve or thirteen by the calendar but much younger in terms of what they could do and what they could understand. They were wide-eyed or shut-eyed, quiet and terrified or screaming and enraged. The more you got to know them, the more you sensed the two to be different sides of the same thing. They'd have struggled, in some cases, if they'd had the wealthiest and most caring homes and parents. Very few of this lot had such homes or such parents. Some would show up first thing with bruises on their faces and arms. If it looked especially bad, we'd get on the phone to the police. When I made those calls, the coppers at the other end – while careful not to say it in so many words – sounded as if they knew the families and had no trouble believing us. But it was just as obvious, from those same tones of voices, how little chance they thought any of us had at making a difference. One of our third years had died a few months before: thirteen, looking underfed and with eyes sunken and grey-ringed like those of an old man. And the worst thing was how it had not surprised me. I just felt like sighing, shrugging my shoulders and getting back on with things – which, I suppose, was just as well because 'getting on with things' was what I had to do. When they heard I was going to be a dad, though, a lot of the roughest kids were really nice about it. Quite a few of the girls had younger siblings and, of course, a lot of them had had no choice but to become 'Deputy Moms' to their frequently drug- or booze-damaged mothers. One such girl, Brenda, thirteen, put together a little booklet of advice for me, a low-fi version of the neat instructions Mom had put in her notes to Frances. Despite the differences in presentation and literacy, the ideas were mostly the same. I took it home and kept it in a drawer of our new-to-us sideboard. Next to Mom's version.

Colleagues were generally nice about it too. They warned me it would 'be a struggle' – our nipper having me up three times a night, then the Third Years to deal with in the morning – but they never doubted I'd be up to it. It was due around February half-term, so, with a bit of luck, I could hope for a week's 'paternity leave' to help Frances get started.

Somebody should have carved a statue of Frances' mum, though. They could have stuck it in Chamberlain Square, Birmingham, outside the big futuristic library, and called it 'Optimism.' For a woman – a big woman – in her sixties, she was striding around assertive as a prime minister – only without the toxic self-doubt you always sensed to be gnawing at Mrs Thatcher. No: Rosemary Chessil belonged in a piece of celebratory art and was already taking to the role of 'Granny' in that spirit. Reg had sense enough to let her play the part in her own operatic way, smiling to himself at the spectacle.

She gave the same treatment to young Brenda's notes for expectant parents as she had to Mom's more detailed and specific guidance, this time punctuating her perusal with cries of 'Aah, bless...'

Frances had got big in the middle. I began to expect that she'd end up having her waters break while half way up from the back yard. Our place – one narrow staircase from the first floor to the bedrooms and the clattery metal thing from the back yard to the kitchen – was not the friendliest for someone struggling to get around. The grim determination I'd see in Frances' eyes as she fixed her gaze on the bottommost of those metal steps! She would not let the bugger beat her! Her eyes, coolly blue at the best of times, got frosty and fierce and I would not have wanted to be on the receiving end of that gaze. Then, one step at a time, up she'd go, grunting a little, obstinately. I didn't allow myself to love the sound; that'd have been too close to loving her discomfort and she'd have torn a right strip off me if she'd thought I was doing that.

No, I'd just stand behind her as she went up, ready to hold on to her if she slipped, saying nothing because, at this stage, it could only be her struggle.

At the top, she'd have to stop for a bit, breathing in, breathing out, breathing in, breathing out, until she'd enough air to start looking for her key to the kitchen door – and it always needed a fair few goes in her pockets and in her handbag before she found the thing: little 'un was gobbling up too much of the blood that was meant for her brain – the cheeky sod.

This was just one of many bits of day-to-day argy-bargy that got turned into a major challenge. Sleep itself could be a war zone: at stupid o'clock, one viciously frosty January morning, I woke up yelling in pain, having just been kicked in the kidneys.

'That,' growled Frances, 'was not me.'

I twigged: her flesh had been between me and the offending little feet.

'How do you think I feel?' she grumbled, before turning over. I couldn't work out an answer. I just prayed that, by morning, she would have stopped throbbing.

At work, I think I impressed the rest of the staff – largely female, of course – by my understanding that, yes, the middle-of-the-night kicking was going to have hurt Frances a bloody sight worse than it had hurt me.

Girl or boy, I hoped it had got its attitude sorted by the time it came out into the real world.

Then, inevitably, I got the phone call. Frances had indeed been halfway up the stairs to the kitchen door when her waters broke. I wanted to give Sir William Sod a right kicking when I heard that – him and his bloody great Law. Anyway, she'd struggled, struggled, struggled to the top, scrabbled around for her keys, finally found them and tried to get them into the doorlock.

Then she'd dropped them and, of course, they'd fallen through the metal grille of the stairhead and down to the grey-slabbed yard below.

In agony, she'd dragged herself back down to the yard, small one getting tangibly crosser within. She'd felt around on the damp stone for the keys and, eventually finding them, dragged herself back up the clattering aluminium to the kitchen door and it was all slower and more painful than it had been the first time.

At the top once more, hands trembling, she'd got the door open and crawled to the lounge to phone her mum. And then the ambulance. Rosemary had driven over, leaving Reg to phone me.

In turn, I'd phoned Mom before rushing to get cover sorted, then motored to the hospital, trying to keep my driving sensible. Mom had all the luck with public transport, as she ever did, and was sitting in the waiting room, cool and self-possessed, as I rushed in. Reg and Rosemary were in more of a tizzy and Rosemary was whispering to the nervously pacing Reg that he should sit down. A nurse turned up and told us that we might have to wait a while. I sat. So did Reg.

And we waited.

And waited.

And waited.

And I looked up at the clock.

And three minutes had gone by.

And I picked up a magazine.

And I put it back down again.

And I looked at the clock again.

And another minute and a half had gone by.

And I could see the way this was going.

So I was sitting on one of those padded benches you get in hospital waiting rooms and my eyes fell to the carpet tiles. And, because my mind was so blanked out with nervous strain like static or white noise, I could focus on nothing but those carpet tiles. I couldn't exactly take in what colour they were: greyish-blue? Or turquoise? Orange? Dark green? But I became lost in the texture of their fibres – the kind of fibres that looked dirty, however much they were cleaned. The kind of tangled, knotted fibres into which ages of dust seemed ground. You could fall into carpet tiles like these. Fall into them like they were a jungle and you were some nutty old Japanese soldier. Fall into them like the war wasn't over...

I *really* needed to snap out of this.

No I didn't.

That was the truth. I did not need to snap out of it at all. Because there was bugger all to do apart from go doolally. So where was I? Oh yes: carpet tiles. Carpet tiles like grasping prehistoric vegetation. Carpet tiles behind which any number of any kind of scaly-faced predators might...

'Mr Griefstick?'

A nurse's face. Right up close to mine and smiling. Smiling very sanely. Yeah – sanity: I needed to remember how to do that stuff. Remember, like, right now... Well, I thought, you gave a quick little grin

– a polite one... No! Not like that! That was more like a nervous twitch. More like... More like... Yeah. That would do. Well – that would *have* to do. And, in this situation – never mind what the situation actually was: you'd only lose the plot again if you dwelt on it... In this situation, you stood up and you tried not to fall over. And you succeeded – that was a bonus! My God, you'd actually succeeded in not falling over... And – *no-ow*... Now you followed the nurse as she led you out of the waiting room, one step at a time. Yeah, steps. Remember how to do them? Only just, because they're tricky buggers, but you just about do...

And you're in the... What's it called again? 'Maternity unit', you think, but that somehow doesn't sound convincing. And Frances is there... Christ, she looks wrecked! What's she been doing? Climbing Everest or something..? She's completely...

Oh.

Oh, yes. Of course.

That.

And there it is.

Pink and little.

Well, it would be little, wouldn't it?

And... bit by bloody bit... my head made it back into the world of the right here, right now. Partly. I still felt... more than ever I felt... *threatened*.

It still didn't seem like we'd completed the job of bringing this little thing into the real world. Somewhere, somehow, there was a final hurdle we were going to have to get over; it was going to be a right bastard and it was coming soon.

I stroked the little head, very much afraid to do so, and looked at Frances' greyed and thinned face as it attempted to push some sort of a smile through all that pain. We said nothing – just looked at each other, then looked back at the little thing and silently worried ourselves sick about how we were going to keep it alive. It didn't seem likely we'd succeed.

After a bit, somebody suggested I go and tell the grandparents. So, like a ball in an arcade machine, I staggered and wrong-turned my way through the corridors, eventually landing back in the waiting room.

Rosemary was there, red-smiled and toothy; Reg, smiling more cautiously behind her. I couldn't see Mom but there was a cool, grey kind of feeling in the back of my neck that told me she was around.

'*Well?!*' Rosemary almost shrieked.

'Er. Yeah.'

'Yes *what?*'

'Well... er... It seems to be doing okay.'

'*Yes?!*'

'Er... Yes.' I sensed she wanted to know more. I struggled to think of anything. 'Er... it's very little. But really... Really, it looks like it's doing okay. It's a kind of... pink colour. I mean... that's healthy, isn't it? I mean... not *too* pink... Not like it's sore or flushed or anything. But... well... yeah...'

Rosemary cast her eyes to Heaven. Reg laughed.

'*Is it a boy or a girl?*' Rosemary roared.

'Oh. Oh. That. Er... I don't know.'

Rosemary gaped.

'It just looks okay. Didn't really think to worry about anything else. And, er, that bit was covered. Covered by a towel. Was it a towel? Er... Don't know. But I think it was a towel. Er... yeah. A towel.'

Rosemary was frozen for an instant. Then she was laughing. Reg was already in hysterics. But the feeling in the back of my neck had just got cooler and greyer.

'Suppose... suppose I should go back and have a look, shouldn't I?' I ventured.

Rosemary nodded vigorously. Reg nodded slightly. The cool grey feeling in the back of my neck stayed cool and stayed grey – noncommittal.

I turned and went a step or two down the corridor. Then I turned back.

'Oh, er... it's got really nice eyes. Blue-green. Like underwater sunlight.' (Where on Earth had *that* come from? Never mind.) 'Er... Right. I'll just go and ask about that other thing.'

...and I shuffled back down the corridor. This time, I found the place more easily. Frances was asleep. The little pink thing was asleep. They were asleep together. I felt that was how things ought to be, though I doubted I had the right to such a feeling. I doubted I had the right to

160

anything, at that moment. I felt weak and full of doubt. I looked around. A nurse saw me and smiled.

'Er..?' I said. And dried up.

'Boy,' she replied.

'Ah,' I said.

'Doing fine,' she said. 'Best leave them to have a sleep now.'

'Ah,' I said. 'Yeah. Right. Ta.'

And I did so.

'Boy,' she'd said. And there was something about even that that frightened me.

It was difficult to get Mom into my field of vision when I returned to the waiting room. She seemed to slip out of sight, to drain away out of the corner of my eye as if caught half way between existence and nothingness. Rosemary was the opposite: she was wide eyed and in my face and wanting to know.

'Both asleep,' I said. 'Both doing fine.' Then, understanding full well that just so much information would not do at all, I took as deep a breath as I could manage.

I was scared to say it.

But I didn't know why, so I made myself say it anyway.

'Boy,' I said.

There were a few seconds of delight on Rosemary and Reg's faces. They were, both of them, surely going through a speeded-up internal montage of buying him his first football kit and teaching him about vegetable gardening and all the other stuff that the knowledge they'd just gained would have prompted.

Then they noticed what was happening to Mom.

I'd been able to feel the greyness in her; now, I could almost see it. And it deepened, it swamped her, it drowned the life out of...

Out of what?

What had I been seeing in her face over the past few weeks, perhaps the past few months? What was it I could now see dying?

Physically, her face wasn't changing all that much. But there was a collapse about the eyes and mouth – a sense of life extinguished, of life and of hope.

I was looking at an absolute extinction of hope that became an absolute extinction of Mom's humanity. The God Squad at uni had used to go on about damnation – they'd hardly gone on about anything else! – but it had never seemed like anything to get worked up over: as almost everyone *was* going to be damned – everyone who didn't go to *their* church – why make a fuss about any single damnation?

But now I was looking at Damnation. And it *was* something to get worked up over and it *was* something to make a fuss about and those prats in the God Squad hadn't understood it at all.

And I had… some way or other… I had to keep it away from Frances and…

From Warren. From *Warren*. That was his name: *Warren*. I had to keep this terrible thing away from him.

'I think I should drive you home, Mom,' I said, softly.

Reg and Rosemary didn't argue. They could see… They could see *something*, though they were both too kind to put a name to it. Mom's power to argue was beyond dead, of course. It was somewhere far worse than dead.

We didn't speak as we drove back to hers. At least, I don't think we did. And we parted in the same absolute silence.

And then I drove back to the hospital.

And Frances, I was told, was awake again and Rosemary and Reg were with her. And when I met them, it was all happiness and laughter and breast feeding. Though Frances' face when she looked at me showed how worried she was.

Two days later, she was back home. With Warren.

There was just the beginning of what would be a bright orange mop on top of his little noddle.

16: Frances Chessil

It came for me like a black fog. People try to give it a name – 'Post-Natal Depression' – but it's not something you can ever put a name to. If you think you've named it, you fool yourself that it's something nameable – something of this world. It's not: it's something that makes this world go away. Truth and logic, love and reason – they all flake off like dead skin and things go back to how they were before: there is only the Black Fog – all-powerful and unspeakable Nothing.

Mum had gone through it and so she understood.

Janice Croviss had been into something like it, I realised, only she'd never come out the other side.

Mum's words were gently comforting, but never making light of what was happening to me. She must, I thought, be explaining things very carefully to Tony, because there was the light of a terrible sympathy in his eyes when he came in to me after each working day. He'd park himself on the sofa, divided from me by about half an inch of space and a light year of black fog and he'd wish he had a bridge to cross that greater distance and to bring me back, to give me strength. If I'd had any love in me, then, I'd have loved him for that. As it was, I could only long for a time when I got the love back and could show him a bit of it. Mum said it would happen eventually. I'd get myself back eventually. I'd exist again, eventually. Eventually, eventually, eventually…

There were times when I could have said 'Bollocks to "Eventually".' But at that point, I was non-existing in a Universe of Black Fog: I could have said 'Bollocks' to anything.

Tony would take my hand and I'd make the effort needed not to tug it away in annoyance. He could feel the need for that effort and, yes, it hurt him. But Mum had done a good job and, to some extent, he understood.

Mum was round a lot in those early weeks. She didn't fuss but put on a manner that was quiet, solemn, concerned. As I said, she'd been through it; she knew.

And I began to sense Warren again. The way I had in that first wonderful couple of days, before the Black Fog descended. I could sense his absolute, universe-bridging Need for me. That need started to bring me back.

Then, one day, Mom didn't turn up. Instead, I got a call from her.

'Frances, I think I'm going down with a cold.'

'Oh,' I said. I felt it as a catastrophe that I would not be able to cope with. My fragile little bridge across the Black Fog was crumbling.

'I don't want to go giving it to Warren, though he's going to be as tough as old boots before long.'

'Oh. No. No – of course not.'

'No. So I'll stay away for a few days. Maybe till a week tomorrow. If it clears up before then, I'll give you a ring. But you know what these things are like…'

Yes. I knew.

'Now, you've got me on the end of the phone here, and I'm not going to be away from it for more than five minutes at a time, so if things are starting to get on top of you – and they will – I want you to phone me, no messing. If I can't come over, I'll send your dad, unless he's gone down with it too…'

Of course. Of course. My mind could see exactly what she meant. Only my mind didn't count for anything right now, and we both knew it.

I made some brave little noises down the telephone line – noises I despised. Then I ended the call.

Upstairs, Warren started to cry and there was half an instant when I – or the Black Fog that had taken my place – wanted to strangle him. But I went up, part-undressed myself and shoved my left tit in his gob instead.

He seemed content enough with that. I said 'content' – but I wasn't really sure. I wasn't happy in myself and I knew he'd be able to smell the unhappiness, to feel it. To taste it.

I wasn't together at all; I was in bits. By the time I'd fed Warren, I was ready to go back to bed.

So I was not up for company of any description; the polite tap at the door couldn't have come at a worse time. It was polite, yes, but it had carried upstairs from the kitchen – strangely.

At least Warren had nodded off after feeding.

I got myself tidied up a bit and went downstairs.

It didn't make any difference that it was Janice Croviss. Anyone would have been as bad.

Oh well. I let her in.

We didn't speak. That didn't seem weird. She just went into the lounge and sat on the sofa. I sat at the little writing desk we'd put against the opposite wall. She looked out the window. I looked at her.

She'd twitched a bit as she'd gone past a mirror that hung in the passage from the kitchen. I remembered she didn't like mirrors. A few weeks back, if you'd not heard Kevin's story, this would have been hard to explain; you could have taken a decade off her age if you'd had a guess and the burn marks had hardly shown. Not now, though: she looked a ruin and the burns were livid.

Perhaps it was the greyness that was worst. I wasn't even sure it was a physical greyness – an actual colour. It was there, though. You could see it under her skin. You could see its toxicity. You could see its deadness.

I'd not have thought anyone could have gone around with such a thing inside them. This greyness, this deadness – surely it would stress its carrier until they broke. You couldn't live with such greyness, such deadness under your skin.

So: if Janice Croviss wasn't alive – what was she?

She was nothing that had the power *not* to wish me harm. Wish me harm and wish Warren harm. Some little crushed part of her, tucked away in her guts might badly wish not to wish us harm, but that part would have no power over the grey nothingness that was in charge of her. The grey nothingness was there. The wish was there. They made Janice Croviss something very dangerous.

I needed to tell her to go. I needed to have told her to go… minutes, minutes ago. Instead, we'd just sat and I'd looked at her and she… or the greyness within her… had looked out of the window at the greyness without.

165

How much time had passed? The light… perhaps… had begun to fade. It was hard to tell with all that thick English winter cloud.

Cars and lorries rumbled outside. The westbound traffic was heading for Bewdley. And beyond that, to Shropshire, to Wales… I had a sudden crazy urge to dash upstairs into the little bedroom, grab Warren, smash through the window and jump out like some comic book hero – landing on the back of a passing flatbed truck and letting it take us far away from this greyness, this deadness, this *Evil*…

Janice Croviss flashed me a look. It was a look of anger, of warning. She'd heard me…

Except that I hadn't spoken.

She couldn't have heard me.

Never mind – she had heard me. She'd heard me and she'd not liked what she'd heard. She'd heard me and she'd not liked me thinking I had the right to use *that* word against her.

Hang on: *what* word?

I shouldn't ask what word. I had no right to ask what word. Only she had the right to ask. And only she had the right to decide how that word (*What* word?) was to be applied. That word… and the other one. I knew the words she meant, didn't I? I knew them. *Those* two words. She alone had the right to administer them. They were the instruments of her mastery.

Yes. I knew them. They were coming to get me, weren't they? Coming to get me and to get Warren. As she commanded, they were coming to get us both. I would not be able to resist them. I would not be able to defend myself. Because I did not have the right to defend myself. Such rights were hers alone.

She stood.

It occurred to me that I'd not offered her a cup of tea.

It occurred to me that this was strange.

It occurred to me that it was stranger still that I should think of it now, after thinking all those other things.

She walked out of the lounge. She walked out of the lounge and down the passage. She walked out of the lounge and down the passage and into the kitchen…

And I heard the door of the kitchen open… And close.

166

Perhaps I heard the neat, step-by-step clatter of her shoes, going down the metal staircase. Perhaps not.

I stood. It didn't mean the same as when she'd stood. Unlike her standing, my standing was of no consequence.

And the greyness I'd seen beneath her skin, boiling icy and deadly away beneath her skin… it seemed to still hang in the air. I ought not to have questioned this. It had every right to do so: it had the right to hang wherever it wanted.

I didn't go upstairs to look in on Warren. I thought I wanted to but I wanted more to keep myself away from him for a little longer. Until that greyness, in its own… in its own time (What *sort* of time?), had dispersed.

I felt wobbly on my feet and, twisting round as I fell, I collapsed into the sofa. The sofa where Janice Croviss had sat. I felt weak, so bloody weak and…

And I was going to be sick.

I dragged myself from the sofa and on to my hands and knees. I began to crawl along the passage towards the loo, but I didn't make it. I was sick outside the kitchen door and collapsed face down into my own vomit.

This shouldn't have been happening now, should it?

It was long minutes before I had the strength to drag my face out of the puke, to get myself into the bathroom and wash myself, to rinse the sick out of the mucky clothes and put them in the washing machine, to get a bucket of warm water and a sponge out of the kitchen and clean the carpet out. My crawling seemed to have spread bits of puke everywhere. Then, as I was emptying out the last bucket of sicky water into the loo, Warren started yelling for his next instalment of protein from my gloomy mammaries.

That took longer than it should have done, too. My milk wasn't up to standard and it was ages before he was satisfied. I had my own Black Fog and to that was now added the greyness. The greyness Janice Croviss had brought with her and had passed on to me. As she had every right to do, of course. I couldn't argue with that. I had no right to argue with that.

So, once Warren was fed, I just took myself to bed and waited for Tony

167

to get home.

17: Anthony Griefstick

'Frances? *Frances?!*'

I was shaking her like crazy. I thought she was dead.

'Whu..? Huh? Oh... Hi, Tony.'

As reassurances went, a faintly croaked *'Hi Tony'* didn't cut it. I couldn't keep the panic out of my voice.

'What's happened? What's been going on?'

Her brows furrowed. It looked like she was having trouble remembering. Or understanding what I was going on about.

'Frances, you really don't look...'

'I was sick,' she said. 'I was sick. I cleaned it up. Not to worry.'

I was worried. I was bloody terrified.

'Don't you... Don't you know what brought it on?'

There was a pause.

'Your mom came round,' she said.

I blinked. And found I had to sit on the edge of the bed: my knees were about to collapse under me.

'Oh,' I said. *Mom came round:* that could have meant a lot of different things – none of them good.

'Was she..?' I dried up, then tried again: 'How was she?'

She scowled, trying to remember. 'She didn't say anything.'

I turned cold. I didn't know what this meant but I knew I was scared of it. And I could feel Mom's contempt for me – for the idea that I had the right to be scared. I could feel that the idea was an insult to her – an insult for which I should be ashamed. Ashamed of myself, as she was ashamed of me. All she had ever felt for me was shame. And now, instead of just me...

I didn't pursue the thought.

'She'll be round again next week,' I said. I didn't even try to work out how I knew this. 'Same time and same day. I'll be here.'

169

'Hope you have a bit more luck,' Frances said, 'getting a peep out of her.'

But we both knew it wasn't the silence that was the problem. It was what was on the other side of the silence.

I expected quite a bit of bother from work, asking for the day off. In any other profession, I'd have got it, but teaching, with its largely female population, has a better understanding than others of post-natal depression and, after all, that was what this was partly about. So I got the following Tuesday off with few questions asked.

'Why don't we move the crib into the lounge?' I asked when that morning came and I was munching my way through a single round of toast. 'So we can keep an eye on him.'

Frances paused. 'Yes,' she said, at last. 'Yes.'

Breakfast over and Warren fed, I brought the crib downstairs. Then we sat on the sofa and we waited.

And waited.

A couple more days, I reckoned, and Rosemary would be confident enough that she'd shaken off the lurgie. Then she'd be round as often as before and we'd all be safe. If something bad was going to happen, it would happen today.

We didn't speak to each other. We didn't have any lunch. We didn't even make a cup of tea.

Frances got up a few times to feed Warren, then put him back in his crib.

In the middle of the afternoon, there was the expected tap on the door.

I went to get it. I'd not seen Mom for two weeks and, though I probably should not have been, I was shocked at how rough she was looking: the old scars put there by Jethro burned more harshly than they'd done since her accident. I wasn't so surprised at her expression: blank, somewhere way out on the far side of contempt.

And we were silent too. And there was a deep, long-lasting feel to her silence that reminded me of the time she'd checked my room before I'd gone away to uni. One way or the other, we'd come to the end of things; we'd have nothing to say to each other after today.

I knew that she needed watching. I knew this without thinking about it. I had as much understanding of why this poor woman was to be pitied as anyone could ever hope for, but I still knew I could not let that understanding foster the illusion that she could be trusted.

Face it, you bloody fool, she's come here to do you harm. To do Frances harm. To do Warren harm. Don't take your eyes off her.

A car outside the front backfired. And I *did* take my eyes off her. And when I looked back, she was stepping from the kitchen into the passage. And, as I followed her, I sensed that something had disappeared from the kitchen table.

She was in the lounge, with Frances and with Warren. Frances seemed to have nodded off and lay unmoving on the sofa. In her hand, Mom clutched a heavy wooden rolling pin.

I felt as if I was standing in the shade of something unspeakably toxic and the shade itself was so corrosive that I was dissolving in it.

For a moment – a moment that seemed to go on for a very long time – I didn't know what to do – I hadn't decided yet. But there was more to it than that.

I couldn't write it, I couldn't think it, all I could do was live it.

I lived it by...

By standing, frozen, and watching the rolling pin come down... come down properly, correctly it seemed, on little Warren's skull. Properly and correctly, I said, because this was the proper, correct and right thing to happen...

And the shade went on forever.

Or by moving more quickly than I thought I ever could and snatching the thing out of her hand. And feeling like I'd committed the last word in evil, in perversion.

But the shade had cleared away.

And, the way I remember it now, there was a moment when both these things had happened. And Warren was dead and I was on the side of good. And Warren was alive and I was on the side of evil.

And then, the way I remember it now, I had the rolling pin in my hand and Janice Croviss was looking at me as if I was the most disgusting piece of scum in the world. And Warren had woken up and was yelling. And Frances had woken up and stood up and could see exactly what had happened. What had happened in this world, at least.

Janice Croviss couldn't see anything anymore. Apart from the fact that the World, embodied in me, had let her down one more time. One last time. Because this would surely kill her.

I couldn't leave it to Frances to say what needed to be said. I looked at her, very briefly, begging her not to try. I turned back to Janice Croviss and attempted to talk over the sickening guilt I felt at the betrayal I'd just committed. After a moment, I managed it:

'You need to leave,' I said, 'now.'

My voice sounded strange to me. Strange in that it seemed to hold neither pity nor moral judgement. Moral judgement could fuck right off out of it.

Janice Croviss left.

Frances looked at me for a moment, after the kitchen door had closed. She began to stretch out her hand to me, then let it fall. It wasn't time for that. Not yet. Instead, she went to Warren, picked him up and cuddled him. She opened her dress and started to feed him.

I collapsed on to the sofa.

Warren was alive. I could hear the sucking noises he was making against Frances' tit. He was alive! A moment before, he'd been alive... but he'd been dead as well. A moment before, he'd been lying dead and I'd known what a dead baby looked like. Known what a dead baby with its skull all scarlet and smashed open by a rolling pin looked like. I had known.

I looked up at Frances and my eyes started to swim in the face of my utter inability to explain what had happened.

'Two different worlds,' I said. 'Two different worlds!'

She sat next to me. I drew back. I didn't feel I should be so close.

Frances just waited, waited for me to get it together enough.

'And in one,' I finally attempted, 'in one, I just stood there. Just stood there and let her do it.'

'But in this one,' she said, softly, 'you didn't.'

'But it was so close!' I said. 'There was so little difference!'

'Little – but enough,' she said. 'In this world, it's okay.'

Later on, she was to tell me that she'd thought of saying 'In this world, I still love you.' But it wouldn't have mattered; what mattered was that she understood – she'd felt it as well. She'd been there with me at the moment when one world had become two. And now, here we were, in a world where I still had her and we still had Warren but Janice Croviss wasn't 'Mom' anymore and never could be, now – if that possibility had ever really existed. And we had to start looking for a frame of Good and of Evil in which I wasn't damned. Which would take a few years. I suppose writing this together has more or less got us there. Because I'll tell you what, Lon: we could never have written it if things had gone the other way.

PART THREE:

THE

RONSARD

BATHROOM

18: Dave Calper

It was the day they closed the bleedin' border.

We'd not expected things to get so bad this side of the election, but with the Ronsardists certain of Number Ten, the Tories were just shitting themselves that if they didn't play along they'd wind up getting banned, like the Greens or the LibDems or what was left of Labour after the WiGIiEs split off. So they'd given the Ronsardists what they wanted and closed it, just to keep on the right side of Charlotte and of Pretty Polly.

The barbed wire fences had been up for months, of course, which made a complete joke of the Tories' claims to be still Unionists. Greyshirt *'Fuck off Jockos'* rallies, *'Fuck off Ulster'* rallies, *'Fuck off Taffies'* rallies or *'Fuck off Cornish Bastards'* rallies were now a weekly event up in central Dudley and in any number of similar provincial towns. So the minefields were being laid and the machine gun towers were being manned, from one side of the country to the other.

Everybody just seemed to accept it – even the WiGIiEs, or maybe especially the WiGIiEs. Now don't get me wrong: I'd always thought I was left-of-centre. Half my mates had been in one Trotskyite group or another, back in the seventies. A few worked their way through membership of each one in turn, until they'd got the set. I'd take the piss out of them, they'd take the piss out of me – the usual pub stuff. But it had started taking a funny turn in the eighties and, by the Millennium, I wasn't talking about politics with anyone much. Now, in 2019, opening your mouth about that sort of thing to almost anyone was asking to get your teeth kicked in.

And when I actually checked out what the WiGIiEs were saying…

'We' is Good. 'I' is Evil.

It just sounds daft, doesn't it? Well, it did to me. But I guess no more bonkers than you'd get off any number of California-style mystical sweat-lodges or believers that God's a gerbil.

They'd been a very tiny sub-section of the Labour Party when they first turned up. Apparently far-left and oh-so-very North London. But they'd grown fast – grown alongside the Ronsardists, for whom they were convenient natural enemies. It wasn't easy to say whether they'd been booted out of Labour or whether they'd left in a righteous huff but by the time we were gone from Europe, they were an independent party. Not that they ever won any elections – apart from a few London council seats, they never seemed to want to: their voting figures were like nothing since the glory days of Screaming Lord Sutch. But with Labour itself banned by the Tory-Ronsardist coalition, the WiGIiEs were all the opposition we had that wasn't far-right (that's to say, further right than the Ronsardists). They were an opposition, though, that could never and would never win political power: any kind of victory would compromise their status as Virtuous Victims. Which suited the Ronsardists fine, so the WiGIiEs were allowed to persist – the perfect example of the kind of 'whining leftie scum' that Charlotte or Danny Cosgrove or Big Mohammed could sound off about to any crowd they wanted to rile up.

A few WiGIiEs, though, had it in for the likes of us: rock bands were too flamboyant, too hedonistic. We represented something they liked to call 'bourgeois individualism' which, yes, did have something to do with the fact that, in her mid-thirties, Lon still couldn't be relied upon to keep her kit on till the end of the show. Their disapproval was getting to be a problem. Over the past few months, when we'd advertised a gig in the area, there'd been hostile WiGIiEs in the street outside the venues. Just enough of them that most places were thinking twice before they booked us.

As if we weren't copping it enough off the Greyshirts…

That particular afternoon, we weren't rehearsing. I'd been visiting an old mate in Tipton – a bloke who'd used to put on gigs in the 1970s and 80s. By now, he had Parkinson's and was going fast. This wasn't quite the last time I saw him but it was the last time we were able to have a good chat. We'd spent the afternoon chewing over old memories and listening to music. Mostly, it had been from his vast Kenny Wheeler collection but we'd squeezed in a bit of Westbrook's *Cortège* too: 'Democratie' had spooked me even more than it usually did. At about four, his missus had spotted he was getting tired so I'd made myself scarce. I walked the long way to the station, so I didn't have to go past a certain mural on the end of a row of burned-out terraces, a soot-stained mural, not looked after since the artist had had his head smashed in. The face of Arthur Tolland, politician, pretend occultist and actual child abuser, painted eight years ago by his soon-to-be-killed grandson: I still didn't like seeing it.

There was noise of some bother down the street.

Oh, bleedin' 'ell, not again!

When I turned the corner, there was the remains of a bunch of WiGIiEs in the road and on the pavement. And a mob of Greyshirts kicking the shit out of them – with big grins on their faces.

Sod all I could do, of course. There must have been seven or eight Greyshirts and there was me with me walking stick. Did I mention I was using a walking stick?

Eventually, the Greyshirts got bored and moved on. By then, I'd got my phone and made the 999 call:

'Yeah. Street attack. I can see six – sorry, make that seven injured. One of them's dead. Definitely. 'Cause it's bleedin' obvious – her neck's bust and her head's at a hundred and eighty degrees!' *(You twat.)* 'No I did not see the attackers. Not clearly.' *(Which was a lie but if I said they'd been Greyshirts, there was a fair chance nobody'd come out. That often happened these days.)* 'Yeah, yeah. I'm not going anywhere.'

I gave the location, then phoned Ith and Dougie. It wasn't out of the question that our goons in grey might be back and, if that happened, I'd rather know I had some heavy duty back-up on the way.

Not expecting to be able to do much, I hobbled my way a bit closer.

One of the WiGIiEs made a noise. Painfully, I knelt down next to her. I had a good grasp of one field of first-aid: drug overdose. With everything else – broken bones, internal bleeding, whatever – I was a non-starter. It'd be the worst possible move for me to try shifting her – I did know that. So I just knelt there – the rain-cold tarmac giving my seventy-eight year-old knees – (There: I've admitted it.) – some serious bother.

'Try and stay still, love. The ambulance is coming.'

She lay there and made soft breathing noises that were quickly getting softer.

And I took a good look at her. How old was she? Nineteen, twenty maybe. A kid. She was a skinhead, like all the WiGIiE girls, and she'd got some nasty tattoos and what must have been self-inflicted scars all over her face – again, typical WiGIiE.

I think she was trying to grit her teeth – trying really hard – but she didn't have the strength left. Still, I could tell she was making a hell of an effort – an effort to believe that this death was what she wanted. Because only death could ever truly destroy the hated *'I'*.

Not just my knees, now, but ankles, feet, hips were all yowling their silent complaints. And most of my spine was very unhappy. Jeeze, there'd be nothing wrong with *me* wanting to snuff it!

But not you, kid, not you.

'I am... I *is* dying!'

Just a whisper. But the fervour burned in it, brighter than ever. And she was such a clever little thing: did you notice how she used that change in the verb to put the loathing across? You had to listen hard to hear the doubt behind it. And the loathing was so abominable, so wrong, so *out of place* in her – but getting to be so right for me.

'*You* don't have to, love.'

She didn't answer. She was too weak.

And I knew she was going and – stupid thing to do – I put my arms around her, lifting her up as I did so, because it didn't matter now and I wanted her to feel cared for just a bit and –

'What you doing?!'

I looked up. One of the other WiGIiEs was on his feet and looking mean.

And I felt her go.

'Ey?'

I let her down and started the difficult process of getting to my feet.

'Ey?'

They'd kicked him about a fair bit, though for a mob with a couple of female bosses, it was weird how the Greyshirts saved their worst doses of venom for female victims. Still, he might be able to give me a thrashing and, having caught a 'Bourgeois Individualist' outsider presuming to offer help to a WiGIiE, he'd be sure he had the right to.

I stood there, swaying a bit from my aches and my pains and, suddenly, I was bone tired and bitter.

He was getting nearer and there'd be no talking him out of it: he was in a bad way himself but, Christ, he had the best part of sixty years on me – I'd be in bits by the time Ith and Dougie turned up, even though Dougie'd have his foot right down all the way from Milton Street.

And then he stopped and his face went very pale. Then he fell. He lay there, groaning and clutching at his guts. Internal bleeding? Very likely.

Ith and Dougie got there a long time before the ambulances. These days, everybody seemed to have the knack of smelling when someone'd been done over by the Greyshirts and almost everybody would make sure they didn't get involved. Self-preservation. Unlike me, Ith did know about first aid – knew a heck of a lot – and she fixed up the living as well as she could. The cops showed up eventually and one of them asked me, of course, if I'd been able to recognise anything about the attackers? I caught the undertone in his voice and gave him the answer he was after: 'No, Officer, it was too dark.' He nodded at me in a way that indicated I was being sensible.

Six or seven years before, I'd have said the coppers round here were an alright bunch. Not too bright, some of them, and very keen to cut corners but, generally, an alright bunch.

How had it all gone so wrong?

Because there was no way I was going to say *'They were a load of Greyshirts, Officer, and I recognised the one. He lives in Wall Heath.'*

No way I was going to say that because I wasn't sure I'd last the week if I did.

Mechanically, not meeting anybody's eyes and trying their best to make themselves invisible, the paramedics got the WiGIiEs – dead and alive – into the ambulances. Truth be told, everybody had that half-invisible look about them – apart from Ith.

Sixty years old and she was still stunning. I didn't think it had so much to do with the physical look of her as with that sheer bloody-minded confidence she radiated. The Dragon Lady: the inverse of the gently blinking little churchmouse who'd come to the shop sixteen-seventeen years ago to find out about her pa. And who'd discovered her own real name, lying around inside her, inside but in plain sight.

She looked hard at the coppers and they wilted under her glare. She gave them her name and address – though they all knew her – and said she'd be happy to help with further investigations. They made quiet, polite noises, wishing that she'd just go away. She didn't go away. She'd clocked the WiGIiE who I'd watched die. Exactly the sort of self-denying little thing Pastor Brian had tried to make of her back in her teens. She had no sympathies with the cause of *We is Good; I is Evil* but she had every sympathy with the poor bastard WiGIiEs themselves.

I wondered how long she was going to last.

It was a serious question. Her mob, 'Stourbridge and North Worcestershire Women's Self-Defence' had been, from the outset, obvious rivals of the Ronsardists. But Harry Ronsard himself had been quietly respectful of Ith, and let his fan club know as much. Now though, it seemed only a matter of time before somebody paid a sniper to do the hit. It'd be that or expend a lot of Greyshirts: she might have been sixty, but I'd seen Ith put her fist through a concrete wall.

For now, she radiated indestructibility. And she was inviting me round for a cup of tea – which I needed: by the time we got to Milton Street, I was in tears.

Luke was out over Kinver with his telescopes: he'd been on Welsh telly the week before as a teenage astronomical prodigy but it hadn't gone to his head. With his thoughts out among the stars so much, he had the keenest sense of his own smallness. He never thought anything out there would notice *him*, so he was as self-deprecating as his mum had once been – only with a core of his quest for knowledge.

Mattie, Luke's twin and his absolute opposite, had put down a book on rhubarb cultivation that must have been a struggle for him to read and gone into the kitchen. He'd have sussed as soon as the front door opened that the kettle needed sticking on. I sat on the sofa with Ith's potentially apocalyptic right arm over my shoulder. Dougie stuck some vinyl on – ambient but not slushy, which was exactly what I needed. The knocking and clattering of Mattie making the tea in the kitchen was just as soothing. That was the thing with Mattie: he hadn't turned out as dim as we'd once feared, but he'd be in the slowest academic lane for the rest of his time at Redhill. On the other hand, he had no end of what got called 'emotional intelligence' these days and 'kindness' a few years before. He was good with plants. And he was good with animals. And he was good with people.

We didn't say much that night. You've known each other the best part of two decades – longer with me and Dougie – and you've a pretty good idea what each other are going to say. So, if you need to save the effort, then save it.

Tea. Too hot to drink at first. Just give it time. And I felt the force in Ith's arm soak into me.

She drove me home. Dougie stayed with Mattie. I was in bed by ten and asleep early enough that I was up with the February sun. And a cold and grey sort of sunlight it was, shagged-out after struggling down through a mile or more of heavy cloud. I got dressed, went into the kitchen and made myself a pot of tea. And did some Marmite on toast: that was as much of a breakfast as I could cope with, these days.

I'd be ready to get the shop open by nine, though I expected no customers any time before eleven. But hang on...

It felt like somebody had already got the fire on in there...

I went in.

Lon was sitting in the big easy chair. She was staring at that book of Lee Icement's art. Specifically, she was looking at the photo spreads of what he'd painted on the walls, on the floor and on the ceiling of Harry Ronsard's bathroom.

She wasn't just looking at the photos: she was living them.

A room of two halves. The ceiling, like the wall that faced you as you went in, gaped with a black so absolute that it ought not to have been found anywhere this side of Cygnus X-1. How had he made it so black? *How?* And it had been on the walls for – what? Four or five years when they did the photoshoot. Shouldn't it have faded a bit? But no: no touch of grey to be seen; it was Dark Star all the bleedin' way.

The floor, like the wall behind you, swirled with a cloud-like grey that seemed to move, to flow. The sort of cloud that hides mysteries.

The other walls mirrored each other: divided diagonally, each lower half swirling with the grey, each upper half gaping with the black.

You felt as if you were standing in a reality that was sinking, ship-like, from utterly unknowable blackness, into the swirling ambiguity of the world we know.

Lon's eyes were fixed on to those images and I knew she was getting drawn into that blackness – as if she knew it, as if she understood it, her gaze the Primal Data, getting drawn across Da'at.

They'd only met once or twice, Lon and Lee Icement, despite them both having been regulars in the shop. He'd been full of his usual, theatrical hostility. She had been cautious and guarded – you'd never have thought there'd come a time when she would be staring so fixedly at his work.

With an effort – a hell of an effort, it seemed, she tore her gaze from the book. 'Hope you don't mind my letting myself in,' she said.

I smiled. 'Wouldn't have given you the spare key if I did,' I said.

She smiled back. Then her face lapsed into that puzzled frown she'd been wearing when staring into Lee's unknowable blackness.

'Dave,' she said, 'have you ever seen a... a book... a book vanish in front of your eyes?'

19: Lon Kyle

My brain felt a size too big for my skull: I'd spent the past day typing. That was to say – a day literally, a whole twenty-four: I'd not paused for food, sleep or the bog – and I'd pissed myself once, maybe twice. I opened my eyes. I was on the floor. I'd fallen from my chair as soon as I'd got the final words safely on to the laptop and I'd been lying for a while, on my left side, which ached.

Get up then. I did so.

And things were different.

I couldn't put my finger on it. Something about the table – the table I'd been lying next to... Something was missing. And outside the window... Something was missing there too.

Something had been there, but wasn't there anymore... Kind of...

A splitting headache! I'd had the HS2 driven through my bonce and it sodding well hurt. But the pain wasn't just from the typing: it went beyond my mind, my brain, my... my anything. It was in the world outside and it was like all the Magick that Dad and Uncle Alex and Frater Magnifico had ever taught me, only more powerful. So powerful it had changed everything about the world. Everything. Absolutely, only...

Only not in a way you'd notice. Or perhaps you would. But only in the little things. Things like...

The side wall of the house opposite was grey, unadorned concrete. It *should* have had...

There were four bundles of paper on the table. There *should* have been...

Things were different and I'd come close to losing my knowledge of how, of why. But I'd not lost that knowledge! An aching side, two numb and throbbing hands and an agonised head were small prices to pay: I'd been able to read the story of how things should have been from a little bundle of A4 paper. And I'd been able to type it up – I'd known I'd have to type it up because I'd known that the little bundle of A4 couldn't stay in this world for very long.

So now I knew there was evil. And resentment. This evil and this resentment were the jagged edges of the last broken third of an old woman. An evil old woman who, given that she was so broken, insisted things be *this* way. *This* way, not the other way... I clicked my computer a few times. There it was – 'Tony and Frances' – an ordinary Word document. A document I had brought here from a different Earth.

How had I done it? Howhow*how?*

And I knew.

The Smethwick gig had been part of it. The hushhush gig at... At The Abyss... At the Lost Sefirot of Da'at... *At The Disused Smethwick West Station!*

Where, on the back wall of the collapsing concrete passenger shelter, someone had graffitied the word 'Data' on to the cold grey concrete...

'Data' – an anagram of 'Da'at', The Voice of Reason had said. The primal information. Able to cross The Abyss, if only because of what we'd done to The Guardian of The Abyss back in 2003. And so I had been able to see the mural that should have been on the wall outside, to read the book that had been given to me by Tony and Frances. By the parents of Warren Griefstick. By the mother who had borne him and the father who'd snatched the club, the rolling pin, out of the hand of his murderer and grandmother... By the parents of Warren Griefstick and, therefore...

By the grandparents of my beautiful beautiful boy!

Who did, after all, exist. He existed. HE EXISTED!

But not on this Earth.

And so this became, for me, an Earth that didn't matter. It was, I equally convinced, an Earth that would be hitting the buffers before very much longer. I wasn't sure where such an idea came from; the question didn't seem important. I had been summoned by *my* Earth, by *my* homeworld, by the world where lived my beautiful beautiful boy!

And that rancid little Janice Croviss thought she could stop me, did she? Thought she could stop me being with my boy?

186

I caught myself grinning. Grinning crazily. I went over to one of the mirrors.

Janice Croviss. Yes, I knew too well that you could expect nothing better of a broken third of a human being. Know her well enough, you could have pitied her. But it was not my function to know her that well. It was not my function to pity. Not to pity her. It was my function to tear through the barriers she'd put up between me and my beautiful boy. Barriers that had been universes thick but which I had made tissue thin.

Tear through them!

And tear through Janice fucking Croviss while I was at it!

And I knew, now, who and what my real enemy had always been. It was a thing that had been sneering at me and belittling me for the whole of my life – but now I was going to give it the kicking it had grown to deserve.

Morality.

It had been a useful servant, in some ways. A useful tool. When people agree not to murder each other, it makes everybody safer. Everybody lives longer. That's the purpose of morality. That's what it's for. But when people start doing things *because* they're the right thing to do, *because* they're *moral*, that's the point when it's got ideas above its station – that's the point when it needs slapping down sharpish. And if it doesn't stay slapped down, then it needs putting down.

Janice Croviss had thought she'd the *moral* right to smash open the skull of her infant grandson. And who's to say she hadn't? Who's to say what's moral and what isn't, once people stop thinking of morality as a tool, like a fire or a wheel or a spanner, and start thinking of Morality as a purpose or a justification. Once people like Janice Croviss start talking about 'The Moral Purpose of Existence.' That's the point where they start thinking they can smash babies' skulls; that's the point when they start thinking they can take away my beautiful beautiful boy!

That's the point when you need to get hold of that uppity little gobshite Morality and kick its fucking head in.

That was what was needed. Somebody had to kick Morality's head in.

'And I'm just the girl to do it...'

I tore my clothes off, showered and dragged myself to bed. When I woke, it was dark outside. I looked at my phone: 5:17am.

I didn't need any more sleep. I dressed, went downstairs and wheeled my bike outside, then mounted it and pedalled through the damp and dewy predawn to Dave's place.

I had a spare key. I let myself in and started to make up the fire.

After that, I looked around for something to read. Or to look at.

And found it: *Satansfist.* Of course.

I couldn't help being drawn to it and I couldn't help opening it at that final montage of photos taken in Harry Ronsard's bathroom.

The images glowed with otherworldliness. The sheer bloody destructiveness of their owner and of their creator was too obvious but, besides that…

Besides that, there was the sense of something, of somewhere, beyond the void left by all that destruction. Something that justified Satansfist's lover – poor wannabe poet Lewis Gladrell – still being banged up for a murder he'd been goaded into… No: commanded to perform – by the man who'd left us this utter blackness. This blackness so much deeper and more appalling than any mere absence of light.

If there was a way through to a different version of the world, this was where I'd find it. Nowhere else.

I shuddered. But I kept staring, transfixed.

I heard Dave come in. He was still and silent for a moment. Seeing me stare at these images frightened him.

And it occurred to me that Dave Calper loved me. Which was odd because, unlike Magnifico or Ith or Charlotte or anyone else I'd ever been able to say that about, there wasn't a trace of sex to it. Weird, that. I wondered how it had come to be?

'Vanished?' he asked when I'd told him what had happened.

'Er…' I replied.

'I'll get you a cup of tea,' he said, helpfully.

'I haven't been taking anything remotely fun,' I told him as he came back with a mug in his hand. The mug was chipped and its outside patterned in wavy yellow, orange and chocolate brown. People told me wallpaper used to look like that in the 1970s. Inside, the liquid was dark copper and dangerous looking. I sipped at it. Whew! Dave may have played the bass like Holger Czukay but he made tea like Lemmy.

'So,' he said. 'Something happened.'

'Yes. Definitely something.'

'And we're not just talking a book, either.'

'No. Not just a book.'

'Anything else you can put your finger on?'

'A bit. And a lot I can't.'

'Well, there always will be, won't there? With stuff like this.'

'Yes. With stuff like this.'

'What did you see?'

'I read this... This book. I say a book, but it was unpublished. Just a sheaf of papers.'

'What was it?'

'It was by... By Tony Griefstick and Frances Chessil.'

'Hang on, they're...'

'Warren Griefstick's parents.'

'I see.'

Dave's voice was even and noncommittal. He was determined neither to accept what I said, nor to dismiss it. He was capable of being either a credulous disciple or the bitterest of sceptics. At that moment, he felt neither was right: he was just there for me, listening.

'It seemed to have turned up on my work table. It was written to me. But there was more... There was...'

'Yes?'

'Outside the window. On the wall opposite my place. The wall... There was a mural on the wall. A huge thing.'

'It's just bare concrete there, love.'

'Yes. I know. But there was a mural there... When the book was on my table, there was a mural there. It was called "Orpheus". But it was... it was...'

My voice faded.

'Lewis Gladrell?' Dave asked, knowing the answer.

I nodded, once.

'Painted by Lee?' he asked again and, once more, I nodded.

'He never did a painting like that, though. Never painted Lewis.'

'I know,' I said. 'I think he only did it two or three years ago. But...'

'Lewis killed him eight years back.'

'Yes.'

'This has the feeling,' Dave started, then hesitated, '...the feeling of looking into a different world.'

'Yes.'

'But not like a parallel universe...'

I paused.

'No,' I said eventually. 'It's not the same as that. Warren's something more... more deliberate. It's like somebody's remade the world. But they've tweaked it, mucked about with it, tried to improve on it in all sorts of little ways and their version's running in parallel to ours, because...'

I dried up.

'Why,' asked Dave, his voice trembling strangely, 'would anyone want to remake the world?'

'Because,' I said, 'This one isn't going to last much longer.'

He looked at me, silently, for a few moments.

'It's going to hit the buffers,' he said, very quietly.

And I knew then that he understood. I'd been a fool not to realise that he'd do so.

'Perhaps whoever destroys it does so accidentally,' he whispered. 'Like, y'know, they're superintelligent but... y'know... they don't always have it together... they're not very well organised. Sort of like your dad...'

'Or like you, Dave.'

'Yeah.' He laughed. 'A race of superintelligent but not very well organised Giant Spiders from the Planet Dave. And when they realise what they've done, they say *'Whoops'* and they recreate the world – which, for them, is a piss-easy thing to do.'

'Sounds a lot like what you or Dad would do,' I said, 'if you had that kind of power – and you made that kind of cock-up.'

'Yeah. I hope so. Only they put in a few tweaks... you know – improvements. To make up for our trouble... Which could lead to there being two versions of the world, in parallel... sort of. But for any one of us to get from one version to another...'

He looked at the thick album of art by Lee Icement – by Satansfist. We both looked at it. It had fallen shut so I reached over and opened it. I flicked through the glossy pages, quickly reaching the photographs at the end – the photographs of the Ronsard Bathroom.

That blackness! There was the Abyss! Lee Icement had seen it and known he would paint it and it should hardly come as a surprise that it had been a piece of cake for him to drag Lucifer Seventheye out of it and remake Charlotte's dad into him!

That absolute blackness and… on the other side…

On the other side was Warren! Warren and our beautiful beautiful boy!

'Lon,' said Dave, carefully.

'I know, Dave.'

'You've got to do what you've got to do but… please… Please try and keep yourself together… In this world… if you can.'

'I'll try.'

Dave understood. He knew I would try. But he knew it might not be possible.

I went back home, sat at the laptop and spent two days reading and rereading the words of Tony Griefstick and of Frances Chessil.

Then I rang Ith. Mattie answered and spoke to me in a voice he used instinctively sometimes: it was a friendly but knowing voice that took people by surprise if they'd been assuming he was dim compared to his brother. He said some inconsequential but warming things, then put his mom on. Like him, she could hear more in what I said than was in the words; crazy how she disbelieved absolutely in psychic power yet went around reading minds every second of her life. We agreed to meet up a couple of days later.

Grey skies of pre-spring, buds just getting started on the trees and there we were in the car park of Stourbridge Junction Station. We hugged, briefly, but not quite as briefly as you can if you've never been lovers. And the strength in those arms was like a warm mountain. I ran my hand through her short hair – grey now; mousy blonde when we'd been together. Then we went and got ourselves coffees from the little shop on the platform. And then…

It only took ten or fifteen to get to Rowley Regis. Ith had expected me to want to go to Smethwick but, no, there was a grave I wanted to take a look at. A particular grave.

And, as we wandered along Avenue Road with the tall redbricks at our right and the tall trees to our left, I tried to explain everything.

It was all par for the course to her: she was the daughter of Alex Chaplain, one of the greatest occult magicians the world has known; she had a demon brother who led her on dream-quests through every possible subconscious landscape; she, with Dougie's help and that of his spirit guide, had cast out the devil Choronzon, Guardian of the Abyss…

And the fact that she believed in none of these things made her power in such realms only the stronger; her dad would have been proud of her beyond measure.

'Whose grave is it that you want to see?' she asked as we entered the churchyard. 'It can't be Warren's. From what you say, his mother won't have wanted him buried with any Crovisses.'

'She might not have had much choice. Janice Croviss was like you. Like you but in reverse. She could make people agree to evil things.'

Ith was silent. Either she felt me to be too fragile to argue with – which might have been true – or she couldn't think of any arguments.

We picked our way through the long, sodden grasses, among the uneven, often broken monuments, across the treacherous ground.

I'd thought I had a pretty good idea of where it had been – that grave I'd noticed weeks before, the one that had attracted me, or repelled me, the one from which Warren had almost seemed to emerge (*Had* he? Or was my memory distorting the experience?) But a crowded graveyard can be a bit of a trickster on the quiet and we were clumping around for the best part of two hours, the grasses seeming to grasp at our ankles like awakening zombies. Then, eventually, Ith said:

'Er… is this it?'

I turned. She was standing by a gravestone, hard up against the north wall. I came up and looked. Her arm went around me. I needed it.

IN MEMORY OF
JENNIFER JUDITH CROVISS
1936-1946
AND
FRIEDA ICEMENT, NÉE CROVISS
1929-1968

No trace of a 'loving' anywhere. Hardly surprising, when it came to Satansfist's granny, but… I was silent. There were two names on the grave. Two names, not three, though there was enough space left on the marble for a third one.

So that evil piece of shit was still out there.

The day after, I started to look for the other grave.

It took weeks. I thought at first I'd ask – make official enquiries – of vicars, undertakers and other folk who knew where bodies were buried. But no – I wound up doing it the hard way. I spent hour after hour trolling through Kidderminster graveyards in search of those names and of a few brief sad dates. The other Wallensteinies and Ith must have worried I was losing the plot. Even Dad thought it peculiar.

Then, one dull Saturday afternoon, I found it.

Never mind which graveyard: it was a more open, windier place than Saint Paul's Blackheath. The gravestone was white marble with gold lettering. It was a big-ish monument – it had to be:

WARREN PETER GRIEFSTICK:
10TH MARCH 1982 – 24TH MARCH 1982
FRANCES HEIDI GRIEFSTICK, NÉE CHESSIL:
2ND MAY 1951 – 3RD JULY 1987
REGINALD HERBERT CHESSIL:
1ST DECEMBER 1919 – 3RD NOVEMBER 1987
ROSEMARY ELEANOR CHESSIL, NÉE RAYBOULD:
8TH OCTOBER 1918 – 3RD JUNE 2004.

All snuggled up together – cold but cosy. Granny Kidderminster had hung on for the longest, of course, determined, surely, to see Janice Slagbitchscum Croviss in the ground before she went herself – then deciding, at eighty-five, that it just wasn't worth the bloody effort.

Had suicide been Frances' way out? Maybe. But she could just as easily have taken to the fags – big time – and trusted them to get the job done. She wasn't the type to get into smack or anything. But, maybe, one day she'd just stopped paying attention to the world and stepped off the pavement into the path of a cement truck.

Reg hadn't hung about long, of course. I bet it had been a heart attack. I bet it had been in his back garden. I bet he'd been trying to force himself to still care about his tomatoes and his runner beans.

So. That had left Rosemary. Granny Kidderminster. Who'd given Warren his ginger hair. On her own for – what? – that had been evil, that had. That had been the most evil thing of all.

And, this time, there really was no naming the thing that had done it. The things that had possessed Sharon Maitland and Charlotte's dad – we'd put names to them. But not this thing. Not Choronzon, not Lucifer Seventheye, no: what possessed Janice Croviss was an utter cold emptiness. An unthinking nullity. A void.

And, suddenly, I realised that I knew why God had done it – done Creation, I mean. I realised that it had been to put an end to that terrible bloody Void. I realised that I understood God –

'Who are you?'

I turned.

An old man. In his seventies maybe. Unbelievable that he'd turned up here at the same time as I – except that, of course, since Rosemary had died, he'd been coming here very often.

'What are you doing here?'

It was a hard, dead voice, as I might have expected. A hard dead voice that, though I'd never heard it before, I knew well. Just as I knew the lines of grief and self-loathing in the face. Of grief and self-loathing rationalised, anæsthetized into evil, in a hopeless and pathetic attempt to make the pain go away. I knew him by the heavy truncheon that hung from his belt – a heavy truncheon that would have shattered the skulls of any number of wretched, masochistic, suicidal WiGIiEs.

I knew him, by the Grey Shirt.

'I said, what are you doing here?'

I looked at him and felt my face go hard – harder than his. So he'd wound up a Greyshirt? Big deal. I'd been trained by Ith: I knew how to plant a kick under his lower jaw that would take his fucking head off.

Because this wasn't Grandad Tony.

194

This wasn't Grandad Tony who made such a fuss of my beautiful beautiful boy, who spoiled him rotten and made us all laugh on Saturday afternoons. This wasn't a man who'd ever got to read his son's books and think most of them were too '*portentous*'. This was only the debris in the wake of the shade, of the void. This was the thing that, maybe for only a second or two, had failed to be himself and had, by his failure, let everything go to shit. This was a protective shell with nothing inside.

I pointed.

'That truncheon,' I said, 'it looks a lot like a rolling pin, doesn't it?'

The flesh of his face turned the colour of a dead jellyfish washed up on a beach – and just as venomous. He didn't know how I knew, but he knew I knew.

I looked into the wreck of a face.

'*That little seedling,*' I said. '*By Christ, it was an evil thing. Tiny, but evil. And now look what it has grown into. Look what fruit it has borne.*'

His face remained unresponsive, dead. I stepped a little nearer. Though I loathed being so close to him, I knew he could save me a lot of trouble.

'So, Mr Applebright,' I whispered, 'where can I find your sack of shit of a mother?'

Once he'd have got that reference – he had been an English graduate. Not anymore though.

'Because,' I whispered, more softly still, 'when I find her, I'm going to rip her guts out through her twat and stuff them down her throat. Or I might, quite possibly, do it the other way round. Decisions decisions decisions – I don't know! But it will be one way or the other. So. Tell me.' I leaned still closer. '*Where is she?*'

In the faintest whisper, he gave me the name of a care home.

I left him.

On the way out of the graveyard, I looked back.

He was staring at the headstone, slumped, empty, motionless. It was as if he'd forgotten I'd spoken to him. He was staring at the headstone as if it were a place both warm and homely, from which he was locked out.

I spent some time getting ready – a week or so. There was a knack my dad had taught me that I knew I'd need: I'd still be solid, I'd still reflect light, I'd still have weight. *But...*

Normal people can't just walk into old folk's homes, can they?

195

Tony hadn't been near Janice since the 80s. There was no sorrow at the care home over that. It wasn't surprising: I'd learned he had a bad reputation, even among the Greyshirts. There was scarcely more sympathy for Janice herself; she'd been silent and inert for the past ten years but before that she'd been, as I overheard it whispered in the lobby of the place, 'a right Tartar.' I could imagine.

Of course, I shouldn't have been let in and, of course, if I'd allowed myself to wonder even vaguely why I *was* let in – then I wouldn't have been let in. But I was David Kyle's daughter and, after a week of the right sort of preparatory meditation, this sort of Magick came as naturally to me as breathing.

I was led upstairs and left in a quiet, lamplit little bedroom with the curtains drawn, though it was broad daylight outside. 'She used to say she preferred it this way,' I was told. Ah.

No pictures on the walls. And no mirrors. She'd always hated and feared them. I had brought one in my tote bag. As soon as the door closed and it was just her and me – I got it out.

Wait, though: before I did anything, I'd just noticed…

There was no sign here of Tony's existence. But on top of the bedside cupboard, there was a small photo, sepia, in an oval frame of dark chocolate Bakelite, or something similar.

Three girls. Three sisters. Two plain twins and one younger and far prettier.

Or was it that she was prettier? Wasn't it rather that she looked into the lens with openness, with friendliness, with no morbid assumption that the world was her enemy?

Because I could see that assumption beginning to fester on the faces of the twins.

I held up the mirror to the face of the bedridden old woman. There was no reaction. I'd expected none: that wasn't the point. The point was to let little Janice get a good look at the foulness she was going to become.

Take a look, little Janice… take a good… long… look…

See, you poison bitch? Even your own self thinks you are a monster! Thinks you are the… most… repulsive… filth!

But she wasn't looking into the mirror. The little girl of the 1940s might have been gazing in horror at the old woman of 2019, but the old woman was paying no attention to the little girl.

I turned from her and put the mirror away. I was drained and disgusted. Then I looked back. Her eyes had come into focus and her head – very slightly – had moved. It seemed she was looking at me. At me – with my face full of murder. She – who'd not been able to look at anything for a long time.

I slumped into a wicker chair and stared into those old old eyes – in which, to my shock, I could see no evil at all.

'Jenny?' A voice ragged as torn fragments of tracing paper.

What..?

'Jenny!' The voice was still ragged but it was brighter. And those eyes – no point trying to deny it – really had got their vision back. She could see me. And the look on her face – if I'd been prepared to accept the possibility of love in this ancient slag, then I could have mistaken it for love.

'No,' I whispered. But I couldn't get my voice above a whisper. I couldn't tell this poisonous thing that I was not the person – the only person – she'd ever loved. I wasn't her little sister and how the hell was she making such a mistake anyway? How could she think a woman of thirty-four was someone who'd died seventy years ago and more? Died at the age of ten!

And her hand had stretched out and taken mine before I'd registered she was doing it. And it was cold and slightly moist and the skin felt thin, the way old people's skin does. It should have been a vile thing but, horrified, I could not help but feel the love in it. The loathsome, hideous love.

'Oh Jenny...' She was struggling to speak now. Did she think she could say something that could justify her murder – yes, it had been murder, don't give me any bollocks about 'accident'! – justify her murder of sweet, gentle Warren and, through that murder, her annihilation of my beautiful beautiful boy?

'None of it was ever real.'

And that was all she had strength left to say. No problem, because that was all I needed to hear. Not just the words, but their disgusting sincerity.

197

None of it had ever been real to her. She'd never cast a poison shade over her son, because he'd not existed. She'd never murdered her grandson because he'd not existed. Existence had ended when Jenny died. As for what was left – they'd never had to take any of it seriously – had they? Had those two remaining Croviss girls? No they'd never had to.

Gradually, the hand let go. I backed away from the bed. The sepia photograph of the three young girls still stared up from the bedside table. And, skin growing greyer with every moment, the face of the old woman relaxed into a blessed smile.

She was dying, was this Croviss Girl. She was dying with an expression of love and blessedness on her face.

No!

This had not been what I'd intended! I'd not come here to redeem her! I'd not come to save the soul of the hydrochloric scum who'd destroyed my beautiful boy! I'd wanted to be like Christine and her dad – to keep Heaven safe from such rubbish!

–You're not suited to the part of Satan, Lon.

Who was that voice in the back of my head?

No no no. I didn't believe this. I did not believe I was being spoken to by the ghost of Jenny Croviss.

– Lon, you believe in absolutely everything.

I do NOT believe in the salvation of the evil slag who...

–Satansfist made a way to see...

And I stood there, staring at Janice Croviss. At dying Janice Croviss. And the voice in my head was silent.

Janice Croviss' breath laboured on, shallow and getting shallower. Wouldn't be long now.

***

Outside, I phoned Dad before I'd even got on my bike.

'Hello,' I said, attempting fake brightness.

'Hello Babalon,' said Dad, not fooled by the attempt.

'I've got a bit of a thing on.' Still trying to come over all bright and chirpy. Still not bringing it off.

'A... thing?'

Thing: the word clanged like a funeral bell. I could turn on all the fake sunshine I liked; Dad would sniff the Black Hole at the back of it; Dad had a nose for black holes. And I was reeking of the buggers.

'You know Zann Street?'

'Of course.' A bit of fear creeping into his voice.

'You know... that... that bloke it was named after?'

A pause. Dad had known this was coming. This, or something like it. *That bloke:* Zann, the German violinist who had created some of the most otherworldly music of the last century, only a few fragments of which had survived, tucked away in the orchestra pit of a cheap theatre. Zann, who had perhaps never been human at all and, according to the account of the last person to see him alive, had ultimately been reclaimed by the terrible region from which he had come.

Dad did his best to change the course of my thought: 'A great musical genius! I sometimes catch a little of him in your playing...'

'I know,' I said. 'The thing is, there's somewhere I really really need to be. And... to get to it... I think I need to... to go through... the place he came from... and went back to...'

A silence. Then, from Dad, a single syllable: 'Da'at.'

I inhaled.

'It's doable, Dad. Nothing's there to stop me anymore. You know what we did to Choronzon. You were there...'

'But Babalon,' he whispered. Then he dried up. He was breathing very heavily – sobbing perhaps. 'I shall never see you again.'

'Not on this side of the doings but... you know...'

I was silent. He knew.

'Don't let them tell you I'm dead,' I told him. 'They'll try to talk you into it. But don't believe them. It's important that you don't believe them. Ask Dave Calper; he'll have sussed it out. He'll say... he'll say... I tried to do a Dave impression through my tears: *"She's only been and gone and done a bleedin' Gandalf, ain't she?"'*

'Babalon!' he tore my name out of himself as if it were by caesarean section. 'I understand, Babalon.'

'I know you do, Dad. Love you to bits.'

The second phone call, much briefer, I made once I'd got back home:

'Hi, Dave.'

''Ello, gorgeous. What's the bother?'

'Well, I might have to… No, I'm definitely going to have to go… away for a bit.'

'Ah.' The same note of distress I'd heard from Dad. Better hidden, though. 'You mean…'

'Da'at.'

He inhaled. He exhaled. He'd known.

'Smethwick West wasn't close enough?' he asked.

'It's a good roadmap, that railway line, but the map's not the territory.'

'You going to… tell Ith about this?'

'No. If there turns out to be… any trouble… getting where I need to go – and she steps in, there might be… collateral damage. I don't want that…'

'I know, love, I know.'

He would, I knew, be on the phone to Ith as soon as this call was over. I didn't blame him: from his point of view, it was the right thing to do. But this meant I had to get moving; it might take them a while to work out where I was going, but they'd do it eventually.

Right now, I've just spent the night typing this out. I shall scribble a little note to Dave, bequeathing him the editorial duties, then treat myself to a couple of hours' kip.

Then it'll be time to pick up the phone once more, to flick through the Contacts and to stop when my least favourite name comes up – the name of the one I tried hardest to save. Tried hardest – and failed. The name of the person I now have to ask to save me – at least to the extent of lending me a set of front door keys.

But I have no doubt I'll be able to talk them out of her.

After that, my next stop will be my last stop – at least on this version of Planet Earth: Satansfist's final and most terrible painting, in Harry Ronsard's bathroom, Barratt Road, Kingswinford.

Because Satansfist had made a way to see. That's what I had heard. From the ghost of Jenny Croviss. And, if not from the ghost of Jenny Croviss, then from who..?

What she hadn't needed to say was that, when it comes to art like Satansfist's, as everybody had learned from what it had made of Harry, to see it was to be it.

Hugz and kissez all round, me lovers,

Lon   xxxxx

20:Adil Muhammed Shah

That day, I'd been on security over The Old Gaffer's missus' – New Cimourdain's. I'd never liked the place. I'd never thought the Old Gaffer had either: when he'd heard about New Cimourdain moving in there with little Siegfried, he was supposed to have looked grim. I'd reckoned that, if he'd been able to speak, he'd have had things to say about it. But his looking grim had been plenty enough for those who'd seen it: trust me, when it came to looking grim, there never was anyone to touch the Old Gaffer. The place was near Enville – which meant it was dead posh, and had used to belong to an Oldbury mob called the Khans: smack-dealers. There were rumours that the Old Gaffer had seen the lot of them off when he was starting out. So, no, it wasn't a place where I would have chosen to live but New Cimourdain had decided she liked it and, if the Khans' ghosts still hung around the place, they were being sensible and keeping their heads down. I couldn't blame them: Old Cimourdain – whose name the Old Gaffer's missus had taken – was one of them blokes as ran the French Revolution. The Khans had been hard but, when I read a bit about him, it sounded like Old Cimourdain's ghost would be able to see off any number of theirs, no bother.

Most of the time, little Siegfried was a good kid. With the Old Gaffer for a dad and New Cimourdain for a mom, he was going to be. But that day he'd been funny. New Cimourdain had left him alone – only for a few minutes. He was sat at a computer and he'd been going on the internet, YouTube, I think. New Cimourdain had all the child restrictions, of course, but the people who do these things, they haven't got a clue. And Siegfried had come across something... Some kind of noise, I don't know what it was. But as soon as I came in the room, I knew it was disgusting. I didn't know why: it just was. It was something, I knew, that needed not to be allowed. As the Old Gaffer would have said, 'It wants stopping.'

But here was his own son, the six year-old Siegfried Ronsard, staring at this filth – worse still, listening to this filth – as if it was his fate.

And sometimes, you know, I wonder if it's a bad thing to teach kids to read. Until they're able to tell what's good from what's bad, I mean. Because little Siegfried looked at the name of the video and, bit by bit...

'We – ather – Rep – ort...'

'Weather Report live,' I put him right. Then, inside, I kicked myself.

I tried – I swear I tried – to find some way of explaining to a six year old why this sort of filth needed turning off. Then it stopped.

Or nearly stopped. The blokes – I suppose I'd have to call them that – who were making their bloody noise, put their stuff – their 'instruments' – down. Then there was a still pic of each of them, in turn, with his name at the bottom of the screen.

When one of those stills came up, Siegfried clicked 'pause'.

'Ja – co – Part – sorry – us,' he tried.

This time, I stopped myself from putting him right.

'What's that?' he asked, pointing at the screen.

'I don't know,' I said. A guitar? Maybe a bass guitar...'

'I got to have one,' he said. And I didn't know what to say to that because, for all the voice was that of a little kid, it was the first time I'd heard him sound like his dad. The first time his voice had sounded like Destiny.

Then New Cimourdain came in.

'Turn that rubbish off, Siegfried' she said, very cool and calm but not sounding as if she was going to be mucked about. The little 'un did as he was told and wandered off; it was time for the kids' shows on the telly.

'I don't know what's getting into him,' she sighed. 'The day before yesterday he was telling everybody he wanted to be called "Ziggy". I told them his father wouldn't hear of it. And I'm sure his father wouldn't hear of him listening to filth like that.'

'Probably not,' I said.

I could understand her wanting the kid on his best behaviour. These were challenging times for us all. Challenging, but promising. I mean, now we'd finally booted out the Jocks, with the Northern Irish guaranteed to follow, all we had to make sure was that the Welsh got the same treatment. And the Cornish. And the Channel Isles. And the Manx.

Yeah, the Manx most of all – dodgy bastards them Manx. Then we could start knocking the country into shape good and proper.

But, locally, things had got mucked up when our top man over at Blackheath had done himself in. District Overlord Griefstick – previously one of the most reliable blokes we had. He'd been getting on a bit and everybody thought it must have been because his mom had died a day or two before, which made sense. But dousing yourself with petrol and striking a match? That's no good way to go whatever it's all about. Anyway, it had made a load of extra work for us.

So, with all that on the go, the last person you wanted to find letting the side down was the son of the Old Gaffer and of New Cimourdain. One day he was wanting to be called 'Ziggy', the next he was wanting to make a noise like that 'Weather Report' filth. We were going to have to keep him out of the way for a bit, because anybody who found out about it was going to have to get put at the bottom of the canal, sharpish. And you can't do that too often, because them canals, they get clogged with stiffs. Believe me – I know.

I looked at my watch: just coming up to five. It was sunny and, outside, the daffodils were out.

My phone went: Gaffer Charlotte. I went through the French windows into the back garden – big massive place with thick privet hedges ten foot high – and I answered it.

'Good evening, Adil.'

'Evening, Gaffer.'

'Siegfried being a bit of a pain?' It was like she had second sight when it came to her little half-brother.

'A bit, yeah, but nothing to worry about right now.'

'Good. I need you here in about an hour.'

'No problem.'

And it wouldn't be. With the Security Team One logo all over my car, you'd be a bloody fool to grumble if I cut you up or went through a red light.

'Good. See you then.'

And she rang off.

Quickly, I checked on the rest of the lads; it was okay – they'd got everything nailed down. Then I had a quick word with New Cimourdain.

She was watching something American on the telly. *Keeping Up with the Kardashians*, I think it was: when she was watching stuff like that, she got a different look on her face – it was like she stopped being New Cimourdain and went back to being Polly Gauvain again.

'Got to nip over head office,' I told her. 'Gaffer Charlotte needs a hand. I've checked on the lads. They've got everything under control, you've no need to worry.'

She looked up at me. She snapped back into being New Cimourdain. Funny thing: when I'd first known her, she hadn't been thin at all. But, over the past couple of years, 'thin' was what she had become – particularly in the face. And, at that moment, something seemed to click on behind her eyes – something very cold and clever.

'I see,' she said. No doubt she'd be on the phone to Gaffer Charlotte as soon as she heard my tyres on the gravel. New Cimourdain always wanted to know the details and she was good at finding them out.

She just gave me a quiet little nod and I bowed out.

The drive over to Birmingham went nice and smooth. I took the Dudley route and it was good to see there was a big bonfire on the go in the car park of the Tesco near Burnt Tree Island. There were fireworks getting let off, though it still wasn't dark, and loads of banners saying 'Fuck off you Jocks!' Better still, there were a few saying the same to the Welsh and one or two saying as much to the Cornish. Now, don't get me wrong: I didn't like the language – the Old Gaffer wouldn't have approved of the language. But, when things were going so good, you had to allow people a bit of celebration, didn't you?

And there was a lot to celebrate. I'd been up the Solway Firth the week before and we hadn't been mucking about: machine gun towers, barbed wire, minefields and guard dogs that would attack to kill. And it was just like that all the way to Marshall Meadows Bay on the East Coast. Great stuff! No way them Jocks weren't going to know we meant business!

It'd be just as good out west once we'd got Offa's Dyke brought back up to some serious, state-of-the-art spec. There'd be the minefields, of course, with laser-triggered alarm systems in case them Welsh bastards tried any funny business. And, just like with the Jocks, we hadn't ruled out having a few tactical nukes stashed not so very far away – though that was all being kept very hush-hush for the moment.

Things weren't so sure in the south-west though. We couldn't get stuck into the infrastructure because nobody knew if the border was going to run through Plymouth or through Yeovil. It all depended on which way them Devon buggers decided to jump. I'd never trusted them Devon buggers.

I parked my Audi in the underground car-park. A couple of big lads – white lads – said 'Evenin', Big Mohammed,' and 'Cheers, Big Mo' as I headed for the lifts. Okay, they hadn't got my name right exactly but I knew the pair of 'em and they'd got the right attitude and they didn't mean no disrespect. There's nobody got nothing to worry about off me so long as they've got the right attitude and they don't mean no disrespect. And I can always tell.

The executive lift picked up the signal from my ID and opened automatically. Inside, the light was soft and turquoise. I was taken up the seventh floor. The music was the same in the lift and in reception: *The Valkyrie*, end of Act Three – a father saying goodbye to his daughter. Forever. It had never sounded so sad to me, never sounded so real – though they always had the Wagner on here at Party Headquarters. Tradition, wasn't it?

I whipped off my mirrorshades as I came up to the front desk, and straightened my jacket. The girl who sat there was new. She dressed smart, though – modest and smart, like women ought to. She waved me through.

Gaffer Charlotte stood up behind her desk.

'Good evening, Adil'

'Evenin', Gaffer.'

She'd got herself well turned out: dark grey jacket, dark grey slacks, hair a bit shorter than I usually like to see in a woman – but that was just to show she wasn't one to be messed about with. There were, I knew, some people who liked to see it in a different light. But only a few of them had ever said as much in my hearing.

And none of them ever got to say it more than the once.

'I'd like you to get over to Barratt Road. Keep an eye on the old place.'

'Sure,' I said. 'Any reason?'

'There's a friend of mine who wants to take a look at the paintings.'

'Okay,' I said.

Thinking I'd been given my orders, I turned to get off but she stopped me:

'One more thing, Adil.'

'Yes Gaffer?'

'If anything… anything odd appears to be happening, I want you to get her out of there. Drag her if necessary.' Her voice sounded stiff and hard.

Now, if there was one thing I'd learned with Gaffer Charlotte, it was that if you had ideas or thoughts come into your head when she was around, you never tried keeping them to yourself. It was the same as it had been with the Old Gaffer: the pair of them, they could sniff out them notions from a mile off.

So: 'Has New Cimourdain been worrying about this?' I asked. 'It seemed to me as she might have been.'

Gaffer Charlotte smiled. Sort of. One corner of her mouth went up a bit: she was as canny with her smiles as the Old Gaffer had been.

'No getting anything past you,' she said. 'Not if you don't *want* it to get past you. You're right. She was on the phone while you were on the way. She must have… heard from somewhere that this friend had been to see me. Anyway, here are the keys. Please be careful with them; I only have one other set.'

'You know I will.'

'I do.'

'What's this friend look like?'

'Very small. Only about five, five-one. Red hair – with a few grey bits. In her thirties. I say very small but she's had a lot of self-defence training. Been with the Stourbridge lot. She can handle herself so… try to keep things friendly with her. Her name's Lon.'

'No problem,' I said.

I went straight to the lift and headed down. I was worried. Lon. That meant Lon Kyle – Babalon Kyle. A lot of the lies people told about Gaffer Charlotte also mentioned Babalon Kyle. So she hadn't been someone I'd wanted to come across at all. Hang on, though, just because those lies mentioned her, it didn't mean she'd been telling them herself. Of course not; get a grip!

All the same, I wasn't sure. It was the name, in part. No crime to get called 'Babalon'. It just showed you'd had a prat of a mom. Or a prat of a dad. Or both. Still, she could have changed it. She had, though – sort of. Shortened it.

I put all those thoughts out my head as I got in the Audi. Just get over there, play it cool and see how things turn out. I sighed and started the engine.

Barratt Road Kingswinford.

It was dark when I pulled up outside the Old Gaffer's house. The place always got to me when I looked at it: if it hadn't been for the Old Gaffer, when I was nineteen, I'd have been back in the nick in no time. Him and Mrs Icement, of course. When I'd got out, it had been him as had turned my life round and that meant I owed him – him and Gaffer Charlotte and New Cimourdain and little Siegfried – owed all of 'em big time.

It was quiet. It was always quiet in Kingswinford: people would be out at work in the day, or asleep at night, or watching their big massive tellies in the evening. They always had the biggest tellies in Kingswinford – massive great tellies. And of course, with tellies like that, they never had much cause to say anything to each other, which was probably how so many of them wound up being such scummers – they never got to practice being with – you know – actual people.

Behind the Old Gaffer's house was the wood. A thick wood – though they'd had to chop a few of the conifers down a year or two back. Thick and silent.

There were a lot of stories about the wood. I didn't know how many of them were true. It was supposed to have been the place where the Old Gaffer had had his accident – the one that had put him in hospital ever since. I wasn't sure I believed that; there was a feeling about that wood – a strong, no-mucking-about feeling – like it was and always would be a place that was on the Old Gaffer's side.

I got out the car.

Babalon Kyle had already arrived. Obvious that, because she'd left the front door swinging open, the daft madam!

Thinking I'd need to have a serious word with her, I walked across the front lawn. Then, just outside the front door, I stopped. I'd started to feel really cold. And – this was the weird thing – the cold seemed to be coming from inside the house. I zipped up the front of my leather jacket and went in.

Yes, it was definitely colder inside the house. The cold seemed to be falling in waves down the stairs.

'Miss Kyle?'

No answer. I could sense she was in there somewhere, but she was staying quiet.

I don't remember touching the doorframe or the bannister at the foot of the stairs. But I must have done. Because what started to happen then can't have been real. Can't have been. Because it had been a long time since the Old Gaffer had straightened me out and I'd not touched a drop of anything dodgy since then. But Kyle was known to be into all that hippy stuff – ganja, mushrooms, kru-shan – so I reckon she must have sprayed or wiped something pretty powerful all over the place. Whatever it was, it was strong enough to be absorbed through the skin and it was well evil. That's the only explanation I've got.

The light was on in the downstairs hall, and on the upstairs landing. The murals on the wall were just like I remembered them. But still, they stopped me for a moment. They always did.

Now people had said some bad stuff about the bloke as had painted them murals on the Old Gaffer's walls – the same sort of stuff as they'd said about Gaffer Charlotte and this Kyle woman. Let me tell you: the blokes in them pictures – they was rock hard. Stripped to the waist, a lot of 'em, big massive muscles and proper oiled up. And, these blokes, they was taking on some of the massivest dragons, some of the evillest-looking zombies you ever saw! And they was dealing with them dragons and them zombies with some of the most big massive swords ever! Shining steel! Seeing them buggers off with powerful, manly thrusts.

So, it stands to reason, it ain't gonna be no wolley woofter as painted them murals in the Old Gaffer's house. No way. Definitely not.

There was a noise from upstairs.

Kyle was in the bathroom.

Now, I'd heard the murals in there were different to the others. I didn't know exactly how because I'd not been upstairs myself – not since that bit had been painted. There was a couple of blokes as had seen them but they didn't seem to want to talk about them much. Which was funny because all of us with the Grey Shirt on our backs had a load of respect for all the other stuff. It was an honour to get an invite just to look at the hall, let alone to be allowed into the downstairs front room. Respect for them murals was as much a part of us as loyalty to the Gaffers or kicking WiGIiEs' heads in. Strange then, that whatever was on them bathroom walls was something you just didn't talk about.

'You alright up there?' I tried again.

Still no answer.

'Gaffer Charlotte sent me to make sure you're alright.'

It was getting colder. And the cold felt weird. It seemed to get inside you too easily.

I started climbing up the stairs…

And…

I get to the top and the bathroom door's on the left. It's open.

I look in and… Kyle's there alright. She's standing. Or is she walking? Walking away from me? But she can't be walking away from me because it's only a few steps to the other side of the room… or it ought to be. From here, just three or four metres away, I can't tell if the wall's there or not. I can't tell if that cold blackness is a wall or… something else. Something like space. But bigger, colder than space. And I can't tell if the bathroom light is on because… because the bathroom light doesn't seem to be there anymore: the whole room doesn't seem to be there anymore. Beyond that doorway… there's just…

Okay, okay, I've got enough about me to think, *somebody's slipped me summat mighty peculiar.*

Below Kyle's feet, where the floor should be, there's only cloud – white and pale grey and swirly swirly swirling. It's like she's walking in the air above sunlit cloud.

But there ain't no sun. There's only…

Oh no.

I try not to look. I really try… not… to… look…

No question now. Where the ceiling ought to be, where the wall opposite the door ought to be, there's just Black.

And it's not just any sort of black. Nobody's ever taught me about this Black – not Dad or Mom, not up the mosque, definitely not at school and not even the Old Gaffer, though I'm absolutely sure he knew all about it, one way or another.

And I think about being a little kid again. And always wanting to do the right thing – be a good Moslem. And then going off the rails and winding up doing time. And how it was the Old Gaffer as took me in hand and stuck me back on the right track. And, after that, I'd got back into going up the mosque and the Old Gaffer had been pleased about that, even though he was a white bloke...

Okay, I know there's been some rough stuff – maybe more than there should have been 'cause, yeah, we have been banging some of them WiGIiEs about summat vicious. But I've always thought I've been about doing what's right. I've never known why but I've always thought I've been about trying to do what's right.

Only now I know why. Oh, I know.

I know why God... Created.

'Cause I tell you, if you could see That Black. That Black that's out there... Outside. Outside Everything...

The Old Gaffer always used to say there was 'Stuff as wants stopping.' And That Black is the sum and the total of What Wants Stopping.

That Black is why Everything is worth it.

And suddenly I want to grab Kyle and drag her back out of That Black. Because she looks like she's just walking into it as if it's the sodding Yellow Brick Road or summat. Like it's summat that'll take her where she wants to go, or to who she wants to be with. She hasn't got a bloody clue, this woman!

So I lean forward and try to reach out to her, try to grab her before she's too far away, but all the time I keep my one foot on the landing carpet...

And I catch myself thinking that this terrible nothing ought not to be sitting here unguarded – not just sitting here in somebody's bathroom in a nice detached house in Kingswinford. It ought to have a guardian...

And, just for a second, I think I can smell summat disgusting and really Haram and I can hear a load of really really bad language.

I force my hand forward. Reach out...

And my hand touches her face. And her face is ice-cold and stiff and she's not breathing.

And I know that it's too late, that she's gone, but I ain't having it, I just ain't, so I grab her and I pull her towards me.

And we're back on the landing and I'm lying there and I can feel the flesh of my face and the flesh of my hands burning with the cold and I know I'm starting to freeze solid like…

Like her.

I tear my arm away from her and look at my hand. The skin of my palm and the inside of my fingers has been ripped off. It was frozen to her. Then I look at her; she's a frozen block of ice.

I know that I'll die if I stay close to her. I try to drag myself away. I get as far as the top of the stairs when…

There's somebody coming up the stairs.

No: two somebodies.

No: a somebody and a…

The somebody gets to the top of the stairs. And I look up. And it's Gaffer Charlotte. She reaches into her long coat and she takes out…

The spatha! The old Roman sword as used to belong to her dad, to the Old Gaffer. And she's holding it like she knows how to use it. She looks at the frozen thing lying on the landing carpet – looks long and hard. Then her face cracks and she's screaming. She turns away and looks back down the staircase. I look back down the staircase too.

Coming up the staircase is this big massive blue dragon.

And its wingspan must be about fifty metres and this makes no sense at all because the staircase is only about a metre across. But, of course, rules like that just don't apply to dragons.

Up it comes, with its teeth and its claws and its blue armoured scales – don't try putting a hole in them with your AK rig, bro; you'd just piss it off.

Only just for a second, it seems like it's not really a dragon but this woman, maybe sixty or so, with short grey hair and bright blue eyes behind thick round specs. And the look on her face when she sees what's lying frozen there is just like Gaffer Charlotte's.

And then she looks at Gaffer Charlotte and her face goes blank. And she looks around her at the murals on the walls and looks back at Gaffer Charlotte as if everything makes sense to her.

Gaffer Charlotte's got the spatha raised and she starts to bring it down. She could bring it down a load quicker if she wanted to, I'm thinking.

But she doesn't want to.

Because, before the spatha's half way there, the dragon draws its foreleg back, bunches its scaly claws and punches. And its fist goes straight through Gaffer Charlotte's chest and straight through the wall behind her into the bedroom on the other side. Like a rivet.

I see the life go out in Gaffer Charlotte's eyes. As her body collapses down the stairs, the dragon turns and looks at me. I never thought I'd see pity in a dragon's eyes; I never thought I'd see tears. Then it raises its big massive wing so that I can get under it and get out. On the way downstairs, I have the feeling that the light behind me is getting brighter. And even with the cold, even with That Black, I have the feeling that this light, it's warm – it's gold. But I don't stop or look round. I've already seen more than it's possible to know.

It was insane for me to try to drive. My hands were pretty much skinless and slippy with blood. By morning, I knew I had to get myself over to A and E somewhere to get them seen to.

All I could say was 'I touched something really cold.' The doc and the nurses weren't impressed.

And then there was all the argy-bargy when everybody woke up and there was a dead body in the Old Gaffer's house – a hole where her heart should have been – and it was the woman who'd been expected to be Prime Minister in a couple of months' – it was Gaffer Charlotte. And when I heard that, I went crackers at the coppers, telling them that, no, there wasn't one dead body; there were definitely two. Because, and this was what really freaked me out...

If the second body wasn't there, then That Black had got it. Must have done.

***

It's not surprising they've had to bang me up. Obviously, it was going to look like I knew something. I told them I didn't. I told them I hadn't got a clue what had happened. After that, it was the long months of waiting while things ground slowly on through the courts, the appeal courts and the Supreme Court.

I hear that the Old Gaffer passed away last week. He'd got that funny bug they say is going round. And that bloke who was supposed to be a mate of the Kyle woman, Calper, he went the same day from the same thing.

Funny thing, I never liked him but old Danny Cosgrove came to visit, day before last. He tried his best and I was very grateful but there was nothing I could tell him to get me out of the frame. He looked pretty gutted about it. Funny thing, he's got to be Prime Minister now but he wasn't looking like a bloke who's in any kind of control; he looked weak – he looked afraid.

So: firing squad I suppose it's got to be. They only brought the death penalty back a month ago – I should be honoured.

Mrs Ith, I'd not ask you to explain any of this stuff to me, even if there was time. But I know you knew the Kyle woman. And I know you knew the Old Gaffer. He had a lot of respect for you. I know you've moved north of The Border but I hope they let me send this to you.

By the way, my dad and mom have moved up there too. With my mrs and the kids. Danny Cosgrove told me he thought it might be sensible. If you could look in on them – check they're alright – well, I'd be grateful.

And I hope you'll understand what's happened. Because I bloody don't.

I tell you one funny thing though: while I was typing this, I nearly trod on a spider. And before I knew what I was doing, I'd got hold of a sheet of paper and waited until that spider was crawling across it. Then I'd picked it up and carried it to a bit of the wall where there was a gap in the tiles: it looked like a good place for a web. And I'd let it go there. And this is funny because, before, when I've seen a bug – any kind of bug – I've crushed it, so I've no idea why for half a second, saving one spider felt like the most important thing in the world.

The End

Thank you to everyone who contributed a title of a book for Lon to edit.

The previous lives of Lon Kyle, Dave Calper, Charlotte Ronsard, Adil Muhammed Shah and New Cimourdain (Polly Gauvain) are told of in *Both* and in *Kingswinford Sunset*.

Luke and Mattie Ith-Cayle will be back in *Cooper's Ducks for Planet Earth???!!!*

Also available from Tenebrous Texts:

Fall of the Petrol Queen – Jon Hartless

In 1904, Poppy Orpington founded Thunderbolt Motors in the hope of manufacturing fast, competitive cars which would be cheap enough for the average worker to buy and enjoy. History shows that by 1908, Poppy's dream had been cruelly destroyed, but what exactly occurred in those four years? James Birkin once again picks up his pen to tell the real story behind the enigmatic Poppy Orpington, played out against a background of rising intolerance and the increasing certainty of war with Kaiser Wilhelm VI's Unified Germany. The weight of history is pressing down and destiny can never be denied.

Tales from the Bookshop – anthology

An anthology from the speculative, alternative and darkly-inclined Tenebrous Texts publishing house, which ranges from humorous to historic, folk horror to noir, comedic to post-fantasy.

This anthology is intended to demonstrate the range and versatility of those authors and writers that Tenebrous Texts works with. From the gentle, prehistoric tale of how the race of giants met their end (imagine this tale being told late at night, around a roaring campfire), to the poignant and 70s-fantasy inspired retelling of the legend of Beddgelert; jumping forwards to the Victorian era of Jack the Theorist; to World War One in the Black Country.

Lore of the Sælvatici – Steven C. Davis

A thousand years ago and more, Sherewode was a very different place from what it is now. Old gods, Hel-borne beasts, cruel Normans plundering and destroying history and justice, while a religious zealot salts and burns the earth, cutting down trees and carving the forest up to construct a Cathedral to destroy Paganism, individuality and more. Into the troubled times comes a reborn archer called Hurnungaz and a ragged band of heroes. A feral god walks the woods, half-stag, half human, the spirit of Sherewode, but driven mad by her own existence. This is Robin Hood for the 21st Century.

Cornix Sinistra – Steven C. Davis

There is a bookshop in Reading. A second-hand bookshop, like many others, a place of strangeness and comfort, a place to escape reality for a while and immerse yourself in another world. But something's not quite right. There are books which don't exist. Worlds which come and go. But beware. If the door sticks, you are not where you were.

Printed in Great Britain
by Amazon